THE SCENT OF MURDER

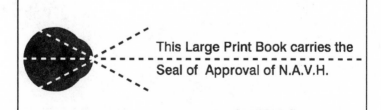

This Large Print Book carries the
Seal of Approval of N.A.V.H.

THE SCENT OF MURDER

KYLIE LOGAN

THORNDIKE PRESS
A part of Gale, a Cengage Company

Farmington Hills, Mich • San Francisco • New York • Waterville, Maine
Meriden, Conn • Mason, Ohio • Chicago

LIBRARY OF CONGRESS CIP DATA ON FILE.
CATALOGUING IN PUBLICATION FOR THIS BOOK
IS AVAILABLE FROM THE LIBRARY OF CONGRESS

ISBN-13: 978-1-4328-6532-0 (hardcover alk. paper)

Published in 2019 by arrangement with Macmillan Publishing Group, LLC/St. Martin's Press

Printed in the United States of America
1 2 3 4 5 6 7 23 22 21 20 19

For David

ACKNOWLEDGMENTS

We have always had dogs in our lives. For those of you who've never let a furry critter share your home and your time, you'll never understand the power they hold over us or the place they stake in our hearts and our memories. For the rest of you . . . well, of course you know how wonderful it is. And how maddening it can be. You remember the puppy years and the constant chorus of "No! Don't touch that. Don't eat that. Don't jump on that." You remember the sometimes sky-high vet bills and the times when your furry friend was sick and you slept on the kitchen floor next to him because . . . well, because you had to. You'll always cherish the walks, the play time, the simple, wonderful friendship of a dog sitting at your side.

And you know that every single minute of it is worthwhile.

Around here, dogs have always been pets

and companions, but there are so many who are even more than that. There are dogs who work alongside law enforcement, dogs who save lives, and of course, those dogs known as human remains detection dogs — cadaver dogs — whose job is to locate the dead.

It is an awesome responsibility and the people who dedicate their time and their pets to it are some of the most admirable I've met. As part of doing research for *The Scent of Murder,* I was privileged to participate in cadaver dog training with the Ohio Search Dog Association, volunteers who give of their time and their talents in the name of helping their communities. Thank you to each and every one of them:

Team leader Ellita and her dog, Tallon

Chris and Forrest and Aspen

Zach and Iggy

Leigh and Pyro

Jennifer and Annie and Big George (I borrowed that name to use in the book, too good not to!)

Martha and Xena

Dan and Forest

I hope I haven't left anyone — human or furry — out! I am grateful for your knowledge, your dedication, and the incredible lesson of loyalty shown by both dogs and owners.

As always, my special thanks to my fabulous brainstorming partners, Shelley Costa, Serena Miller, and Emilie Richards; to my agent, Gail Fortune, who worked so hard to make this book a reality; and to my family and my own furry companions. When I was writing *The Scent of Murder,* Ernie and Lucy were in residence. Now it's Lucy, a mixed breed with a shady past and a whole lot of fur, and Eliot, our Airedale puppy, who share our home and our hearts.

CHAPTER 1

It had rained that afternoon and the sidewalks were still wet. When the last of the evening light hit them, the slate squares reflected Jazz Ramsey's neighborhood — streetlights, and the neon signs that flashed from the windows of the trendy pubs, and a watery rendering of St. John Cantius church, an urban Monet masterpiece, its tan brick walls and bell tower blurred.

Even though it was officially spring, the wind off Lake Erie was wicked. Jazz bundled her shoulder-length brown hair into a loose ponytail and pulled up the hood of her sweatshirt, then hunched further into her North Face jacket. She stopped at a corner, waiting for the light to change, and was pleased when Luther sat down at her side even without a command.

"Good dog," she was sure to tell him at the same time she breathed in the combined smell of damp earth and the discarded bag from Taco Bell crumpled near the curb.

To Luther's credit, he ignored whatever bits and bites of Mexican cuisine might still be in the bag. But then, he'd been trained to follow different scents. When the light changed, he trotted along when Jazz crossed the street, his pace as brisk as hers, and the way he pricked his ears and cocked his head, she knew he sensed the exhilaration that vibrated from her hand through his leash. Luther knew it was almost time to get down to business.

Here, College Avenue started its downhill trek into the Cleveland Flats, the city's once-booming industrial heart. These days, Clevelanders were more likely to work in health care or IT than in foundries and factories, but one hundred years ago, this was the route thousands of workers took each day from their homes in blue-collar Tremont — it was simply called the South Side then — to the fiery furnaces that produced America's steel.

"We're not going far," Jazz assured Luther at the same time she noticed the couple who stumbled out of the Treehouse just up ahead made sure to give the massive German shepherd a wide berth. "Just over here," she told him once they'd passed the open door to the bar and the blaring music that seeped onto the street wasn't quite so loud. "Over to the new condos."

They stopped outside a sturdy brick building nearly ninety years old with solid walls and a slate roof. By the end of summer, Jazz imagined there would be gleaming glass in the window frames where there was plywood now, and window boxes, too, no doubt, and cars parked outside that reflected the status-conscious success of the young professionals she'd heard were already lined up to buy.

But not tonight.

Tonight the building was empty and dark and she had it all to herself.

It was the perfect place to put Luther through his paces.

Still hanging on to the dog's leash with one hand, Jazz fished the key from her pocket with the other and silently thanked Ken Zelinsky, the site supervisor, who'd agreed to give her an hour's time inside the building.

It wasn't easy to find urban training sites for a human remains detection dog.

She swung open the door and slanted Luther a look. "So what do you think?"

Luther sat, his tail thumping out a rhythm of excitement on the front stoop, and before she unhooked his leash, Jazz did a quick run-through of what she'd learned from his owner. Luther was a little over two years old, good-natured. He could be as playful as any pup, but he had a serious side, too. Like now, when he had to work.

"He's a smart dog," Greg Johnson had insisted when he begged Jazz to help with the final stages of Luther's training. "He just needs some reinforcement from a really good handler. That's you, Jazz."

It was.

Or at least it used to be.

These days, Jazz was feeling a little rusty. She was out of practice, not in the mood. It was one of the reasons that, after hemming and hawing and finding excuse after excuse, she'd finally agreed to Greg's request. She needed to shake herself out of her funk, and to her way of thinking, there was no better way to do that than with a dog.

She stepped into the long, narrow entryway of the building with its rows of broken mailboxes along one wall, and shut the front door behind her. The eerie quiet of years of neglect closed around her along with the smell of dampness and decay, rotted wiring and musty tiles carried by an errant breeze. Feeling her way, she unsnapped the leash from Luther's collar and gave him the command she'd devised for all the dogs she worked with because it was less ghoulish

14

than saying "Find the dead guy!"

"Find Henry!" she told him, and she stepped back and out of Luther's way.

Like all HRD dogs, Luther was that rare combination — independent enough to go off on his own and loyal enough to owner and handler to need praise. But he didn't know Jazz well, and smart dog that he was, he wanted to be certain. He glanced over his shoulder at her.

"You know what to do, Luther. You don't need Greg here to tell you." She swept a hand along her side. "Find Henry!"

In fact, what Jazz hoped the dog would do was clear both the first and second floors in record time and head up to the third floor where that afternoon she'd hidden a human tooth (a donation from her mother, Claire, who, at the age of fifty-two, had decided she wanted the kind of sparkling smile she'd seen on so many models and had begun to see an orthodontist). Human teeth contained enough scent to attract a properly trained dog's attention. If Luther was on his game — and she hoped he was because she hated the thought of telling Greg his dog wasn't ready for the grueling volunteer work done by dogs and handlers — he would locate the tooth, signal by barking three times, and chomp on the treat she would use as a reward while she secured the scene and made a simulated call to the cops, just as she would do if they made a real find.

"You gonna get a move on or what?" she asked Luther, her voice falling flat against the pitted plaster. "Find Henry!"

In a flash of black and sable, the dog took off down the darkened hallway.

After nearly ten years training and handling cadaver dogs, Jazz knew the ropes. She couldn't give Luther a hint about where to go or what he was looking for so she kept back, letting him work, refusing to influence him by her demeanor or her movements. She heard his claws scramble on the tile floor somewhere in the dark up ahead, flicked on her high-powered flashlight, and followed.

Some dogs, like pointers, are air sniffers. Some, like bloodhounds, keep their noses to the ground. No matter their breed, cadaver dogs, by virtue of their work, have to be proficient at both. They are trained as trailing dogs to pick up the scent that has fallen from decomposing bodies onto the ground, and as air-scenting dogs as well, so they can detect any smell of decomposition that's carried on the breeze. By the time she located him in a back room of what had once been a four-room working-class apartment, Luther was hard at work.

His eyes focused and every inch of his muscular body at the ready, he drew in a breath then hurried back and forth, side to side, through what had once been a kitchen, in an attempt to catch the strongest scent.

Not here. On the third floor.

Jazz knew better than to say it. Part of an HRD dog's gift was to eliminate one area so dog and handler could move on to the next. Luther was doing his job, and he was doing it well. She had to remember to compliment Greg on his training methods.

Nose to the floor, his ears pricked, Luther cleared the kitchen and headed into the back bedrooms. Jazz kicked a piece of fallen tile out of the way, but she kept her place. She would wait quietly until the dog emerged from the back rooms and when he headed out into the hallway, she would follow.

At least that was her plan.

Until Luther barked.

Once.

Twice.

Three times.

CHAPTER 2

"As soon as I heard the word *dog*, I had a feeling I'd find you here."

Jazz had been staring into the cup of coffee one of the cops had put into her hands. Her head came up, and she swallowed the sudden tightness in her throat. She ignored the flash of awareness that zinged through her and pasted on a tiny smile. After all this time, it was the only way she could face Nick.

She turned toward him and refused to let the blast of memory and that old, familiar tingle knock her for a loop. "Are you talking about my personality or my volunteer work, Detective Kolesov?"

He was as cool, calm, and collected as ever. She wouldn't expect him to be any other way. Nick tipped his head in the direction of the two cruisers with their light bars rolling. "How long have they been here?"

She remembered every minute of what

had happened since Luther signaled his find, but she checked the time on her phone, anyway. It gave her something to do. "I made the call at eight forty-two. They arrived at three minutes to nine."

"That's a pretty quick response."

"It can get lively around here on a Saturday night. My guess is they were close."

"Is the site secured?"

"It was when I walked out of the building." There was no trash can nearby so she dumped her coffee on the postage stamp–sized bit of grass outside the soon-to-be-expensive-condos building and set the paper cup on the sidewalk. "Unless your guys messed it up, it should be just as I left it."

He nodded but didn't speak. Instead, Nick glanced around, from the groups of curious people gathered beyond the yellow crime scene tape that had been strung from the stop sign at the corner all the way around to the bar next door to the padlock that hung from the door of the building where Jazz had done her search.

"You had a key."

It wasn't a question, but she answered anyway. "I had permission from the construction company people to come and use the building tonight."

Luther sat at Jazz's side working over the

tennis ball she'd given him as a reward for a job well done, and Nick gave him the briefest of looks. "Where's Manny?"

She managed to keep her voice level and her shoulders steady. "Luther's training," she told him.

"I'm going to assume you're not the one who put the body there for the dog to find as part of the exercise."

If he was going for funny, it didn't work, and maybe Nick realized it because he had the good sense to at least make a stab at looking embarrassed. It was not something he'd ever done well. When one of the uniformed cops came out of the building and talked quietly to him, Jazz allowed herself a closer look at Nick. It had been a little more than a year since she'd seen him, and she wasn't sure if it was a good thing or a bad thing that he hadn't changed one iota.

Crisply pressed khakis, a white shirt stained red and blue with the flashing colors of the roll-bar lights, a sport coat with a tiny checked pattern in it, brown and black, maybe, but it was hard to tell in this light. His sandy-colored hair needed to be cut. It was close to trim time when it curled behind his ears.

Nick finished with the officer before he looked her way again. "I'm going to need a

20

statement."

She had expected as much, though she hadn't expected Nick. In fact, she'd been hoping someone else was on duty that night, that Nick was doing whatever it was Nick did on Saturday nights. With whoever he did it with.

"Of course," she told him.

He studied the area the way he did everything else, slowly and thoroughly, like there was going to be a test, and his gaze stopped on the bright lights of a nearby pizza place. "We could sit down inside and talk. I haven't had dinner. You hungry?"

She wasn't. She wasn't forgetful, either, even though he must have been. They had gone to Edison's on their first date, and they'd shared leftover cold pizza the next morning for breakfast.

"I need to stick around. Luther's owner is on his way to pick him up."

"The dog didn't mess with anything at the scene, did he?"

"You know I wouldn't let one of my dogs do that."

"You wouldn't let Manny mess with the scene. I don't know this dog." One hand out, Nick took a step closer to Luther, but when the shepherd swung his head around, Nick changed his mind about giving him a

21

pat. "You want to start from the beginning?"

She did, because once she started, she could get it over with. "Luther and I arrived at eight thirty. We had permission to be in the building. The site super and his wife are having dinner down the street. He said he'd come by for the key when they're done."

"Good." Nick nodded. "I'm going to want to talk to him. If the front door was locked —"

"There was a breeze." Though it had barely registered at the time, Jazz remembered now and a shiver skittered over her shoulders. "There was air movement inside the building. I noticed it when we walked in. And if the whole place was boarded up and locked tight, there shouldn't have been, right? Maybe there was a piece of plywood missing from one of the windows. Or another door somewhere left open?"

One corner of his mouth pulled tight. "Back door. It looked as if it had been pried open and it's closed now, but not all the way. At least that's what Officer Franklin just told me. You might have been in there with the perp."

It was something she hadn't thought about, something she didn't want to think about, so she refused to consider it. "Luther would have let me know. I let him have the

22

run of the place and he found —"

"What?"

She made sure to turn away from Nick before she squeezed her eyes shut, bracing herself against the memory.

"I thought . . ." When her voice cracked, she swore under her breath, lifted her chin, and turned back to Nick. "When the beam of my flashlight first hit it, I thought it was a mannequin. But Luther wouldn't have signaled if it was."

"And you took a closer look."

The image was burned in her brain, not as frightening as it was horrific. Maybe the way to deal with it was to talk it out.

"Most of what we do is practice and preparation. You know that. I haven't actually found a body in a couple years."

He'd been writing down everything she said in a small notebook he had taken out of his pocket, and his head came up. "A couple years ago? You never told me —"

"You never had time to listen." It was as much soul-baring as she was willing to do now. Maybe ever. "That time it was an old man named Henry. He'd wandered away from assisted living. It was February, cold. There was eight inches of snow on the ground. When we found him —"

"You and Manny."

"When we found him, he looked peaceful. As if he'd just sat down and fallen asleep."

"This woman didn't look like she was sleeping."

Another question that wasn't. Jazz wished she hadn't tossed her coffee. "She was supine," she said so he could make note of it. "On her back."

"I know what *supine* means."

"Of course you do." She cleared her throat. "Her head was thrown back and at a funny angle. That's how I was able to see the ligature marks on her neck. Her skin was paler than it should have been. I thought —" Shrugging made her look helpless, but she couldn't stop herself. "I don't know what I thought. Even for a dead person, her skin color looked unnatural. Too white. Too chalky. Until I saw that it was makeup."

Nick paused, his pen poised over his notebook.

"The paleness. She looked pale because of makeup," Jazz said because she knew he was waiting for clarification. "Lots and lots of white makeup. It was on her face and on her arms and legs, too. Between that and her black clothing —"

"Black clothing. White makeup. Sounds freaky."

"Sounds like the goth kids back in high school. Her nails are painted black. Her eyes are ringed with black shadow and liner and she's got on enough mascara to paint a house. Her nose and her left eyebrow and her chin are pierced." Jazz realized that somehow she'd gone from speaking about the victim in the past tense to the present. It should have been the other way around.

"She's got tattoos on both arms," she added, though Nick would see as much for himself in a bit. "A skeleton, a rose, a vampire or some such. She's wearing a black skirt. Tight and short. And high black boots with tall heels, one of them is cracked off and lying twelve inches or so from the body. Black cami, no coat. Silver rings. Maybe seven or eight of them. All the typical stuff, skulls and fake rubies and spiders. And a necklace, a silver cross. It's big and cheap."

"Think that was what was used to strangle her?"

She shook her head. "If it was pulled hard enough to cause the bruising on her neck, the chain would have broken for sure. Besides, the marks on her neck are wider than the chain. Oh, and there's a backpack in the room. It might be hers. It isn't dusty, so it hasn't been there long. And it's black."

He tapped the notebook with the tip of his pen. "You're good with details."

"It's part of the training. You know that."

"I do know that. What I don't know —"

"Jazz! Jazz! Over here." Somewhere beyond the flashing lights, she heard her name called and looked into the sea of staring faces in time to see Greg Johnson jump up and down and wave his arms. "I couldn't get close. I had to park down the street. They won't let me through."

"Dog's owner?" Sometime while she was watching Greg, Nick had stepped up beside her. When she shivered, she told herself it had nothing to do with him. It was late. She was cold. She'd had a shock. "I guess I'd better go over there and get him or we'll stand here all night with the dog."

Greg Johnson was a retired high school math teacher. He was short, compact, and still limber enough to easily slip under the yellow crime scene tape when Nick lifted it to allow him into the restricted area.

"Good boy, Luther." Greg praised the dog and Jazz didn't take it personally. It was important to reinforce Luther's training. Greg scratched Luther's ears and, when she offered it, he took the leash out of her hands.

"You okay?" he asked when he was done with the dog, and before she could answer, he pulled her into a brief, fierce hug.

"I'm good," she assured him and re-minded herself. "Luther did great."

"We'll need your contact information." Nick poked his notebook between Greg and Jazz, and Greg wrote down what was needed. "You can take your dog home."

"We'll talk." Greg put a reassuring hand on Jazz's shoulder, then, with Luther trotting beside him, he disappeared into the crowd.

"Who knew you were going to be here tonight?"

Jazz had been watching Greg and Luther and she flinched at the sound of Nick's voice. "Who knew —"

"Did anyone know you'd be here tonight with the dog?"

"You mean did somebody put a body here purposely so we could find it?" Maybe not the dumbest question she'd ever heard, but mighty close. There was no use pointing that out to Nick. He was just doing his job.

She told herself not to forget it, and not to let the past cloud her attitude or her answers.

"I told Sarah I was training a dog tonight."

His sigh was barely perceptible. "Of course."

"It's called sharing. It's one of the things

you do with best friends." She hadn't meant to snap, but it had been a long evening.

Maybe Nick knew it, too, because he backed off. "Did you tell Sarah where you were bringing the dog?"

"What, so she could stop by and drop off a body?" Sarcasm was lost on him, so there was no use even trying. Jazz gave in with as much grace as possible. It was never easy for her. "No. I told Sarah I was doing training in the neighborhood tonight. That's all. And I wouldn't have even bothered except she and some guy named Rob who she's dating were going to a Cavs game with some other guy they want me to meet. They said I should join them for a drink after the game." She bit her lip. Sharing with a friend was one thing. Sharing with Nick was another altogether.

Since she couldn't give herself a good, swift kick, she said, "I didn't tell her where we were training."

"Did you tell her you'd meet them later for a drink?"

"No." Jazz had always been self-conscious about her five-feet-two, and Nick towered over her. She never let that stop her from lifting her chin and looking him in the eye, and now was no exception. "I figured I'd finish with the training and go home and grab a beer. I'm not interested in meeting Sarah's friend."

"How about that Greg guy?"

"I already know Greg. We're in training group together."

"Did you ever meet him for a drink?"

She didn't even bother to censor the curse that fell from her lips. "He has grandchildren, Nick. And a wife he adores. And believe me, I'm not interested. And it's none of your business, anyway."

"Just trying to get a clear picture of the situation."

"The situation is you've got a body to deal with." Back in the day, she knew Nick would have quirked an eyebrow and said something about dealing with her body, and though she hoped he had better sense now than he had then, she couldn't be sure. She had to get them both back on track. "No, I didn't tell Sarah where I'd be training tonight."

"Did you mention it to anyone else?"

"She didn't know the location, but I told my mom I was taking a dog out."

It must have been a trick of the light, but she could have sworn Nick looked a little uncomfortable. He'd never give it away with a facial expression. She knew better than that. She could read his discomfort in the way he suddenly held his hands. A little loose, a little below his waist. Like he was getting ready to juggle what he was sure was going to be a wave of emotion.

An ambulance pulled up, its lights adding to the carnival atmosphere, and he waited until it stopped, two paramedics got out, and he waved them into the building. "I'm sorry," he said once they were inside. "About your dad."

She knew it was bound to come to this. That explained the tightness that stretched her back muscles, the sensation of a fist slamming into her stomach. "You saw it —"

"On TV, online, in the newspaper. When a fire captain is killed fighting a fire, it's pretty big news. I'm sorry. Your mom must be —"

"She's devastated, but she's dealing."

"And you?"

Jazz had already reached down to pat Luther's head when she remembered the dog was gone. Force of habit. People stumbled over their words. They blundered when it came to their feelings. Dogs always knew what to do. She could always count on a dog.

People, not so much.

She stuffed her hands in her pockets. "Speaking of my mom, I'd like to get my training bait out of the building."

Some other time, some other place, some other cop, she would have laughed when his top lip curled. "Should I even ask?"

"It's just a tooth. I put it up on the third floor this afternoon."

"And this afternoon there was no body on the first floor?"

"I can't say. This afternoon I didn't go into the room where Luther found the body. But the guys working on the building were still here. Maybe six or seven of them. They would have seen something if there was something to see."

"Maybe."

She turned toward the building. "Can I —"

"Where's Manny?"

In the image that flitted through her mind when she thought of Manny, he was always smiling in a goofy, golden-retriever way.

"Lymphoma," she said. "He died the same week my dad did. Can I go inside and get my bait?"

"Sure." He stepped up beside her. "But I'm coming with you."

As much as she wanted to, she knew there was no use arguing with him. He would come anyway, and she would waste what little energy she had left.

Side by side, they entered the building.

31

The cops who'd arrived first had called for an evidence team, and the three officers who'd responded — two women and a man — had brought portable lights and a generator with them. The apartment at the end of the hallway radiated unearthly light.

Like there was an angel in there.

Jazz was not the fanciful type. She shook away the thought and flicked on her flashlight, heading for the stairs. "Be careful," she warned Nick. "Some of the risers are a little rickety."

Together, they navigated around broken ceramic tile, bits and pieces of fallen plaster, and the carcasses of three rats and got up to the third floor.

"I put the tooth behind a loose wallboard," she told Nick, and she retrieved the container it was in, put a lid on it, and tucked it in her pocket, then shined her light on Nick where he stood in the doorway.

"I should have come to the funeral," he said.

"I didn't have a funeral for Manny."

"I mean your dad's funeral. I should have come to your dad's funeral."

"It probably wasn't a good idea."

"Then I did the right thing."

She wasn't sure she'd go that far.

The room had once been a living room,

but it wasn't big, and Nick, with all his height and the way he stood, hands on hips, filled the doorframe. It was appropriate, somehow, for the two of them to finally talk here in a place that was falling apart.

She wasn't big on metaphor, but this one was pretty hard to miss.

Jazz shifted from foot to foot. "I'm sure you have a lot of work to do."

"Yeah." He didn't move from the doorway. "I need to talk to the officers downstairs and do a sketch of the crime scene and write a report."

"Looks like you won't get dinner."

"Probably not. You going home to have that beer?"

"Yeah, I think I will."

"If you want someone to drive you home —"

She hoped to God he wouldn't volunteer, that he'd have the sense to send one of the uniformed officers, but she wasn't going to take that chance. "I'll walk."

When she stepped forward, he stepped back. A minute later, they got back to what was left of the lobby just as Officer Franklin — a big guy with broad shoulders and a deep voice — came out of the back apartment carrying a small black purse with silver skeleton heads embroidered on it.

"I found this in the backpack," he said. "There's identification inside."

Nick reached into his pocket for a pair of latex gloves, slipped them on, and accepted the purse from the officer. He opened it and pulled out a driver's license, reading as he did, "Victim's name is —"

"Florentine Allen."

Nick was never surprised. It wasn't in his personality and it sure wasn't in his job description. When he looked from the license to Jazz, he snapped his jaw shut, and she had to force down the spurt of satisfaction at one-upping him that nearly made her smile.

"You didn't tell me —"

"You didn't ask."

"So what you're saying is —"

"That her name is Florie Allen. Yeah. I knew her."

CHAPTER 3

"Why didn't you call me?"

If there was a poster child for art teachers, Sarah Carrington would fit the bill. Curly blond hair (this week with a hot pink streak) that was always in her eyes. Ankle-brushing skirts bought from a Web site that supported women textile workers in underdeveloped countries. Bangle bracelets. Earrings that swept her shoulders. She was middle-sized, closing in on middle-aged, the divorced mother of two kids who, thanks to her example, were the only gluten-free vegans at their elementary school.

Sarah was the total package — incredibly talented, devoted to her students, loyal to a fault.

What she wasn't — ever — was early to school on a Monday morning.

Automatically, Jazz checked the time on the computer on her desk outside Sister Eileen Flannery's office.

"It's seven fifteen."

Sarah dropped her tote bag on one of the chairs in front of Jazz's desk, flopped into the other, and popped off the lid of her Starbucks cup.

"You should have let me know what was going on Saturday. You should have called me."

"You were at the basketball game on Saturday."

"Come on, Jazz, this is more important than basketball."

"I didn't want to bother you."

"Well, I wouldn't have minded. Rob turned out to be a loser. And it doesn't matter, anyway, because you're trying to change the subject. If not Saturday, you could have called yesterday."

"Yesterday I was . . ." There were some things Jazz couldn't explain, even to her best friend. One of them was how she'd spent most of that Sunday either picturing how she'd found Florie or dissecting (and second-guessing) every word she and Nick had exchanged.

"My mother stopped by." It was the way she'd spent the time in between the picturing and the dissecting and the second-guessing, and she knew Sarah would understand.

"Of course she did. I would have stopped by, too. If you had bothered to let me know what was going on. You must have been terrified."

"I was . . ." Because she didn't know what she was, she let the words fade and float to the high ceilings in the building that was once a Russian Orthodox seminary and now housed St. Catherine's Preparatory Academy. How could she explain that all she'd felt when she found Florie — all she felt now — was a deep sense of sadness? If there was anything the last year had proved to her, it was that the universe had a way of stretching her thin, of testing her and then laughing at her when she fell short of the mark. Nick. Her dad. Manny.

And now Florie's murder.

There was only one way to deal, and it wasn't with the tears and angst of her father's side of the family. It was her mother's Polish side that won out, and thanks to the genes she shared with those tough Eastern European ancestors who'd faced war and famine, prejudice and hardship, there was only one thing she could possibly say.

"I'm fine," she told Sarah.

"Well I'm not. It was Florie Allen."

"Yes." As she did every day, Jazz had

brought her lunch to school. She tucked the bag containing a salad and an apple into the bottom drawer of her desk even though she knew she wouldn't have the heart to eat it. "I found her."

"I know." Sarah couldn't sit still. She slapped her knees, got up, sat back down. "It was in the paper, Jazz. It was on the news."

The news was something Jazz had avoided all weekend. "Did they mention St. Catherine's?"

Sarah shook her head. "Not that I heard. But that's not surprising. Florie graduated . . . was it two or three years ago?"

Jazz had been wondering the same thing, but in between her mother arriving in a flurry of hugs, and her mother fussing, and her mother taking over Jazz's kitchen so she could make a pot of chicken soup, she hadn't exactly had much of a chance to think about it. She logged onto her computer and accessed school records restricted to everyone but the principal — Sister Eileen — and Jazz, her administrative assistant.

She keyed in Florentine Allen's name.

"Two years," she told Sarah, reading the information from the screen. "Well, it will be two years in June. It gets to the point where one year fades into another and it's hard to remember." She scanned the rest of Florie's record. "She was a good student."

"And talented." Maybe it was because she'd come to school early so she could corner Jazz and pump her for information that Sarah hadn't bothered with lipstick that morning. Her lips were as pale as her skin, and when her bottom lip trembled, her chin did, too. "I always liked Florie."

"The way I remember it . . ." Jazz tapped a pencil against the desktop. "Florie was a popular student. Wasn't she yearbook photography editor?"

"She had a good eye for design."

"And she got a college scholarship, right?"

Sarah's golden brows dropped over her eyes. "The North Coast School of Photography and Design. Pretty prestigious place. She was a scholarship girl here, too, right?"

Sarah knew better than to ask, and Jazz knew better than to answer. In the fifteen years since it had opened, St. Catherine's, just down the block from Jazz's Tremont home, had earned a reputation as one of the city's most prestigious college preparatory schools. The school encompassed grades seven through twelve, and a good many of its students came from families who could afford the sky-high tuition that paid for the latest technology, the best teachers, and an academic reputation that was second to none.

But some of them, girls who passed the entrance exam but showed financial need, were given a full ride. Sister Eileen, who had been the guiding force behind the school since day one, believed there was nothing to be gained from creating an in-school class system and had established a strict rule — no one knew who paid tuition and who didn't.

No one but Eileen and Jazz.

She slipped into the chair behind her desk. "You know I can't tell you that. And what difference would it make, anyway? Florie's been gone for two years. I wonder how she was doing at North Coast."

"Not so good, I don't think." When Jazz looked at her in wonder, Sarah raised her hands in a gesture of innocence. "Hey, I keep track of my art students. Or at least I try. Florie and I used to talk right after graduation, and she was always . . ." Sarah let her hands fall back down on her lap. "Florie was Florie. You know how she could be, wisecracking and sarcastic, and funny enough to make you bust a gut." Her voice cracked, and Sarah took a minute to compose herself.

She cleared her throat. "But the last time I talked to her, I asked about school, and she danced around the subject and never gave me a straight answer. I'll admit it made me curious. You know how I like to stick my nose where it doesn't belong." Sarah didn't give Jazz a chance to confirm or deny and it was just as well because yes, Sarah did have a way of minding everyone's business but her own, and Jazz was tired of reminding her. "I checked with someone I know at North Coast. He said he's heard Florie was having problems. Academic problems. She was always such a smart kid. I wondered what was going on."

"You weren't about to let that pass you by without checking it out." If Jazz was feeling more like herself and less like the woman who hadn't slept since Saturday, she might have smiled. Typical Sarah.

Sarah grinned. "Damn straight! I called Florie. I texted. I emailed. I never got a reply. Florie fell off the radar."

"Something was up with her." It was so obvious, Jazz didn't have to say it, yet something about the words helped her feel as if she was at least trying. Trying to do something. Trying to understand. Trying to make sense of what would never make sense, even if she did have answers.

She got up and crossed the room. The architects who had refurbished and reconfigured the seminary into St. Catherine's had been wise enough to keep its old-world character. Jazz's office had fifteen-foot-high ceilings, ornate plaster moldings, and bookshelves that filled one wall and closed with leaded-glass doors.

When she first started working at the school, she often wondered why Russian Orthodox priests — or anyone else, for that matter — needed such elaborate furnishings, but four years in the admin office and Jazz had long since stopped speculating. Like so many other buildings in the neighborhood, St. Catherine's was a mixture of bygone beauty and modern convenience, with state-of-the-art science labs, a chapel where they all attended monthly Mass, and a library Jazz hardly ever went into, one that Sarah claimed was one of the city's forgotten wonders.

But then, there was a lot about Tremont that was a little different from the rest of Cleveland. The neighborhood had once been home to thirty-six different churches, and the why of it was no surprise — many of the immigrants who flooded the area to work in the nearby factories kept the customs and the languages of their home countries. They stayed within their own ethnic groups and, street by street, the South Side grew up around them. The Poles had their own church, their own stores, their own doctors and pharmacies. So did the Ukrainians, and the Lebanese, and the Slovaks, and the Greeks. In the midcentury, when the neighborhood was bisected by a new freeway system and the descendants of those immigrants fled to the suburbs, they left a slew of schools and churches and social clubs behind, and when the next wave of people moved into the area — Southern whites and Puerto Ricans and African Americans — there were more than enough big, empty buildings to go around. Some, like the one Jazz had been in Saturday evening, were turned into pricey housing. Others were restaurants, wine bars, boutiques, art galleries.

And St. Catherine's.

Still at the bookshelves, Jazz ran her finger along the spines of fifteen years' worth of yearbooks and pulled out the one that featured Florie's graduating class. Since the senior girls were pictured alphabetically, Florie's photograph was one of the first.

Her hair was honey brown, not the charcoal black with red streaks that Jazz had seen on Saturday night.

She had no piercings or tattoos. At least none that showed.

What Florie Allen did have were brown eyes and a wide smile, tawny skin, straight teeth, a dimple in her left cheek.

"Class Treasurer," Jazz read the words printed under Florie's picture. *"Habitat for Humanity volunteer, Choir, Art Club. Plans for the future art school, brilliance, and changing the world!"*

She snapped the book shut.

"The world changed her instead," Jazz said. "When I found her, she was dressed in what we used to call goth. Black clothes, lots of piercings, plenty of tats."

"None of which means she wasn't still a nice kid."

"I didn't say that." Jazz slid the book back in place and closed the glass bookcase door. "I just said she'd changed. I wonder —"

The first bell of the morning rang, and Jazz headed back to her desk. "You'd better get a move on if you're going to get to your homeroom on time," she told Sarah.

"I've got plenty of time." She waved a dismissive hand. "And you haven't told me nearly enough. Were you listening to what I said, Jazz? I said the story was in the paper. So was the name of the lead detective on the case."

Jazz sat down and, though her desk was just as she'd left it when she walked out of the school on Friday, neat and orderly, she rearranged her notepad and her mouse and the nameplate that said jasmine ramsey in block letters. If only it was so easy to put all the emotions that seeing Nick again had churned up back into the tight box where she'd kept them in check over the past year. "So?"

"So, bad enough you didn't call me about Florie. I can't believe you didn't call and tell me you saw Nick."

"Who says I did?"

Sarah grumbled a word she shouldn't have used inside St. Catherine's. "If there's one thing I remember about Nick Kolesov, it's that he'd never let someone else interview the person who found a body. Not when he's in charge of a case. You talked to him, all right."

"I talked to him."

"And?"

"And nothing." Jazz's phone rang and she answered and took down the information from a mother calling about a girl who would be out sick that day. "There's nothing to tell, Sarah," she said when she was finished.

"Right." She stood and grabbed her tote

45

bag. "There was a time you would have told me he was a son of a —" She whispered. "A son of a bitch."

"And have I said anything today to contradict that?"

"It's not what you're saying, it's what you're not saying."

"He showed up. He interviewed me. He took my statement. I left."

"End of story."

"Yes, end of story. It was end of story over a year ago. You know that."

"Did he say what he's been up to?"

"I didn't ask. Because I don't care."

"Did he ask what you've been up to?"

"He didn't. Because he doesn't care."

"You don't know that."

"I do. And I know the second bell is about to ring." Right on time, it did, and Sarah took the hint. She was out of the door in a flash, but not before she gave Jazz the kind of look that clearly said best friends should be more open. And less evasive.

"We'll need to make some sort of announcement."

Sister Eileen Flannery entered a room the way she did everything else, quickly and efficiently. There was little time for dawdling in Eileen's day, and less time to waste on people or projects that weren't a direct

46

benefit to St. Catherine's, the all-girls school she'd started and nurtured for fifteen years, the one she hosted fundraisers for and talked up every chance she got. To anyone who would listen.

Eileen was nearing retirement age, but no one who didn't know her well would ever guess that. Her hair had dulled from its once-coppery glory to a color that reminded Jazz of nearly spent embers. It was cut short and stylishly, as was the navy suit she wore with the Toms shoes she claimed were too casual to be seen outside the walls of St. Catherine's but were the only shoes comfortable enough to get her through the miles of hallways she walked each day.

Before she breezed into her office, she stopped at Jazz's desk, and Jazz didn't need to ask who she was talking about, what she was talking about. She and Eileen had the uncanny knack of always being on the same wavelength, and this day was no exception. But then, the news of what happened over the weekend hung in the air of St. Catherine's like a pall. "She was one of our girls, and we can't let her passing go unnoticed."

Eileen didn't need to elaborate.

Jazz picked up a paper that she'd put on her desk on Friday before she left school. "We can add something about Florie to today's announcements."

The way Eileen tipped her head told Jazz she had her approval. "And let's leave a minute after for prayer. It's the least we can do." She turned and started for her office, then stopped and spun back toward Jazz. "Are you okay?"

Twelve years of attending Catholic school, and another four years of working at one. Jazz found it impossible to lie to a nun. "I'm coping."

"And you're doing that how?"

She shrugged and hated herself for it. "My mother made a pot of chicken soup for me."

"That's your mother coping, not you."

Jazz made up her mind in an instant. "I'll go for a run after school. Five miles is coping, right?"

"It is." Eileen pulled open her office door. "But talking is, too. Promise me you'll remember that."

Jazz had no doubt of it.

Even if she had no plans to do it.

It was a shame that though her head knew as much, her gut (or whatever part of her anatomy was responsible for producing the sense of apprehension and restlessness that filled her all that day) wouldn't ease up.

By the time sixth period rolled around and the girls were finished with lunch and there wouldn't be another surge of activity out in the hallways until the last bell rang, she had made up her mind. Yes, running was coping, and for all Jazz knew, so was talking out the feelings that made it seem like her insides had been filled with ice water since Saturday night.

But something told her an even better way of coping might be found in asking questions.

And even more importantly, finding answers.

She rapped on Eileen's door and stuck her head inside her office. "Are you busy?" It was a silly question because Eileen was always busy, but that didn't stop the principal from waving Jazz in while she finished the phone call she was on.

Eileen's office was even more elaborate than Jazz's. It had the same kind of glass-enclosed bookcases, the same high ceilings and windows that looked out on the street and Lincoln Park beyond, but there was a fireplace behind Eileen's desk and an Oriental rug on the floor in shades of blue and cream and green that had been given to the school by a generous donor and didn't fit in any of the other offices.

The principal finished her call. "What's up?" she asked.

Jazz wasn't sure where to start. "It's about Florie."

Eileen sat back, her head tilted, ready to hear more.

"Have you seen her since she graduated?"

"No, I haven't, but I've certainly heard about her."

It was news Eileen had never shared with her. "Recently?" Jazz asked.

Eileen reached for the calendar on the desk and paged through it. "Yes. Just after the last board meeting."

"A month ago? You never told me that Florie had changed from the kid we knew into some kind of vampire chick."

"The person who ran into her . . . well, when she told me the story, she didn't mention that Florie looked like something out of a scary movie." Eileen found the date she was looking for and tapped her finger against the page, satisfied to have her facts straight.

She sat back. "Did you realize what was going on when Florie was here?"

"Going on? Here in school? As in . . . ?"

"As in certain girls in that particular class not getting along with each other."

It was the same story in every class, and Jazz wasn't surprised. Some girls were just plain mean. Others were easy targets. Some of it could be explained by hormones or petty jealousies or, sometimes, Jazz swore, by the phases of the moon. St. Catherine's had standards, and a zero-tolerance policy when it came to bullying. But girls could be sneaky. And cruel.

"They don't all get along," she reminded Eileen.

"And I wouldn't expect them to. We're trying to educate intelligent women here, not robots. But Florie's class . . ." She allowed herself a sigh. "Those girls took it to a new level. There was a wave of threatening text messages —"

Jazz sucked in a breath. "I didn't know."

"No one knew. No one but me. I'm sorry I kept you out of the loop, but I wanted to handle it myself."

"Did you?"

Eileen chuckled. "Not very well, as it turns out. Oh, I pretty much kept a lid on things, I kept the girls from going at each other openly, but I'll tell you what, I was so relieved when those girls graduated and got out of here! I've never seen anything like it. They were like a pack of coyotes."

"And Florie was one of them."

"She was in one of the packs. Yes. Not that they had any sort of formal organization. You know how girls are, one day they're best friends with this person, the next week they can't stand that girl and they're best friends with someone else. The only thing that remained consistent was Florie and Grace Greenwald. They were friends at first, all through seventh and eighth grades. And freshman year, too, I think. Joined at the hip. Then during sophomore year, something changed. Big time. It went downhill from there."

Jazz remembered Grace, blond, pretty, full of herself. Grace had never had an opinion that she wasn't ready to share with the world.

"Grace has a sister who's still here," Jazz said, even though Eileen didn't need the reminder. Eileen knew every girl in the school, and if any one of them was ever in a bad mood, Eileen not only knew it, she knew why.

"Dinah is the polar opposite of her sister," Eileen said. "She's sweet, one of those girls who is so quiet, you barely know she's around. But she's as smart as can be, a real math whiz."

"And not nearly as overbearing as Grace."

Eileen's laugh was all the answer Jazz needed. "Grace and Florie were gone on the same graduation day, thank goodness."

"It was a couple years ago," Jazz reminded her.

"Yes, it was. Except last month . . ." To emphasize the point, she tapped her calendar again. "Last month after the board meeting, some of the trustees went to Ohio City for a drink." Ohio City was the historic neighborhood next door to Tremont. It was just as trendy, just as busy, just as jampacked with restaurants and bars and the crowds that patronized them.

"I was all set to join them," Eileen added, "then I got the call about that pipe that burst in the science lab."

Jazz remembered the incident well. Eileen had been called by the security company that got the alarm, Eileen called Jazz, and they both spent most of the night at the school dealing with plumbers and soaked science equipment.

"The next day, I talked to one of the other board members, Laura Kerchmer. Seems she and the others stopped in at the pub at Great Lakes Brewing, and according to Laura there were two girls there who got into an epic fight."

"Grace and Florie?"

"Well, Laura didn't know that. Not at first. She's new to the school, remember, so she wasn't around when Grace or Florie

53

were here. The other board members were seated in a different room, and Laura passed through the bar on the way to the ladies' room. That's how she saw what she saw. And she says she never would have paid much attention to any of it except she heard one of the girls say those magic words, 'St. Catherine's.' "

"And after that?"

"Laura listened up. And that's when she heard their names. Yes, it was Florie and Grace. She said it took about two seconds for them to be in the room together before they started going at each other."

"It's been two years since they graduated."

"Yes, but they were both attending North Coast now, so chances are they've seen each other plenty since they left here. According to Laura, smoke started coming out of Grace's ears the second she clapped eyes on Florie and the two of them went at it like cats in an alley. One of the restaurant workers had to break things up. He escorted Grace out the front door and Florie out the back."

"Then what happened?"

The way Eileen smiled, one corner of her mouth pulled tight, Jazz knew she was feeling just as helpless as Jazz had felt since Saturday night.

"After that," Eileen said, "Laura went back to her drink. By the time she left the pub, both girls were gone. And it was a month ago and that's a long time, but . . ."

Her cheeks darkened, and Eileen looked out the window, and Jazz knew the principal didn't need to say another word. They both knew what Eileen was thinking, and there was no use giving voice to words that were so poisonous.

One month ago, Florie and Grace were still at it like the hateful teenagers they had once been.

And now, Florie was dead.

CHAPTER 4

Jazz knew there were telltale signs.

Before a back draft turns a smoldering fire in an enclosed space into an explosive inferno, the smoke coming from the structure morphs from black to a sickly grayish yellow and puffs through cracks and under doors, huffing in and out as if there were a dragon breathing in the bowels of the building, daring anyone to step nearer. Windows vibrate and rattle. They get coated on the inside with pitch-dark soot.

Every firefighter knows this. With all his experience and all his smarts, Captain Michael Patrick Ramsey certainly did. At a time like that, the worst thing that can happen is for oxygen to be reintroduced into the structure.

He knew better than to enter the house on Bridge Avenue. Oxygen feeds a fire, and when air rushes across the superheated surfaces of a closed room, the results are instantaneous.

And deadly.

That evening, like always, thinking about the scene that played out just across the street from where she stood made Jazz's insides knot. The lot was empty now, a tangle of overgrown grass and weeds. But it once held a house much like the ones on either side of it.

Two stories plus an attic. Maybe the house had roses tangled around an arbor like the pristine Victorian on the right, with its gingerbread trim and yellow front door. Maybe, like at the house on the left, there was a stroller parked in the middle of the front walk, a van with a busted-out back window in the drive.

Four adults and five children made it out of the house alive that night.

Her dad did not.

When she bent at the waist and fought to catch her breath, it wasn't because she'd run the two miles from her home in Tremont to the equally gentrified Ohio City. Heck, she helped coach the cross-country team at St. Catherine's. For Jazz, running was relaxation and meditation. It kept her in shape to work with the dogs.

A year earlier, every single time she ran, she ended up at the vacant lot. But then spring melted into summer, and summer burst into the fiery shades of autumn, and autumn froze and then melted again and . . .

She didn't run to this spot as often as she used to. Sarah told her that was a good thing, it meant she was getting a handle on her grief. Jazz wasn't so sure. She thought maybe it meant she was starting to forget.

And she didn't ever want that to happen.

She crossed the narrow street. The fire had happened a little more than a year before and there was no way she could still smell the smoke that hung in the air the way it had the morning after the blaze when Jazz and her mom and her brothers, Hal and Owen, stood right here on the slate sidewalk with their arms linked, holding each other up in the face of a pain made even more impossible when they heard the word *arson*. Still, Jazz was convinced the acrid smoke was stuck in her lungs. Sometimes she swore she could still feel the grit of the ashes in her eyes and taste the salt of her tears on her lips.

He was fifty-two years old, and he was her best friend. He was her hero.

And he knew better than to walk into that house.

A car zipped by, its radio blaring Lil Wayne, and the vibration of the bass line shook Jazz out of her thoughts.

She hadn't come to Ohio City to think about the past.

There was something she had to do.

She didn't bother to give the vacant lot one last look. She would be back. Besides, by now she knew where every empty beer bottle on it winked in the sun, and she turned her back on them and on the weeds and on the memories that would always burn with all the intensity of the back draft that killed her father. A couple blocks away, she went north, looped around another corner, and stopped in front of the home of Larry and Renee Allen.

Thanks to the massive Italianate crammed onto the double-wide lot on the left, its garden already in full springtime yellow daffodils and early red tulips, the Allens' house looked like the wallflower at the ball. The house needed paint. The driveway was cracked and overgrown. The wooden steps she climbed to the sagging front porch were cockeyed, the gray paint nearly worn completely away in spots.

Florie's parents weren't expecting her.

She still couldn't decide if that was good or bad, and not knowing made her queasy. Jazz ran a hand over her hair, took off her sunglasses, and tugged her loose-fitting tank

top into place before she pressed the doorbell next to the aluminum screen door. For
the hundredth time since she decided to
come, she wondered what she would say to
the Allens. What words could possibly
penetrate their grief?

It took a few minutes for the inside
wooden door to open. When it did, she
found herself looking through the screen at
a man with close-cropped dark hair and a
paunch that rounded the orange T-shirt he
wore with jeans. He didn't invite her in. In
fact, he didn't even ask who she was. He
blinked, squeezed into the pie slice of
doorway, and stared.

Jazz swallowed her misgivings. "Mr. Allen?
I'm Jasmine Ramsey. I work at St. Catherine's. I was in the area and I stopped by to
tell you how sorry I was about Florie."

"What?" The question came from somewhere behind Larry Allen. A woman's voice.

"Someone's here asking about Florie." He
raised his voice and a second later, a woman
wedged herself into the small space between
Larry and the door. She was short and
round, and her dishwater blond hair hung
around her shoulders. Like her husband,
Renee Allen looked at Jazz through the
screen door.

Jazz studied them, too, wondering if they'd

60

look less careworn without the crisscross of fine metal over their faces.

"I came to offer my condolences," she said. "Florie was a great kid. I'm very sorry."

Larry Allen had a wide nose and he smelled like cigars, but even that wasn't as strong as the musty odor that seeped from the house. Jazz wondered what could smell so dank and heavy on an evening when the skies were blue and a crisp breeze snapped the buds of the maple tree on the perfectly manicured lawn next door.

It was completely inadequate, but the only thing she could think to say was "If there's anything I can do . . ."

Larry glanced at his wife. She looked down at her powder-blue fuzzy slippers.

"You work at the school, huh?" Larry asked.

"I'm Sister Eileen's administrative assistant. I think we met once." She wasn't sure. In fact, she thought they probably hadn't. She would have remembered Renee's watery blue eyes and Larry's missing front tooth. But it seemed like the right thing to say. "Maybe at one of Florie's cross-country meets."

"That Eileen, she's the one who gave us the money to send Florie to that school."

"Eileen doesn't give the money, not directly." Jazz wasn't sure why, but it seemed important to point this out. "The decisions on scholarships are made by the board and a committee of teachers, and —"

"You think she'd give us more? Funerals are mighty expensive."

Jazz caught her breath. Was that all there was behind Larry and Renee's blank expressions, the thought of how much and from where? Where were the tears Florie deserved? Where was the ache, the anger, the despair?

Where was Jazz's own sense of compassion?

The thought knocked some sense into her. If there was one thing she'd learned from her father's death, it was that everyone dealt with grief in their own way. It wasn't her place to judge.

It was, though, her chance to see what she might get in exchange for the promise of considering their request.

"I can talk to Sister Eileen," she told them. "But speaking of that . . . When was the last time you spoke to Florie?"

Larry pursed his fleshy lips. "The cop who came around, he asked us that."

Jazz didn't need to ask which cop. "And what did you tell him?"

"It was maybe three, four weeks ago."

When Renee spoke up, Larry flinched. "She called one day."

"What did you talk about?"

Renee lifted her scrawny shoulders.

"What did Florie say?"

She wrinkled her nose.

"Did she want something? Need something?"

It might have been a trick of the evening light and Jazz's slightly blurred view through the screen on the door. She could have sworn Renee's top lip curled. "Same as always. Florie was always looking for money."

Larry grunted. "Like we have any to give her. I told her that, and she got all mad. Said she'd figure out some other way to get what she needed."

"Did she say why she needed the money?" Jazz wanted to know.

"Like I said," Larry snapped. His cheeks darkened. His eyes popped. "We didn't have any to give her and she knew it."

Jazz automatically stepped back in the face of his fury.

She tensed, watching Larry's barrel chest rise and fall, listening to the sharp intake of his breath.

And she decided there was nothing to be gained by making either of the Allens angry.

Clearly, money was a touchy subject, one far more likely to get a rise out of him than talking about his daughter's murder.

She pulled in a breath. "Florie was very talented."

At his sides, Larry's hands curled into fists. He clicked his tongue. "She took pictures."

She managed a smile. "Florie's pictures were special, weren't they?" She hoped she didn't sound as perky to the Allens as she did to herself, then realized it probably didn't matter much. What was important was to get their conversation back on even footing. If it had ever been there in the first place.

"We've got a few of Florie's photographs hanging in the hallways at St. Catherine's. She had an eye for light. She used it to create a mood. There's a picture of trees she took when she was just a sophomore. Sunlight filtering through the leaves. It's a black-and-white photograph and every time I see it, I imagine how blue the sky above the trees is, and how the summer breeze feels."

Larry shifted his weight from one foot to the other. "Anybody can take pictures. All you need is a phone."

She wasn't about to argue the point. Jazz

64

cleared her throat. "You said you hadn't talked to her for a few weeks. Florie didn't live here?"

As if they weren't quite sure, the Allens exchanged looks before Renee shook her head. "She shared a house with a few other kids over near school."

"It's all been in the paper," Larry said, and as if media attention was some sort of honor rather than the intrusion Jazz knew it to be, he inched back his shoulders. "A couple of the TV stations came by and interviewed us. What did they expect us to say?"

Even though those same TV stations had shown up at her parents' house in the days after her dad's death, Jazz still couldn't even begin to imagine. "There's nothing you can say." She didn't bother to mention that she knew this from experience because her experience wasn't theirs, and she didn't want to patronize them. "I'm sure whatever you said was the right thing."

"I thought maybe that's who you were." Larry looked her up and down. "When you first came to the door, I thought you were that What's-Her-Name, you know, the skinny chick with the long hair. The one on Channel Three."

Just to go along with him, Jazz looked

down at her blue shorts and her purple tank top and laughed. "I have a feeling reporters dress better than this. But maybe they ask the same kinds of questions. Did they ask about the last time you saw Florie? When was that?"

"Halloween," Renee answered instantly, then just as quickly corrected herself. "No, it was around Christmas. Maybe."

"I know that was a while ago, but did she say anything about anyone being angry at her?" It was too blunt, but there was no other way to put it. "Was there anyone who might have wanted to hurt Florie?"

Larry narrowed his eyes. "You say you work at the school? Why do you care? Why are you asking the same things that cop did?"

Legitimate questions. Too bad Jazz didn't know the answers.

"I don't mean to pry," she told them, because that, at least, was true, "but at St. Catherine's, we think of the girls as family."

Not the whole truth. That had more to do with the bruises on Florie's neck, the broken heel of her boot lying next to her body. It had to do with how Jazz hadn't been able to sleep, not without waking up startled, certain she'd heard Luther bark three times.

She squeezed her eyes shut.

The Allens' daughter had been taken from them, just like her dad had been taken from her. For that, if nothing else, she owed them the truth she hadn't even faced up to herself.

When she opened her eyes again, she found both the Allens watching her carefully.

"I thought if I understood more about what Florie was up to, if I heard more about what she's been doing, I thought I could try and make some sense of what happened to her," she told them.

Renee hung her head.

Larry settled his weight on his back foot.

Jazz felt heat rise in her cheeks.

"I'm sorry." She stepped back, closer to the tipsy stairs.

"I'm sorry for your loss and . . . I'm sorry I bothered you."

"You gonna talk to that Sister Eileen?" Larry wanted to know.

She couldn't believe she didn't know better than to leave well enough alone. "Do you have any idea what Florie could have been doing in that old building in Tremont on Saturday night?" she countered.

Larry puffed out his cheeks and Renee clasped her hands at her waist.

"It just seems strange, that's all," Jazz said. "I mean, the building is being rehabbed, but right now, the walls are practically falling down." She stopped herself before she said any more and they realized she'd been there. "It seems like a weird place for Florie to hang out."

"Like I said . . ." When Larry moved back, there was no room for Renee at the door. She had no choice but to melt into the shadows behind him. "We haven't talked to Florie for a while."

"Yes, of course." Jazz scraped her palms against her shorts. "There's no way you would know."

"And Sister Eileen?"

She had bothered them enough. "I'll talk to Sister Eileen," she told Larry, and Renee, too, though she wasn't sure if Renee was still anywhere around. Larry had moved to his right and closed the door so much that she could only see a strip of his jeans and shirt, just a patch of his mouth and nose. "I can't say for sure, but there might be money in the St. Catherine's emergency fund that could help pay funeral expenses. I'm not making any promises, of course, but —"

In the end, *but what* didn't matter because Larry closed the door.

Jazz wondered briefly if he'd come back,

but she knew he wouldn't. She turned and went down the steps and for the first time, she realized there was a woman on the sidewalk watching her.

"You're here about the kid, right?" The woman was short and thin and had a cascade of dark, wavy curls. She poked her chin in the direction of the Allens' house. "Florie? Are you a reporter?"

"Did you know her?"

"Sure. I live right here." The woman walked not toward the Italianate, but in the other direction and a block of yellow stone row houses. On the tiny front porch of the closest unit there was a Pack 'n Play portable playpen, and the woman glanced at it long enough to check on the baby in it.

"I work at the high school Florie attended," Jazz told the woman. "She was a nice kid."

The baby up on the porch started fussing and the woman went and got him. He was maybe a year old and he reminded Jazz of the old men who played bocce in Lincoln Park on Saturday afternoons. Three chins, no hair, chubby legs. The kid had a round head, a nose too big for his face, and eyes that, Jazz hoped, could somehow be uncrossed before he started school and was the butt of too many cruel jokes.

The woman held the baby over her shoulder and patted his back. "I sure am going to miss the money I made off Florie," she said.

Jazz was so busy staring at the ever-growing wet stain on the back of the baby's pants, she hadn't been paying attention and she snapped to.

"Money? Florie paid you money?"

"Twenty-five dollars. Each and every time."

"Each and every time you did . . ."

The woman laughed, and now that he'd quieted, she flipped the baby around and propped him on her hip. He promptly let out a long string of drool.

"Every time I let her take Lalo here."

"She babysat and paid you to do it?"

"Nah, nah, though now that you mention it, I guess that is kind of what happened. She never stopped to see them when she was in the neighborhood, I don't think." The woman glanced at the Allens' house. "But after I had the baby, she'd come by and talk to me once in a while and sometimes she'd ask if she could take Lalo out for the day. It was always a treat to get some alone time, you know? But Florie, she wasn't babysitting. Not exactly. Sometimes she'd take Lalo to the park or over near the Market where there are places to sit outside.

70

And every time she did, she gave me twenty-five bucks. You know, as a kind of a payment. Because she was taking pictures of him."

Jazz thanked the woman and walked away, more curious than ever about what the last years of Florie's life had been like, and what she was up to that brought her to the abandoned building where she'd been strangled.

And why on earth a girl who was apparently desperate for money would pay twenty-five dollars to take pictures of the homeliest kid on earth.

CHAPTER 5

The doorbell rang as Jazz was rinsing the last of the shampoo out of her hair.

It was Tuesday, and just a little after six in the morning. Even before she stepped out of the shower and grabbed her terry-cloth robe, she knew there was no way anyone made a social call at that hour.

"I'm coming," she yelled as soon as she had a towel around her head and the bathroom door open. "Wait a minute. I'm coming!"

She got downstairs and to the front door in record time, then stopped, surprised.

"Sorry." Looking more than a little embarrassed, Greg Johnson mouthed the word through the window on the front door. At his side Luther thumped his tail on the front porch, thrilled to see Jazz.

She opened the door. "What's up?"

"I'm sorry, Jazz. I should have called. It's just . . ."

Though it was a cool morning, his jacket was open, and Greg hadn't combed his hair. She stepped back and out of the way so he and Luther could come into the house.

"What's wrong?" she asked.

Greg scratched a hand along the back of his neck and, now that they were inside, he dropped Luther's leash. The dog had visited before. He headed straight for the corner next to the couch, the place he'd napped the last time Greg and his wife, Toni, dropped by.

"It's my mother," Greg said. "In Florida. We just got the call a couple of hours ago. She's had a stroke."

Jazz put a hand on his arm. "You want to sit and catch your breath? Coffee?"

Greg shook his head. "Thanks, no. Toni's out in the car and we're headed to the airport and . . ." When he looked over at Luther, the tips of Greg's ears turned red. "If there was anyone else I could ask, Jazz, you know I would. But the kids are both living out of town now and Toni's sister has terrible allergies and can't have Luther around and . . ."

"And you want me to watch him for a couple of days."

Since he didn't have to come right out and ask, Greg let go a breath of relief.

"Could you?"

Jazz glanced over to where the dog had already made himself at home and pretended to have to think about it. "I don't know. It looks like he's going to be an awful lot of trouble. What do you think, Luther?"

The dog wagged his tail.

"Settled!" Jazz smiled. "If there's anything else I can do . . ."

"I'll call." Greg zipped back out to the porch and grabbed the Whole Foods tote bag he'd left there when he came inside. "Here's his food and his toys and his favorite blanket and his vet's phone number, but hopefully, you won't need that." He handed the bag to Jazz. "I owe you big time. I know it won't be easy for you having a dog around again, and with what happened the other night, I don't want you to look at Luther and think about . . . well, you know."

"No worries. Believe me, I'm not spending my time thinking about what happened Saturday," Jazz told him, even though the abandoned building and Florie Allen were pretty much the only things she had thought about these last few days. "It will be nice to have somebody around to talk to."

"And I'll call." Greg stepped to the door. "As soon as we're settled, I'll call and let you know what's happening and when we'll be back."

"Go!" At the same time she shooed him outside, she waved to Toni waiting in the car. "Me and Luther, we're old friends. We'll be fine."

She waited until they drove away before she turned to her houseguest. "Breakfast?" she asked. "While you eat, I'll make coffee, then we'll go for a walk."

As it turned out, she walked Luther twice before she went to the school that day. Sure the dog knew her, but dogs are smart and he sensed that something was up; his owners had dropped him off and driven away. Jazz knew that getting rid of some of his nervous energy was better than leaving him in the house all morning to pace and worry. Since she lived within walking distance of St. Catherine's, she checked on him at lunchtime and promised a longer walk and a little training disguised as play when she got home from work that afternoon.

Until then she had plenty to do. The school year was winding down, but that didn't mean St. Catherine's schedule was any less jam-packed. That day Jazz called the caterer to make final plans for the National Honor Society dinner. She checked and rechecked the summer camp schedule because she needed to send it to the printer and it had to be perfect. St. Catherine's welcomed girls from all over northeast Ohio for summer sessions in everything from drama to chemistry, computer programming to oil painting. A typo in the brochure would reflect badly on the school.

When her eyes ached and her back cramped and she needed a break from proofreading, Jazz touched base with Matt Duffey, who would be conducting a workshop for the cross-country girls in a week or so, and because Eileen was away at a must-attend meeting, she called each and every member of the board of directors on her behalf about freeing up money from the school's emergency fund to pay for Florie's funeral. She would leave it to Eileen to tell Larry and Renee that everything was taken care of, just as she'd leave it to Eileen to set a date for a memorial for Florie at St. Catherine's.

All that, along with the early-morning surprise Greg had brought her in the form of Luther, had made it a full and rich day, and it was still a couple hours before the last bell.

There was a coffee maker in her office on a table near the windows that looked out over Lincoln Park, the eight-acre green

76

space in the center of the neighborhood, and she went over and flicked on the machine.

Nothing happened.

She turned the machine off, turned it on again, and, when nothing happened again, she went in search of coffee.

At that hour of the day, she was pretty sure the closest place to find it was the school cafeteria.

Like all of St. Catherine's facilities, the cafeteria where its six hundred students congregated each day was a mixture of utilitarian and dignified. Thanks to a generous donor, the room that had once been the refectory of the Orthodox seminary had kept its rich oak-paneled walls and oak tables, but the service area gleamed with stainless, the lighting was bright and state of the art, and there was a sound system that allowed the girls to program their favorite songs and listen to them while they ate. At this time of the day, with the last lunch period over, the room was empty and clean and set up for the next morning's rush. Sister Eileen was a firm believer in not allowing the girls to have coffee before classes started, but there was always juice and bagels and yogurt available in the morning.

Listening to her own footfalls echo through the massive room, Jazz moved toward the open doorway at the end of the cafeteria, but before she could step into the kitchen, she was met by the roadblock that was Loretta Hardinger.

Loretta was as much a fixture at St. Catherine's as Sister Eileen was. She'd been hired by Eileen before the school officially opened, and it was Loretta who oversaw the transformation of the cafeteria from dark and grim to sleek and modern. Loretta ordered the food and devised the weekly menus. She hired cafeteria staff, she oversaw the students who worked there because each and every girl at St. Catherine's had to take a one-week turn at the serving counter and another doing cleanup, and she made sure that shipping invoices lined up with orders and that St. Catherine's was getting the best prices from its suppliers.

Loretta was nearing sixty, taller than just about any woman Jazz had ever met, and as solid as a brick wall.

It was a fact known from one end of St. Catherine's to the other that Loretta took no nonsense from anyone. But beneath her gruff exterior, it was whispered, there was a heart of gold.

The trick was getting to it — fast — before

Loretta lost what little patience she had.

"Looking for something?"

Jazz was the administrative assistant to the principal and, as such, second in command, and still, every time she talked to Loretta, she felt like a freshman.

She looked up from the white apron Loretta had looped over her neck to Loretta's beefy arms, her square chin, her snubby nose, her small, dark eyes, her halo of grizzled gray hair.

"Coffee?" Jazz squeaked.

"Don't tell me, that fancy coffee maker of yours went south again." When Loretta laughed, Jazz swore the silverware in the drawers vibrated. "Say what you want, but my old percolator never gets cranky and decides not to work like that fancy-schmancy machine of yours. Come on." She stepped back so Jazz could walk into the kitchen. "I just put on a pot."

The kitchen was as no-nonsense as the woman who ran it, with an industrial-sized refrigerator, a couple sinks each big enough to float the *Queen Mary,* and a stove and grill where hundreds of lunches were prepared each day. The center of the room was taken up by a prep counter, and across from that was the large rectangular opening through which Loretta could keep an eye on the line out front — along with each and every girl who went through it. The kitchen was immaculate, the floor spotless. Loretta wouldn't have allowed for anything else. The chalkboard that listed the menu (in pink letters that particular week) was already propped against the wall and ready for the next day. CHEF SALAD. CHICKEN AND BROWN RICE. VEGETARIAN CHILI. Eileen was as concerned about the girls' diets as she was about their minds, and Loretta obliged.

"Here you go." Loretta handed a cup of steaming coffee to Jazz. "Black, right? No sugar."

Jazz pulled in a breath of the delicious aroma. "Perfect!"

Loretta glanced toward the stools near the prep counter. "You got time to sit?"

Loretta probably wanted to go over invoices, or ask what Jazz had heard from the supplier who'd been promising them a deal on a bulk purchase of paper napkins. It was work related, so of course Jazz agreed. Besides, if she took her time, she could get another cup of Loretta's coffee, and yes, though Eileen swore by the expensive (and donated) machine in Jazz's office, Jazz knew better. Loretta's coffee was awesome.

"What's up?" she asked Loretta.

There were no invoices out on the prep table, and Loretta didn't go into her office at the back of the kitchen to get them. Instead, she sat down and, with one finger, traced an invisible pattern over the counter.

"Been meaning to talk to you," she said. "Wanted to yesterday, but you know how Mondays are around here. Never got the chance. I heard . . ." She looked up at the fluorescent fixtures that hung above their heads. "You were the one who found her."

Jazz had heard much the same from every teacher she'd run into in the last day and a half. By now, she had her response memorized. She set down her coffee. "I did."

"That must have been . . ." Loretta wasn't sure what it must have been, which is why she let her words trail off.

Even after all this time, Jazz wasn't sure what it must have been, either, so she didn't even try to finish the sentence.

"Did you know Florie when she went to school here?" she asked Loretta.

"Did her turn here in the kitchen." Loretta had poured a cup of coffee for herself, too, and she spooned sugar into it, then added a glug of half-and-half. "Oh, yeah. Like all the girls, Florie did her time."

"A lot of them complain."

Loretta grunted. "A lot of them need to

81

get their heads out of their my-daddy's-got-money asses and see what the real world is like." She didn't excuse her blunt assessment. Jazz didn't expect her to. Loretta didn't waste time on apologies.

"Florie wasn't one of them?"

Loretta pressed her lips together and shook her head. "Never one bit of moaning or complaining out of that girl. It was like she . . ." Gathering her thoughts, she looked around the kitchen. "It was almost as if she liked it here."

"But she never talked about going to culinary school. Or did she?"

"Oh, I don't think it was the cooking she liked. Though come to think of it, she was such a good worker, I did let her help out at the stove sometimes. That's not something I do with most of these girls. They're not responsible enough and they don't want to get their hands dirty." Loretta made a face. "Florie wasn't like that. She did what she was told to do, and my goodness, how she loved to clean up."

Over the rim of her coffee cup, Jazz smiled at Loretta. "That's got to be unusual for any teenaged girl!"

"You bet. But Florie . . ." Again she looked around, and Jazz imagined she was picturing Florie scrubbing the counters. "It was almost as if the thought of long, bare counters and freshly scrubbed pots and pans made the girl's day. Weird, huh?"

"She was a photographer," Jazz commented, and then because she didn't want Loretta to think that meant she thought Florie was inherently weird, she added, "Maybe the light reflecting off the metal appealed to her. Or the look of things when they were clean and orderly. With her eye for detail, who knows what kind of beauty she saw in everyday things."

Loretta's shoulders were as big as a semi. They sagged. "And now she's gone. Just like that."

Loretta's coffee cup was empty; Jazz's was not. She offered to get them both another cup anyway, and left Loretta alone long enough to compose herself.

When she came back, she handed Loretta the coffee. "What else can you tell me about her?"

"Florie?" Loretta pursed her lips. "She was a scholarship girl."

"That's not something we're supposed to talk about," Jazz reminded her, but had to ask, "How did you know?"

Loretta didn't sip her coffee, she took it in gulps. When she set down her cup, it was already half empty. "It's not like I'm telling tales or anything, and I'd never say it to anyone but you."

"Good thing. You know how Eileen feels about —"

"Yeah, yeah. I've been hearing that song for so many years, I've got all the words memorized. I'm only mentioning it because with Florie, well, it was so obvious. You know, she never had any money."

"For . . . ?"

"For nothing. Girl didn't have money for clothes. She didn't have money for makeup. Her books and her tuition and her uniform, sure, they were all included in her scholarship, but I'll tell you what, that girl didn't have two nickels to rub together for anything else."

The thought was like a punch to the gut. Jazz sat up. "You should have told —"

"You think Florie wanted word to get around about stuff like that?" Loretta shook her head. "Me and Florie, we handled it."

"Meaning?"

As if she was afraid someone might overhear, Loretta looked around and even though they were alone, she lowered her voice and leaned closer to Jazz. "Once in a while, I'd bring her some clothes. You know, when my girls didn't want them no more. Not that my girls and Florie had the same taste!" Loretta chuckled. "Oh, I could see it, all right. Sometimes I'd tell Florie to come into the kitchen when there was nobody around, and I'd give her a bag full of clothes and she'd look through it, and . . ." Her chuckle turned into a full-fledged laugh. "Oh, that girl could look real sour when she didn't like something!"

"But she took the clothes, anyway?"

Loretta nodded. "She did. And once or twice when she was here outside of school time for a dance or to watch some drama-club performance or whatever, I saw her wearing them, too. I think her parents, they don't have much."

Jazz thought back to her conversation with Larry and Renee, how they couldn't pay for a funeral, how Florie had recently asked them for money.

"You haven't . . ." It was Jazz's turn to trace a nervous pattern across the counter. "Florie didn't stop by recently to see you, did she?"

"As a matter of fact, she did. How did you guess?" Her hands on her knees, Loretta sat back. "Said she was in the neighborhood working on some project for school."

It was the first Jazz had heard there was something that brought Florie to Tremont. "Did she say what it was? Where it was?"

"I asked, but Florie, she wasn't interested in chatting. Showed up out of nowhere and left again just as fast."

"Just like that?"

Loretta looked down at the floor. "After she asked me for money. And it's not like I got no heart or anything," she added quickly. "But what the girl was asking . . ."

"What was she asking?"

"Ten thousand dollars." Even now, Loretta could hardly believe it. "I told her she was nuts. I mean, really, if she had asked for a month's rent, well, it would have been tough, but I would have come up with something. But ten thousand dollars! She might as well have asked for the moon."

So a few weeks earlier, Florie had asked her parents for money and when that didn't work, who knows who else she may have hit up. Was Loretta Hardinger her last-ditch effort? Jazz remembered what Florie told Larry and Renee when they, too, were unable to help. "And she said if you wouldn't help her, she'd get the money some other way."

"How did you know?"

"Just a guess," Jazz assured her. "Only, did she say what she needed the money for?"

"I asked. I mean, especially once she said how much she wanted. Can't nobody blame me for being curious."

"And Florie said what?"

"Blew me off. Just like that. Imagine, coming around hat in hand, then refusing to answer when I asked what the money was for. But then, by that time, I think she already knew there was no way I was going to help. How could I? Who's got that kind of money laying around?"

"So after you said no —"

"She just turned around and walked out. Gave me one of those little over-the-shoulder waves. You know, like the girls do. Like she'd see me another time. Only now she won't, will she?"

The last of the coffee in her cup was cold, but Jazz finished it anyway. She didn't want to offend Loretta, and besides, the bitter coffee helped wash down the lump in her throat. She'd already gotten off the stool and pushed it back into place when she thought of something Eileen had told her.

"Did you know?" she asked Loretta. "About Florie and Grace Greenwald?"

"You mean Little Miss Oil and Little Miss Water?" Loretta's expression was sour. "I knew they didn't get along."

"Do you know why?"

Loretta put both her hands to her waist, a Buddha in a white apron. "You think that

Greenwald girl is a suspect?"

Suspect.

It was a word Jazz had never considered, a concept that felt foreign. She was just asking questions, wasn't she? She was just looking to make sense of a senseless act.

And yet, Grace and Florie were enemies. They'd fought. Recently. And Florie was dead and Grace just might be . . .

"Do you think there's any chance Grace could have killed her?" she asked, breathless.

Loretta pressed her lips together, and when she blew out a puff of annoyance, her nostrils flared. "How did you get here?" she asked Jazz.

"Here? You mean how did I get the job here?"

Loretta nodded.

It wasn't a hard question, but it didn't have an easy answer. "I wanted to be a firefighter."

"Like your daddy."

"And both my brothers. My dad was all for it, but my mom . . ." Back when it all happened, there had been enough hard feelings. Jazz didn't need to bring them to the surface. She got rid of them with a shake of her shoulders. "Mom said having a husband and two sons in the department was enough for any woman. I was young and . . . I caved." It was as simple as that. "I went to community college, found out I enjoyed administration courses, worked in the office at a furniture store, then at a preschool."

Even though she hadn't meant it to, her expression must have revealed exactly what those two years at Little Tots were like, because Loretta grinned.

"That place was too noisy for me," Jazz confessed. "Too much wailing. Too much drama."

"And the fire department, that would have been nice and quiet and boring?"

Jazz grinned. "These days if I had to choose, I'd probably join the department no matter what Mom said. But if I had, I might never have time for the dogs. I started with search and rescue, because that's what my dad did. Then I moved to human-remains detection."

A shiver cascaded over Loretta's shoulders. "You don't need to say another word about that."

Jazz wasn't surprised by her reaction. Plenty of people weren't comfortable talking about what Jazz did in her free time, or the locked ammo box of human remains (bodies donated to science) she kept in a fridge in her garage.

Jazz looked over at Loretta. "How did you come to St. Catherine's?"

"The hard way." Loretta stood, and when she did, she towered over Jazz. She grabbed both Jazz's cup and her own from the counter and held them in one meaty hand. "Washing dishes, mopping floors. I was working over at that retreat house on the west side when I met Sister Eileen. We got to talking and she, well, you know the woman's mind works in mysterious ways. She offered me this job and I've never looked back."

"And we're lucky to have you." Jazz meant every word of it. "But what does that have to do with Florie and Grace?"

The tiny smile that played around Loretta's mouth wasn't so much about amusement as it was forbearance. "You know all about the Greenwald family. Grace's little sister, Dinah, is a sophomore. Their daddy is on the board of trustees. And their mother, she heads the big fall fund-raiser. Does everything from sell the tickets to hang the crepe paper."

"Yes, Mr. and Mrs. Greenwald are among our biggest supporters."

"Uh-huh."

And with that, Loretta turned and went

into her office. She closed the door behind her.

CHAPTER 6

She recognized the sound of Luther's husky barks when she was still down the street.

Squirrel, Jazz told herself.

UPS guy, pizza delivery nearby, cloud floating over the house.

Dogs were dogs, and dogs heard things and smelled things no human could imagine.

Luther was just being a dog.

Only from the sound of things, he was pretty serious.

Jazz hefted her tote bag up onto her shoulder and quickened her pace, crossing to her side of the street where Jefferson met the parking lot of the old Tremont School. Once upon a time, the building was the largest elementary school in Ohio, built to serve the needs of the immigrant population pouring into the area. These days it housed a Montessori school in one portion of the building and miles of empty hallways in the other. Not that Jazz was complaining. Usually the school crowd had come and gone by the time she got home from work, and that meant she and Manny had often gone to the empty parking lot to toss a ball around or work on training commands.

A mostly empty school was a good across-the-street neighbor.

Except for that afternoon, when Luther's rough, demanding barks pinged back at her from the brick walls like rifle shot.

Jazz got out her house keys and scrambled around her SUV parked in that most prized of Tremont real estate, a driveway. Back when row upon row of workers cottages had been built, there were few cars around. These days properties with driveways were golden, putting parking at the nearby restaurants and bars at a premium. Jazz never failed to thank her lucky stars that she not only had room for her car, but a tiny backyard where Manny used to romp, protected from the traffic out on the street. She rounded the SUV, headed for the back door, and just where the porch steps met the sliver of lawn in front of the garage, she stopped, stunned and disgusted at herself for letting it show.

As if he had every right to be there, Nick Kolesov strolled into the yard from the far side of the house. His hands were in the pockets of his pants. The knot of his green tie was loose. A breeze caught the front of his navy sport coat and blew it open to reveal the shoulder holster and gun he wore on his right side and the badge clipped to his belt.

"You are home!"

Jazz looked to the house, and yelled, "It's all right, Luther. Good dog!" before she turned her attention to Nick.

"What are you doing?" she asked.

"Your car is here. I figured you were home. I thought maybe you were avoiding me."

"So you decided the way to make me not avoid you was to creep around my yard and look in my windows?"

She was pretty sure she didn't even want to hear whatever excuse he was going to come up with, so she climbed the three steps to the back door. As hints went, it was about as unsubtle as they came.

Nick ignored it completely.

He stood at the bottom of the steps and eyed her on the pint-sized porch, his head tilted back, his eyes impossibly blue in the late-afternoon light.

"I wasn't home." She squeezed her eyes shut, annoyed at herself for even trying to explain. "I just got home. I walked to work."

"That explains the car. It doesn't explain the dog. Luther, right?"

"You looked in the windows!"

"Hey, I'm curious. Comes with the territory."

"And I've got to take Luther for a walk."

She unlocked the door and went inside for dog and leash, and whatever she was hoping, those hopes were dashed when she got back outside and Nick was still there.

"I'll come with you," he said.

"Of course you will."

"What's he doing here?"

"Luther?" Jazz looked down the leash. "Looks like he's peeing on the pansies Sarah brought over last week and insisted on planting even though she knows every living plant dies in my yard."

"Yeah, that, but I mean, what's he doing here?"

She'd planned to walk the other way, the longer way around the block, but at the sidewalk, she turned to her right. It wasn't fair to shortchange Luther and go back inside immediately, but she wasn't about to prolong this particular encounter with Nick, either.

"What do you want?" she asked.

"I was in the neighborhood." He side-stepped a broken bottle on the sidewalk. "I thought I'd stop by and see how you're doing."

"Really?" She thought about asking why he hadn't cared in over a year, but there was no use in pointing out the obvious. "I'm fine."

"Of course you are."

"If you expected me to be fine, why did you have to stop by to ask how I was?"

"Like I said —"

"Curious. Yes, I know."

They turned the corner. Here there were modest, working-class houses on both sides of the street, the slate sidewalks overshadowed by oaks and maples that in a few weeks would burst into shades of green after the long, dull winter. Like in other parts of the neighborhood, many of these houses had been scooped up by young professionals, painted in coordinated colors with names like slate and antique gold, sage and sand, decorated with seasonal flags and fountains and metal sculptures, and one of those caught the last of the afternoon light and winked at Jazz.

Some of the other houses along the street — like the one Jazz owned, which had once belonged to her grandparents — had been in Tremont families for generations. They might not be as color coordinated, their gardens weren't as pristine, but there was history in every board, and thinking about it always made Jazz feel like no matter how many millennials flooded in, Tremont would always be the same, rock solid and hardworking.

Luther stopped to sniff the trunk of a maple tree.

"Want to explain what you're doing here?" Jazz asked Nick.

"Working, of course."

"On Florie's case?"

"Oh, so now you're interested?"

She was. Too interested. Jazz reminded herself to cool her jets. There was nothing to be gained from Nick knowing she'd been asking questions. Especially since before she left school that afternoon, she'd sent an email and agreed on a time to get together with Grace Greenwald later that evening.

"Of course I'm interested." She kept her gaze on Luther, and when he spotted a cat across the street, she gave him a little tug, all the reminder he needed that what he was thinking was unacceptable. "I knew Florie. She went to school at St. Catherine's. She was on the cross-country team."

"That's why I thought I'd give you a

heads-up before tomorrow's paper comes out."

He pulled a folded piece of paper from his pocket and handed it to Jazz.

It wasn't the first photo she'd seen of Florie in the days since the murder. The story was on the front page of both Sunday's and Monday's *Plain Dealer.* By Tuesday, it had been relegated to the second page, along with a story about how the police were looking for leads and hoping for leads and following leads. Nick had been quoted once.

"We're making progress on the case."

Only something told her if they were, he'd have better things to do than lurk in her backyard.

The stories Jazz had seen in the last two days had all featured the same picture of Florie, the same one Jazz had found in the yearbook. This photo, the one he said would be in Wednesday's paper, was different — Florie in pallid makeup, her eyes rimmed with black, her lips painted purple, her nose pierced.

"Where did you get this article?"

"I've got connections."

Jazz didn't mean to do it, but she couldn't help herself. She glanced at the byline on the story. *Tamara Starks.*

She bit back the question she was tempted to ask about how connected the connection was, exactly, and skimmed the story instead.

Her eyes caught on a phrase and her head came up. "Cleveland Horror Film Festival? Florie worked for a horror film festival?"

"She did."

Her gaze slid back to the pretty face that was nearly unrecognizable beneath the makeup.

"Well, that explains how she looked, doesn't it?"

"It does."

"What did she do for them?"

"It was part-time, temporary work. The festival kicks off in a couple weeks, so until then, they're doing all sorts of promotional events. It's a low-budget organization, this is their first year, and they're actually going to have movies playing in theaters throughout the area. There's a skeleton staff, no pun intended, and Florie was what they called their 'brochure bitch.' It's what the guy at the festival told me! She handed out flyers and schedules, tried to spread the word."

"And she dressed the part." Luther pulled at the leash, and Jazz started walking again, thinking through the implications of what she'd just learned. "You think the clothes she was wearing were more of a costume than a fashion choice? Does that mean she was working the night she was killed?"

"Maybe you're the one who should be the detective." Nick didn't dole out compliments often, but Jazz knew better than to be waylaid by the warmth that curled through her insides at this one. Maybe he knew better than to expect her to; maybe that's why he stopped, reached into his pocket, and pulled out a photograph. When she stopped, too, he handed her the picture.

"That was taken by the cameras outside the casino downtown," he explained and pointed to the figure near the center of the picture. The photo was grainy, but Jazz clearly saw that in the midst of the crowds crossing Public Square, the four-block open plaza in the heart of the city, there was a slim woman dressed all in black, a streak of color like blood in her hair.

"Florie."

Nick nodded. "According to Parker Paul, the executive director of the festival, her job Saturday evening was to stake out Public Square and hand out as many brochures as she could. It makes sense that she'd be all dressed up."

"Which means she wasn't some kind of weirdo." For some reason the words were reassuring, though Jazz couldn't say why. Maybe she just wanted to remember Florie the way she'd been back in school, to think of her not as hungry and desperate as Loretta pointed out, not as strange and spooky as the newspaper wanted the world to believe, but as sweet and talented and funny.

"This picture proves she was on Public Square at . . ." Since Nick had already taken back the photograph, Jazz had no choice but to lean closer to him to get a look at the time stamp. She told herself there was no way the aroma of his aftershave — tobacco and cedarwood — could make her dizzy, and just to prove it, she breathed in deep and stayed strong. "Five fourteen. We know she was downtown then."

"And dead by the time you found her just a little before nine."

"So how did she get to Tremont?"

"She didn't own a car," he told her. "And so far, we haven't found anyone who loaned one to her."

"That means she took public transportation. That shouldn't be hard to check. She was young and pretty and she'd be tough to miss in that outfit."

"Exactly what I was thinking. But we canvassed the buses and the Rapid. Nada."

"Then she walked. It's what, about three

miles from downtown over to Tremont? Not exactly close, but she was young and fit. Although in boots with heels that high . . ." The thought made Jazz's feet ache.

"I wondered about that, too. I had a couple officers knocking on doors all day today. No one between here and there claims to have seen her."

"But she had to be somewhere. What did she do between leaving Public Square and showing up at that old building? And what was she doing there in the first place? I had a key. She —" Jazz thought back to Saturday night. "That door that was open at the back of the building? Do you think Florie got in that way? Seems weird that she'd even want to be in that building when there was nothing inside but dirt and decay."

"The media's going to make a big deal out of the horror connection," Nick said, sidestepping her questions in a way that said more than any real answer could. "You know how it is when it comes to these sorts of stories — the more sensational, the better. I was just wondering if maybe there was more to it for Florie than just working at the festival. Can you think of anything you saw Saturday night, any sign of . . . I don't know, something weird that would show she was doing more than just dressing the part for her job?"

"Pentacles painted on the walls? Black candles? Guys in hockey masks? No. There was just Florie. If there was anything else, your guys would have found it."

"Unless you didn't want them to."

She had started walking again and was just about to step off a curb, and Jazz froze and spun to face him. "You think I tampered with the crime scene?"

"I didn't say that."

"You didn't have to."

He scraped a hand through his hair. He'd gotten a trim since Saturday and it was, apparently, a natural and immutable law that even when he mussed it, his hair ended up looking as good as it had before he touched it. "You know how it is, I have to cover all my bases. I don't believe you'd ever do anything like that, but I've got to make a note on my report that I asked you about it. My lieutenant dropped a few heavy-handed hints. She thought —"

Jazz pinned Nick with a look. "She thought what?"

"She knows you work at St. Catherine's and I might have mentioned how much you love the place. She thought if you saw anything that connected Florie to something

that would shed a bad light on the school
—"

"Like what? We sacrifice chickens in the basement?"

"Hey, the woman's got a job to do. And so do I. You know what I mean."

"I know you can sometimes be a total jerk."

"I know it, too. Hey, it's one of my charms. At least I'm self-aware."

"So self-aware, you didn't think it was any big deal to come over here and accuse me of tampering with evidence."

"It was only for my report. Only so I can say I asked. So I asked. I actually came over here because the Cleveland Horror Film Festival has offices next to the ice-cream place over on Professor. Like I said, I was in the neighborhood and —"

"And you just stopped by to say hello and ask how I'm doing and insult me while you were at it. To question my professionalism and my ability to handle a crime scene."

"It's all part of my job."

"Yeah. Your job."

Her heart beating double time and her blood whooshing in her ears, Jazz broke into a run and, thinking it was all part of the fun, the dog loped along at her side. Nick's job had always been the problem. His job.

His long hours. His mule-headed commitment to finding the truth and giving perps their due. Sure, it was all admirable. It made him a sort-of superhero.

But it was hell on a relationship.

She was already back at her driveway, running a hand along Luther's back and fighting to catch her breath when she heard Nick call to her from across the street. "You know I didn't mean it that way. I have to get my ducks in a row."

"Your ducks are jerks. You're a jerk," Jazz muttered.

Nick trotted up the driveway and leaned against the SUV. "You know I didn't think it was possible that you touched anything. Hey, maybe I just wanted to see your reaction when I asked."

"Because you couldn't predict my reaction."

"Sure I could." A smile tickled the corners of his mouth. "I just like to get a rise out of you."

"It worked."

"It did. So now I can complete my report. I'm thinking of adding something like, 'When the witness was asked if anything at the scene was touched, her answer was —' "

"Hell no."

"Can I quote you?"

105

"Absolutely."

"And now that we've got that out of the way, can I apologize for having to ask? I was thinking of dinner tonight."

It was the second time since Saturday he'd tried to tempt her with food. With the gift of his precious time.

"I . . ." She swallowed down the words she was afraid would sound too much like *sure, why not.*

"I can't. I've got something to do. I'm meeting someone tonight."

"A date?"

Her sigh rippled the air. "One of the girls from school." It wasn't exactly a lie. Grace Greenwald had once been one of the girls from school.

"Then how about a rain check?"

She took the steps up to the back porch two at a time, the better to put some distance between herself and Nick and the past.

When she stuck her key in the door, she looked at him over her shoulder. "How about when hell freezes over?"

"Damn." One corner of his mouth thinned and he shook his head and followed her up the stairs. "Come on, Jazz. What we had, was it that bad?"

When she turned the key and shoved the

door open, her smile was hard-edged. "Even after all this time, you haven't figured it out yet, have you? And I thought you were a smart guy. Don't you get it, Nick? It wasn't that bad. It was that good."

CHAPTER 7

From what she'd heard from Eileen and Loretta at St. Catherine's, Florie Allen and Grace Greenwald were mortal enemies. The irony wasn't lost on Jazz. Years of picking and poking at each other in high school and both girls had ended up attending North Coast, Grace as a video major, Florie in photography.

Thinking it through — because it was better than thinking what an idiot she'd been to open up to Nick and point out what he should have known all along — Jazz did another turn through the area at North Coast where she and Grace had agreed to meet, the building where the photography majors each had a small cubicle studio that included a desk, filing cabinets, and half walls where they hung their work.

From the dizzying array of photographs displayed, she could see there was no lack of talent at the school.

There was, however, a lack of Grace Greenwald.

Arms folded over her chest and one foot tapping out an aggravated tattoo against the tile floor, Jazz took another look around at the groups of students huddled over their work, chatting.

No Grace.

She was just about to head over to where three girls were taking turns holding a framed photograph at arm's length and talking about things like perspective and color saturation when the doors closest to where she stood popped open and a young man with a showy head of dreadlocks rambled into the room. He wore skinny jeans, had a backpack slung over one shoulder, and had the sort of intent look on his lean face that told her he had someplace to be. It didn't keep her from stopping him.

"Excuse me, do you know Grace Greenwald?" she asked him.

"Grace? Sure." His fingers were long and slim and he used them to push his tortoiseshell glasses further up the bridge of her nose. "I just saw her downstairs."

Jazz exhaled, forcing away her irritation. "Oh, good. She's on her way."

"I don't think so." The kid slipped the backpack off his shoulder and set it on the

109

floor. "Grace said she was heading to Little Italy for dinner."

"But she can't be. We were supposed to meet tonight. Here."

He tucked his chin, the better to look at her over the rims of his glasses. "Do you know Grace? That girl does what she wants, when she wants. About three minutes ago, she told me what she wanted was linguini with clam sauce. My guess is you won't be seeing her anytime soon."

It meshed with Jazz's memories of Grace, a girl who'd never let things like the convenience of others get in the way of her own desires.

She chewed her lower lip, thinking through the problem. "You know Grace. Did you know Florie, too?" she asked the young man.

"Damn shame." He shook his head, and his dreads swept his shoulders and the crisp white cotton shirt he wore with a knitted red bow tie. "She had real talent."

"You're a photographer, too?"

He was young and canny as gifted kids so often are. Without missing a beat, he pulled a business card from his pocket and handed it to Jazz. "Khari Jemper," he said. "I specialize in portraits. If you ever . . ." He brushed one finger over the phone number and email address on the card. "I'm just starting out so I'm not too picky. I do weddings, baby pics, bar mitzvahs. Anything you need."

It brought up the memory of what Larry and Renee Allens' neighbor had told her. "Florie was taking photographs of one of the neighborhood kids," Jazz told him, then realized she needed to explain. "I knew her from high school."

He narrowed his eyes and studied her the way only an artist could. She had always thought her eyes were a little too close together, her nose a tad too small for a face as round as hers. Of course he would notice. Thank goodness she hadn't taken after her dad when it came to hair. Michael Ramsey had streaks of gray before he was forty. But maybe that had more to do with having three kids than it did with genetics. Still, Jazz wasn't delusional. When she looked in the mirror, she saw what Khari no doubt saw — the small lines at the corners of her eyes that weren't there even two years ago, the ones that surely told him she was older than Florie.

"I didn't go to high school with Florie." Since she knew Khari was trying to work out the math, she smiled. "I work there. And Florie . . . well, like I said, she was taking pictures of a neighbor's baby."

He wrinkled his nose. "She never said anything to me about it, but hey, when it came to sharing . . . well, you knew Florie. She could be really good at keeping secrets."

"Do you think that's what got her killed?"

Khari had large dark eyes, and they widened. "Oh, come on! You're making it sound like something out of some TV show and it was, what, a mugging or something, right? It had to be. Nobody purposely kills a girl like Florie."

Except somebody did.

Rather than make this young man uncomfortable facing the truth, Jazz turned the conversation in another direction. "Did everyone like her?"

His bottom lip caught between soldier-straight teeth, he considered the question. "We all pretty much get along."

"Even Florie and Grace Greenwald?"

His heartbeat of hesitation was enough to make her realize she'd caught him off guard. He knew it, too. "You heard about it, huh?" he asked.

"I've heard . . ." Jazz weighed her options and decided that in this particular case, dodging the truth might be the best of them. "I've heard a lot. About Florie and Grace. I know a lot from their high school days. But lately . . ."

"Lately." Khari whistled low under his breath. "Well, I can't say I know any of this firsthand, of course, but everyone around here is talking about it. Florie and Grace, they were working together. They were making a commercial. The video students were calling the shots. But Florie was in on the project, too. I heard she was looking to earn some extra credit."

The doors behind them swung open again, and Jazz and Khari stepped to the side and out of the way when a couple strolled through, their arms linked.

"What kind of commercial?" Jazz asked him.

"For that horror film festival."

"The one where Florie worked?"

"Yeah. That's what I heard. Tanya, she's the one who was the producer on the project, she told me Florie hooked the school up with the festival people, you know, so the students here could get some real-life experience and the festival people could get a commercial made without spending too much money. Everybody was so excited. Sounded like a blast."

From the tone of his voice, she knew she didn't need to ask. "It wasn't?"

"Well, I guess it would have been if Grace

wasn't on the team. Or if Florie hadn't been there to shoot stills."

Jazz could only imagine.

"They fought."

"Like the Jedi versus the Empire." Khari shook his head. "Tanya says it started up the moment they got to that old building in Tremont for the shoot."

Jazz's heart skipped a beat. "The building where Florie's body was found?"

"Place that's being turned into condos, right? Yeah, that's the one. I went along when Tanya and the others scouted some sites, so when I saw the pictures of the building online with the story about Florie, I recognized it right away."

"So she had a reason to be there." The words left Jazz on the end of a breath of disbelief. "Why?"

"Why? You mean why that building?" He lifted one shoulder. "The video team, they talked about shooting in a cemetery, but let's face it, that's pretty much the same old, same old. Then one day we were walking around Tremont and saw that old building and knew it would be perfect. Dark, dingy, falling down. I bet they got some great footage. It was creepy, all right." A shiver snaked over his slim shoulders. "When I found out that's where they found

114

Florie's body, it got even creepier."

"So what kinds of things did Florie and Grace fight about?" Jazz wanted to know.

"At the shoot? According to Tanya, everything! Grace was in charge of the lighting, and the first day, Florie bumped into one of the light stands and knocked it over. She said it was an accident."

"Was it?"

"Tanya didn't think so. Grace didn't, either. She went nuts on Florie."

"And Florie?"

"Went all nuts right back. It was all anyone around here could talk about, them sniping and arguing and messing with each other. Florie was there to take pictures the festival could use for their publicity campaign. And she'd step into the video shots. Or talk while they were filming."

"And Grace?"

"Just as bad." Khari's mouth twisted. "Made sure she messed up plenty of Florie's pictures. It didn't come to blows," he added quickly, just in case she got the wrong idea. "Not that I heard, anyway. But a couple times, the other students had to step between them and break it up. That commercial should have taken a day, maybe two, to shoot. Instead, what with all the interruptions and all the backbiting, they spent

115

like four days over there, and by the time it was all done, even the kids who are best friends couldn't stand to be in the same room with each other. An atmosphere like that, it's toxic. They took some time off. They regrouped. I hear things are good now. They're editing the commercial."

"When did all this happen?"

"When did they film?" Khari thought about it for a moment. "Last week. No, no, the week before. Remember how it was nice for a couple of days? That's when we went out and scouted locations. I know they filmed right after that because Tanya and me, we were supposed to grab dinner one evening and she was stuck at the shoot. She was really pissed when she missed dinner."

Khari's phone rang, and he pulled it from his pocket and checked the number, answered, and told the caller, "Wait a sec," before he turned back to Jazz.

"If you're looking for more information . . ." He scanned the room and pointed toward the far wall. "I saw Tate Brody over there earlier. He teaches in the video department. His students were the ones making the commercial."

Jazz thanked him and took off in the direction Khari indicated. She skirted a couple groups of students who were hard at work, rounded a corner, and slammed into a man who was just walking out of one of the studios.

"Sorry!" Automatically he put out a hand to keep Jazz from tumbling down.

Just as quickly she put a hand on his arm to keep him from falling.

They laughed at the awkwardness, dropped their hands, stepped back to give themselves a little breathing space.

"Are you Mr. Brody?"

He was fortyish, dressed in chocolate-brown pants and a red sweater that brought out the mahogany highlights in his curly hair and the day's stubble of beard that dusted his chin. He had a framed photo under one arm. His smile revealed a dimple in his left cheek. "Tate, please. Yes, I'm Tate Brody."

"I'm . . ." She stuck out a hand. "Jazz Ramsey. I work at St. Catherine's. I'm here about Florie Allen."

His grasp stayed firm, but his expression sobered. "My condolences. I haven't seen anything in the newspaper about a funeral or a memorial service. If you've heard —"

Thinking about what Eileen had heard from Larry and Renee when she told them the school would help with funeral expenses, Jazz slipped her hand from his. "I hear the family is doing something private. But we're planning a memorial at the school. Keep an eye on our Web site. I'm sure you're aware, the students and staff at school get to be like family. It's tough for everyone to have to go through something like this. That's why I stopped by this evening to talk to Grace Greenwald. She attended St. Catherine's, too."

"I saw her downstairs a while ago." He shifted the photograph from one arm to the other. Its back was to Jazz, brown paper with *FA* scrawled across one corner of it in purple marker. "She said she was going to dinner."

"Yeah. I'm sorry I missed her. But as long as I'm here . . ." Jazz looked over his shoulder and into the cubicle he'd just left. There was a piece of paper hanging above the desk scrawled in the same purple marker that was on the back of the picture. The sign declared the cubicle FLORIE'S PLACE.

"Is this where she worked?"

"Yes." He stepped back to allow Jazz a better view, but rather than settle for that, she went inside.

Like the other cubicles she'd seen, Florie's was small. The desk was empty except for a pack of eight-by-ten Pepto Bismol–pink envelopes decorated with white polka dots.

The top of the file cabinet had a stack of photography magazines on it. The half walls . . .

Jazz closed in on the pictures that hung there.

"We have a number of Florie's photographs at St. Catherine's," she told Brody while she looked over a black-and-white picture of a streaming waterfall. There was nothing dramatic about it — it wasn't stories high; there were no rocky cliffs anywhere in the shot. Still, Jazz was drawn to the way the water misted and fizzed around the cascade, the way it puddled around the ferns that grew along the shore. The light came from the right, above the trees that rimmed the falls, and here and there, sparkling bits of it reflected against the water, like shards of broken glass.

"She's even better than she used to be."

Behind her, she heard Brody make a sound that might have been assent. She turned to find him with his lips pressed into a thin line.

"They all have talent," he said. "They wouldn't be here if they didn't. But Florie . . . She wasn't one of my students, I'm in the video department. But I've seen her work. She had a lot of potential." He glanced over the rest of the pictures hanging above the desk, and Jazz did, too.

One of them was the portrait of an elderly African-American woman, her chin firm and her mouth set, her eyes staring into the camera in a way that said she'd seen things and she knew things and she'd never back down, not from anyone.

Another was a picture of a tabby kitten curled into a red-and-blue-plaid blanket.

There was a blank spot on the wall directly above the desk, and Jazz looked from it to the picture tucked under Brody's arm.

"Don't get the wrong idea." He held up the picture and flipped it over so Jazz could get a look. "Yeah. I just took this photo off the wall, but I have permission."

The picture was a sixteen-by-twenty-inch display of colors and textures framed in black wood. There was an image of what might have been a door in one corner, the brass numbers of the address a blur against the red paint. There was a car in the center of the photo. Or maybe it was an animal of some kind.

Jazz leaned nearer for a better look.

The entire picture was a mishmash of hallucinogenic colors, manipulated images, streaks of light, and smudges of body parts.

It was bewildering.

And amazing.

"Florie's?" she asked.

"She was experimenting with special effects and digital imaging. And I'm not stealing the photograph or anything. Just so you know," Brody added with an uncomfortable laugh. "I spoke with Florie's parents. I told them that of all Florie's projects, this was the one I thought was the most special, the one that said the most about her. They told me I was welcome to it. And the cops, they were here, but they say they're done with Florie's studio now."

Of course. Nick would never be so careless not to come by and have a look.

"So you're . . ." Brody tucked the photograph back under his arm. "You're here for . . ."

"Actually, I just wanted to touch base with Grace. After what happened to Florie . . ." She let it rest at that.

He made a sound that was half grunt, half derision. "I doubt you'll find Grace is especially broken up about Florie's death. If you know Grace, you know she thinks first, last, and always about Grace."

"And what about the commercial the students were filming?"

He rolled eyes the color of November storm clouds. "You know about that, huh? I wasn't there for most of it. Didn't want to

121

be. I wanted the students to take charge and make their own decisions and work it out for themselves. Then I heard what was happening between Grace and Florie, and I'm afraid I finally had to step in. If I didn't, I have a feeling they'd still be there, duking out every frame of that video."

"I'll watch for it on TV." Over her shoulder, Jazz offered him a smile, then moved on to examine a photo of a champagne cork flying from a bottle, sprinkling the air with bubbles.

"It's a happy picture," she said.

"Florie used to be a happy girl."

She spun to face him. "Used to be?"

His mouth twisted. "I don't suppose it matters now. If Florie was still alive . . ." The words caught, and he collected himself. "She was . . ." Brody cleared his throat. "She wasn't coming back to school next semester."

This was news. "Did she say why?"

"No secret there." Brody scratched a hand through his beard. "Her grades were off. She'd lost her scholarship."

Which was why Florie had gone, hat in hand, to her parents and Loretta Hardinger.

She remembered what Loretta had said, about how Florie wouldn't want anyone to know how desperate she was, so she didn't mention it. What difference did it make now, anyway?

"She was always such a good student," Jazz said instead.

Brody nodded and a curl of dark hair tumbled onto his forehead. He brushed it back with one hand. "It's a small school so, naturally, we all know each other. These last months, I couldn't help but notice that Florie seemed . . . preoccupied."

"Because of her job with the horror film festival?"

"I doubt it. She told me . . ." As if the weight of the memories it carried were too much to bear, he set Florie's photo down. "Florie and I would sometimes chat and we always got along. Her advisor knew it and he thought maybe I could get through to Florie, so he asked me to talk to her. I met with Florie a number of times during the semester. I saw what was happening to her grades and I thought if I kept in touch, if I checked in with her now and then . . . well, I didn't want things to get out of control. I knew she was working for the film festival, but when I asked if it was taking too much of her time, she insisted she was only doing a few hours a week."

"So there must have been some other reason her grades were off."

"And I'm afraid I have no idea what it was. She never said. But then, girls like Florie, they have their secrets."

It wasn't the first she'd heard much the same words, but before she had a chance to consider them, Brody bent to retrieve the photo. "I do know it's a shame she'll no longer be able to share her talent with the world."

Another look at the array of photos on the wall and Jazz had to agree. There was insight in Florie's work, a sort of sixth sense that let the observer look beyond the subject, into the subject. Like looking into the eyes of the elderly African-American woman.

Ready to leave, Jazz surveyed the cubicle one last time and stopped, caught by a small square of paper pinned on the wall near the desk. It was something torn from a newspaper, its edges frayed and jagged, and from this distance, she couldn't see much more of it than the letters in boldface type across the top.

Looking for a Divorce Attorney?

"Ms. Ramsey?"

Jazz snapped out of her surprise just in time to see Brody step back to allow her out of the cubicle. She thanked him for his time and headed to the door, one question pounding through her brain.

Why would Florie Allen need a divorce attorney?

CHAPTER 8

Tanya was short, skinny, and as pale without makeup as Florie had been with it troweled on. When Jazz left the building, she and Khari were outside smoking.

Jazz closed in on them as soon as Khari waved from over by a bike rack in front of the building, pointed down to the girl at his side, and called out, "Tanya!"

"You supervised the video shoot," Jazz said as soon as she was close enough. "The commercial for the horror film festival."

Tanya took a drag on her cigarette, sucked in a lungful of smoke, and released it from one corner of her mouth in a stream that frothed like hot breath on a cold day. "I was the producer. Yeah." Another puff and she dropped the butt and stomped on it with one black-and-white Converse Chuck Taylor.

"What can you tell me?"

When Tanya wrinkled her nose, the stud

in it winked at Jazz. "It was a pain in the ass."

"Because of Grace and Florie."

"She knows all about it." Khari finished his cigarette, too, and went over to a tall cylindrical receptacle where he snuffed it out and discarded it. "This lady, she knows how they were fighting."

"Then there's nothing else to say." Tanya shrugged. "It was ugly, and I'm glad it's over."

"But you're still working on the commercial."

"We're editing." She dug a lip gloss out of her purse and uncapped it. "And without Florie around, let me tell you, it's a breeze. It better be. The commercial starts airing next week and we need to finish up."

"I just wondered . . ." Jazz's shrug was a mirror of the one Tanya had just given her. There was still so much she didn't understand. Like if Grace could possibly be involved in Florie's murder. And the ad she'd seen pinned to the wall in the studio upstairs. "Was Florie ever married?"

Tanya laughed. "I would have heard about that. Especially since I know she had her eye on my man Khari here." She wound her arm through his. "What do you think?" she asked him and bumped his hip with hers.

"Was some married chick hitting on you?"

He grinned. "Hardly. In fact, there was a whole group of us sitting around one day talking about things like life after graduation, and Florie, I remember how she said that from her experience, she'd never seen anything good about marriage. She swore she was never getting married."

Tanya smeared on the gloss and tucked away the tube. "Not that anyone here knew all that much about Florie, anyway. She wasn't around much lately."

"Where do you think she was?"

"I can't say." Tanya made a face. "Grace is my roommate and when you're friends with Grace . . ."

"You can't be friends with Florie." Jazz didn't need her to explain. "Do you know if Florie lived on campus?"

Tanya shook her head. Her hair was the color of corn silk, long and straight and shiny in the light that oozed down from above the building's main entrance. "She shared a house somewhere, not with anyone from here at school."

"Did she have a boyfriend?"

"That's what that cute cop wanted to know." Grinning, she slanted Jazz a look. "You work with him?"

"No. But I know him. Well, sort of."

"He got a girlfriend?"

Jazz let go a sigh that was too revealing. "Believe me, you don't want to go there."

"And he'd never treat you as good as I do!" Since he knew she wasn't serious about Nick, Khari wrapped an arm around Tanya's shoulders. "I'm springing for falafel tonight. Tanya . . ." He gave Jazz a wink. "Tanya loves falafel."

"So Nick . . . er . . . Detective Kolesov, did he ask about the building where you shot the commercial?"

A chill breeze whipped across the plaza, and Tanya leaned in closer to Khari. "Sure. He wanted to know all about our production schedule. You know, when we started filming, when we finished."

"You were done before last Saturday, right?"

"Well, mostly."

Jazz perked up. "You weren't?"

When Tanya and Khari started walking, Jazz fell into step beside them. "Our work was done," Tanya said. "At least we thought so. But Brody, he's so cool! He's got a great eye and a real feel for what's going to work and what isn't. He loved the footage we got, but he suggested we shoot some B roll. B roll, that's —"

"The extra film that's edited into a video

to show different scenes and try to make things more interesting." Jazz felt self-conscious explaining herself to kids who slept and ate and breathed their art. "I took visual arts as an elective in college."

"Yeah, well . . ." Clearly an elective in visual arts didn't carry much weight with Tanya. "Brody thought B roll would help. You know, it would add a little more atmosphere, make things a little darker, a little spookier."

"Was he right?"

The look she shot at Jazz made Tanya look years older and wiser than she was. "He's the one who's going to grade us at the end of the semester, does it matter?"

They stopped at the curb, waiting for the light to change.

"So you shot B roll."

"We didn't." The light turned green and they crossed the street together. "Brody's got a heart, you know? Not like some of these other instructors who keep piling on the work. He looked at what we had on Friday, and that's when he suggested the B roll. He also said he was sure we had better things to do on a weekend, so he offered to do it himself."

"Tate Brody shot the B roll last Friday?"

They were outside the Falafel Café, and

Khari paused, his hand on the door. "Not Friday," he said. "It was Saturday."

"And he shot the B roll —"

"In the same building where we shot the footage for the rest of the commercial," Tanya said. "The one where they found Florie's body. I told the cop that."

And Jazz was sure Nick was plenty interested.

Rather than mention it, she dug a little deeper. "That cop, he was probably thinking what I'm thinking. Florie wasn't a video student. She had no reason to be there."

Khari and Tanya exchanged looks.

"Maybe not officially," Khari conceded. "But she was there. I know it for a fact because I saw her leave her studio that afternoon, and she told me that's where she was going after she worked her film festival job. She told me to make sure I mentioned it to Tanya. You know, because she figured Tanya would tell Grace. And Florie, she wanted them both to know Brody had asked her to come along and shoot some stills and use them in the publicity campaign. She was trying to get to Tanya and Grace. You know, by showing them that Brody had singled her out."

Khari and Tanya went inside the restaurant, and Jazz continued on to her car, wondering about the divorce attorney, the B roll, Grace, and why the professor had never bothered to mention that he'd been with Florie the night she was murdered.

Before she got to the car, she stopped and wondered something else, too.

By all accounts, Florie was strapped for cash, and she still paid her parents' neighbor to take pictures of homely, gooey baby Lalo. And yet . . .

Jazz's sigh rippled the cool night air.

After all that trouble and all that money, there wasn't one single picture of Lalo in Florie's studio.

"Maybe he killed her!" Only Sarah could say something so horrifying and do it with a smile. Her eyes gleamed, and her nails — painted a luscious shade of mango — tapped out an excited rhythm against the mug she cradled in both hands. "Maybe that's why that video instructor never said anything about how he was with Florie the night she died."

"Seems a little too easy, don't you think?" Jazz counted down the seconds five, four, three, two, one. . . . The last bell rang and a moment later, the hallway outside her office echoed with footsteps and high-pitched voices. The school day was officially over, and she sat back and watched the girls in their gray-and-navy-plaid skirts and powder-blue blouses stream past her open door. "Besides, you don't think Nick would have let a fact like that get by him, do you? If I found out Brody was here in Tremont on Saturday, you can bet your bottom dollar Nick knows it, too. If it meant anything, he would have done something about it by now."

"Like arrest this Brody character."

"He's not exactly a character." Jazz thought back to her talk with Brody. "He's friendly, he's good-looking. You know, all artsy-fartsy the way you creative types can be." She grinned at her friend. "The kids . . . well, Tanya, anyway, she couldn't say enough nice things about him."

"Which doesn't mean he's not the killer."

"Which means . . ." Annoyed at herself for feeling defensive about the inquiries she'd been making and more defensive than ever because of it, Jazz got up and closed her door so she could change out of her black pants and lightweight peachy sweater and into black capri-length leggings. She tugged a red T-shirt over her head with ST. CATHERINE'S PANTHERS written on it in yellow block letters. "What it means is Nick will take care of it. Nick always takes care of everything."

Sarah turned in her seat, the better to frown at Jazz over the rim of her tea mug. "He didn't take care of you."

"It wasn't his job to take care of me. It was . . . it is my job to take care of me."

Sarah rolled her eyes.

On the way back to her desk, Jazz gave her a pat on the shoulder. "I'm good, Sarah. You know I'm good."

"You were good when Nick wasn't around. Now that he's back —"

"Except he isn't." Jazz hadn't told Sarah she'd found Nick in her yard when she got home from school two days earlier. At the time she figured it would spare her this exact conversation.

"Nick's doing his thing and I'm doing mine. And that's that." She smoothed her pants over a hanger and folded her sweater. "I'm just asking some questions, just trying to get some answers so I can put the whole thing behind me. What Nick's doing . . . well, that's a whole different thing."

Jazz dropped into her desk chair and slipped on sport socks and sneakers.

"Kind of the wrong season for cross-country, isn't it?" Sarah asked.

She was right. Cross-country was a fall sport. "Trying to make sure the girls on the team stay active and don't lose interest over the summer."

"This time of the year, that's a lost cause. All they can think about is prom." Sarah let out a groan that ended in a good-natured laugh. "Oh God, do you remember your prom? I remember satin and ruffles and big shoulders and bigger hair. If my boys ever find my prom pictures, they'll tease me about them until I'm in the nursing home."

"I had fun at my prom." Jazz double-tied her shoelaces. "Except now . . ." She gave it a moment's thought, then dismissed it as unimportant. "I don't even remember the name of the guy I went with. Kevin. Kyle. Connor?"

"Not the love of your life, eh?"

It brought up an interesting point. "Who do you suppose was the love of Florie's life?"

Sarah pursed her lips. "I chaperoned the year of her senior prom. I don't remember her being there."

Maybe because she couldn't afford a dress.

It was another of Florie's secrets better left unspoken, so Jazz didn't mention it.

"If Nick knows about Florie being in the neighborhood with Brody to film B roll last Saturday, I wonder where he's going with the information."

"He didn't tell you?"

Jazz locked her desk drawers and gathered her things so she could take them down to the gym. "When would he have done that?"

"You haven't talked to him?"

She smiled around the lie. "I haven't. Now if you'll get out of my office . . ."

She was saved from booting Sarah out into the hallway by a sharp rap on the door.

"Matt! Come on in! You're right on time, I was just going down to the gym."

Matt Duffey was dressed as informally as Jazz in jeans, sneakers, and a golf shirt striped with gold and a brown the same dark-chocolate shade as his buzz-cut hair.

When he hurried over to give Jazz a quick hug, he stripped off his Ray-Ban Aviators. "I was afraid I'd get here too early and have to wade through a sea of teenage girls."

"Matt . . ." Jazz motioned toward Sarah. "This is Sarah Carrington. She teaches art here. Matt is —"

"Very happy to meet you." He closed in on Sarah, took her hand, and smiled in a way he never smiled at Jazz. But then, Matt was a firefighter and she'd known him forever. He was a little older than Hal and Owen, stationed in a different part of town, but she'd always thought of him like another brother. When Jazz saw the way Sarah smiled at Matt — a little too widely, a little

136

too bright — she wondered why she'd never thought to introduce them before.

"Matt's doing a workshop for the cross-country team," she explained. "On orienteering."

"Jazz's idea," Matt conceded. "She thought if the girls got involved in an outdoor activity it would keep them active over the summer."

"And if they learn to take care of themselves outdoors, they'll have some confidence if they should ever get lost during a race," Jazz said. "Then Matt won't have to get Buddy and go looking for them."

The confused expression on Sarah's face didn't last long. "Let me guess, Buddy is a dog."

"Search and rescue," Matt told her.

Jazz smiled at the memory. "My dad loved Buddy."

"And Buddy loved your dad because your dad always had the best dog treats. I think, of all of us, Buddy was the saddest the day your dad retired Big George and stopped coming to the weekly trainings."

Big George was a chunky mixed breed with bad breath and poor social skills. Thanks to Michael Ramsey's patience and training, he was also the finest search-and-rescue dog Jazz had ever had the privilege to watch work.

"George is as happy as a clam," she assured Matt. "He sleeps on Mom's couch and slobbers on everyone who gets close. He's enjoying retirement."

"You'll have to bring him out to training some time. Buddy would love to see him. And speaking of loving to see someone . . . ." He turned his thousand-watt smile back on Sarah. "Do art teachers like to get out?"

She was not a giggler, which was why Jazz paid attention when Sarah's voice suddenly took on a little lilt. "Are we talking hiking through the woods or something a little more civilized?"

"Hiking through the woods is good, but if martinis are more your thing, there's this place right down the street and —"

"All right, you two." Grinning, Jazz waved her hands to get their attention. "Matt's got a workshop to teach."

He had the good sense to at least look repentant, but that didn't mean he was about to give up. "Compass work, map reading. I hear art teachers are really good at that sort of thing."

"Oh, no!" Before Sarah could say anything that would ratchet up the flirting, Jazz grabbed her arm, hauled her out of the chair, and turned her toward the door.

"Sarah's too much of a distraction. She's not allowed in the workshop."

"Fine." Sarah knew how to play the game. When Matt wasn't looking, she raised her eyebrows in a way that said she was interested. "I'll just go home and read about orienteering," she said, heading for the door. Once she was there, she looked at Matt over her shoulder. "That way we'll have something to talk about over those martinis."

He was still smiling when Sarah left.

"Why didn't you tell me you had a friend that gorgeous?" he wanted to know. "I can't believe I've never met her before!"

Jazz couldn't believe it, either. "Well, she was in Europe with one of our overseas study groups when Dad died," she told Matt. "So she wasn't at the funeral. And I guess . . ." She shook her head. "I guess it just never happened."

"Well, kiddo, you should have made sure it happened. She's great!"

"She's got kids."

"I like kids."

"She's a vegan."

"I can be ecumenical."

"You have a lousy track record with women."

Matt was short and compact. He crossed his arms over his broad chest and pursed his lips. "I do. But she's the one who will make me change my ways. I can feel it in my bones. That's why you're going to give me her phone number."

"Not until I ask her if it's all right."

One corner of his mouth pulled tight. "I knew you were going to say that."

"So . . ." Jazz gathered her things and let Matt walk out of the office before her. Eileen was gone for the afternoon, off at a meeting of community leaders, and Jazz locked the door behind her. "What's up?"

"The usual. You? No. Wait." They were in the hallway near the freshmen lockers, and Matt stopped. "Florentine Allen. I read about it in the papers."

"You remember her?"

"From cross-country, sure. We did that first-aid class for them, remember? When I heard the name, it didn't ring any bells, but then in the newspaper, I read that she was a photographer and they showed her school picture and then I remembered. The news stories, they're making it sound like she turned into some kind of freak."

"She was working for a horror film festival." The thought of how the media twisted a story to make it more interesting didn't sit well with Jazz. "The clothes and the makeup, they were all part of her costume.

I saw some of her recent work. She was as talented as ever. She wasn't a weirdo."

"And I didn't mean to bring up a sore subject." He offered a one-sided smile. "I gave Hal a call when I read the kid went to school here. He said you're the one who found her."

Jazz looked away. "I'm all right."

"I'm sure you are. Let me guess, your mom brought food."

She was grateful to him for lightening the mood, and they continued on down the hallway toward the gym. "She made soup. You know my mom!"

"I know finding a body isn't easy. If you need to talk —"

Jazz pushed through the gym doors and stopped. "Oh my gosh, Matt. I'm sorry. I forgot. I shouldn't have, but I did. You found Darren. After . . ."

They both knew the details and they didn't need to bring them out into the spring sunshine that spilled through the windows high up on the walls of the gym. Darren Marsh was a young firefighter who'd committed suicide three years earlier at the station where both he and Matt worked. When Darren hadn't shown up for dinner, Matt went looking for him. Even though it was clear there was no hope for Darren,

Matt had administered CPR. He'd continued it, desperately, frantically, until his fellow firefighters finally pulled him away.

"I'm sorry." Heat rushed into Jazz cheeks. "Here I am acting like I'm the only one in the world who's ever found . . ."

"A dead person. You can say it. And hey . . . you aren't acting like that at all. You're not whining. But then, you wouldn't. I asked how you were, you told me you're doing all right. I believe you. Only . . ." Matt looked her in the eye. In the weeks after her dad's death, she'd depended on him to do her thinking for her, to help her dodge the media that always seemed to be waiting outside her parents' home, and to navigate through the despair and anger and grief that had threatened to swallow her whole. Matt was just far enough outside the circle of the family to listen and offer advice objectively, and just close enough to understand. He was dependable and honest and loyal to a fault.

"After what happened with Darren, I saw this shrink over on the east side," he said. "Now don't go brushing me off," he added quickly, because of course that was exactly what she was going to do. She was going to remind him she was fine. She was going to lie about how she wasn't having trouble sleeping. She wasn't going to tell him she'd been asking questions about Florie's life and Florie's death because finding the answers was the only thing that was going to bring her peace.

Matt touched his forehead to hers. "When you're ready, I'll give you his number."

"When I'm ready . . ." She backed away from him. There was no use giving the girls already gathered in the gym something to gossip about. "When I'm ready, I'll let you know."

"Good enough for me."

"Only, Matt . . ." Matt moved the way he did everything else, in rapid, efficient steps that showed the world he didn't have the time or the patience to mess around. He'd already started toward the group of girls waiting on the other side of the gym when Jazz latched onto his arm.

"You're right about Florie," she said. "She was a good kid. So how does it make any sense, Matt? How does a good kid end up dead in an abandoned building?"

CHAPTER 9

To Jazz's way of thinking, there was something a little off-kilter about the offices of a horror film festival being right next door to a place with a sign that featured a cone topped with a scoop of hot-pink ice cream.

But then maybe that's why the festival people chose what had been an empty storefront on Professor Avenue to house their offices. Warped sense of humor? Juxtaposition of cheerful and carefree with creepy-crawly? Jazz couldn't say. She only knew that she had fifty minutes before she had to get back to school and she had to make the most of her lunch break.

Standing across the street, her gaze moved from that pink ice cream outside one building to the larger-than-life poster in the front window of the other, a poster that featured a blue-skinned man dressed in black and silver who had claws for fingernails and pointed teeth. Creepy-crawly, sure, but she crossed the street anyway. The sign taped to the front door, CLEVELAND HORROR FILM FESTIVAL, ENTER IF YOU DARE!, also advised that, if she dared, she had to go around to the back to get in.

She went to the right, down an alley so narrow she needed to sidle along, her back to the tall wooden fence that marked off the boundaries of the outdoor patio of the bar next door. It was Friday and the party crowd had started early. She heard glasses clink, smelled cigarette smoke.

Like so much of Tremont, the film festival building was old and built of red brick. At least on this side of it, there were no windows. Up ahead, where the three-story building ended, there was a little more room to move, a little more space to breathe. She stepped into it, turned to her left, and caught her breath.

The man standing there not six inches from her reminded her of the monster on the poster out front. His eyes were rimmed with black. His cheeks and his nose and his left eyebrow were pierced. His earlobes were plugged with wooden discs the size of pennies. He was dressed in black and, though it was a warm afternoon and Jazz had left her jacket back at St. Catherine's, he was swaddled in leather — boots, pants, jacket.

A tattoo of an octopus crawled from the scooped neckline of his black T-shirt, its tentacles reaching up and around his neck and nearly meeting the tattoo on his left cheek, a hand, inked in black. Like the permanent mark of a punishing slap.

"What do you want?"

She was so mesmerized by the way the sun glinted off his shaved head, it took her a moment to remember.

She poked a thumb over her shoulder toward the street. "The sign up front says to come around to the back."

If it was a test, she apparently passed.

He took a step back and, instinctively, Jazz let go a breath she hadn't realized she'd been holding and, with a smile, did her best to chase away the chill that snaked up her back.

"I hoped I could talk to someone from the festival about Florie Allen. I've heard she worked here."

His eyes were nearly as dark as his clothing, his gaze as pointed as the bits of metal in his cheek. "What about her?"

She remembered what Nick had told her about the festival. "Are you Parker Paul, the man in charge?"

The man with the tats chuckled, the sound low and rumbling, like thunder.

"Yeah, Paul, he can tell you about Florie. He's inside."

She stepped around the man, ridiculously relieved when she found the back door open, went into the building, and closed the door behind her.

She did her best to convince herself that she stood still for a minute so she could let her eyes adjust to the lack of light there in the back hallway, but she'd never been a very good liar. She reminded herself that she'd never judged people by their looks, that just because the guy outside looked scary didn't mean he was. But that didn't slow the sharp rap of her heart inside her ribs. She took a quick look over her shoulder just to make sure the door behind her stayed shut and went in search of the film festival offices.

The way she remembered it, the building had once been — back when she was a kid and those kinds of things still existed in neighborhoods — a shoe store. Following the sounds of fingers on a keyboard, she ignored the stairway that led to the upper floors and walked through what must have been, then and now, a storage room. No more Keds. No more saddle shoes. These days, the dark, cavernous room was crammed with things like mannequins without heads, stringy phony spiderwebs, and foam gravestones where leering skulls were frozen in eternal, gaping smiles.

What looked like a body laid out on a board turned out to be a dressmaker's dummy wearing a black cloak. Eager to get away from it and the way it made her think of Florie, Jazz stepped through a curtained doorway and from the gloom into the light that spilled from the front display windows. There, the same poster of the same monster that glared at passersby outside glared fiercely at her from the wall on her left. Directly in front of it, a woman with a gray bouffant and blue jeweled glasses, pointed at the top corners, tapped frantically at her keyboard.

"Hi!"

The woman looked up, but only long enough to frown. "I don't suppose you're from the Geek Squad, are you?"

Jazz stepped closer to the woman, whose computer sat on a red card table that tilted slightly to the left. There was a plastic axe on the floor at her feet, its blade coated in fake blood, and there was a life-sized pressboard coffin behind her. "Sorry. Having problems?"

The woman pounded the keys another time. "Our mailing list is stuck inside this damned thing and I can't get it out. It's frozen." Just for good measure, she thumped the keyboard a few more times.

"Maybe if you just let it . . ." Jazz swallowed the advice. It was clear the woman wasn't going to listen. Instead, she said, "I'm looking for Parker Paul."

The woman leaned forward, the better to scowl at her computer screen, at the same time she raised one hand long enough to wave in the general direction Jazz had just come from. "Upstairs. First door on the right."

Jazz didn't bother thanking her, but went through the back storage room, her footsteps in counterpoint to the clacking from up front. In another minute, she was upstairs and outside a closed door with a piece of paper taped to it. This one did not instruct her to enter if she dared. Instead, it simply said EXECUTIVE DIRECTOR.

She knocked, and heard a hurried "Come on in" before the same voice said something else, lower and quieter.

She found Parker Paul behind a desk, his cell phone in one hand. He raised a finger to tell her "Just a minute," and continued on with his conversation.

"It's like I told you, Veronica. Publicity, publicity, publicity."

Whatever Veronica said in reply, Paul's bushy eyebrows lowered over his eyes like woolly bear caterpillars settling in for a long winter nap. "It's too good an opportunity to pass up." His voice was sweeter now, more melodic. "I've got the passes for you, and I promised you an exclusive interview with Ralph Remington, didn't I? Heck, Veronica, he's the scariest dude to come out of Hollywood since that *It* clown. We're lucky he's going to be here for opening night. The interview will make a great feature."

Paul listened for another moment. "You'll run with the story I sent over this morning?" A smile cut across his wide, unremarkable face. "You're a doll! I knew you'd see it my way."

Still grinning, he ended the call and sat back, satisfied, in a chair that squeaked. "Let me guess, you're a reporter."

"Publicity, publicity, publicity." She echoed what he'd said to Veronica. "I know how important that can be. It can't be easy getting a film festival off the ground."

"You got that right." He sat up and his chair protested. "What can I do for you? No! Wait! You want to know all about Florentine Allen, right? About her association with all that is dark and macabre."

Jazz's stomach went cold. "That's what

you were talking about? On the phone just now? You're using Florie's murder to launch some sort of PR campaign?"

Paul was a man of fifty or so, short and stocky. He stood and smoothed a hand over a beige shirt, a rounded stomach, and a gray tie dotted with tiny black bats. "What do you want to know about her? I mean other than about her work with us here at the festival and all that is monstrous and terrible?"

It was a shame there was no guest chair in Paul's office. Jazz's knees were suddenly weak. Her stomach bunched and she was just as glad she hadn't had a chance to eat lunch. "You're the one who gave the newspapers that picture of Florie in her goth makeup."

"What can I say?" His shrug was nonchalant. "It was one of the shots we're using on the brochure." There was a stack of them on his desk, and he handed one to Jazz. "You know the old saying, there's no such thing as bad publicity."

The front of the festival brochure featured the poster she'd seen downstairs. The inside listed the movies (*Creature from the Black Lagoon, Scream, The Exorcist,* and others) and the times and theaters where they'd be shown. The back . . .

She flipped the brochure over and caught her breath at the sight of Florie's picture staring up at her. Yeah, she was in costume. And she was wearing makeup. And there was purple lipstick on her lips and purple eye shadow smeared over both her eyes. But . . .

"She was just a kid."

Even to her own ears, Jazz's voice sounded small and wounded.

Maybe Paul noticed. He squeezed out from behind the desk and went over to the windows that looked out at the street, and he refused to meet her eyes. "Did you tell me who you are and why you are here?"

"You didn't ask. You were too busy gloating about your PR coup."

He turned and leaned against the windowsill, his arms crossed over his chest. "It's a tough world out there. For any business. It's even harder for anything that has to do with the arts."

Jazz thought about the phony axe and coffin downstairs, the mannequins whose heads had been lopped off. "Are horror movies art?"

"The good ones are." Paul wiggled those caterpillar eyebrows. "They get our blood racing and our pulses pounding. They heighten our senses. You know how it is, you're watching a scary movie and suddenly you're listening a little more closely for every sound around you. You're straining your eyes to see through the dark. Hey!" He cocked his head and studied her. "Aren't you writing any of this down?"

"I'm not a journalist, Mr. Paul. I'm a friend . . . I was a friend of Florie's." Sure, she was a lousy liar. That didn't mean she couldn't give it a try. "Her parents asked me to stop in." Lie number one. "They knew she was working for the festival." Lie number two, because Larry and Renee seemed oblivious to the details of their daughter's life. "And they're anxious to get a more complete picture of what she might have been doing that last day. That's why they sent me." Lie number three, and it was a biggie. Jazz swallowed around the realization and went right on. "I was hoping you might be able to help."

That, at least, was the truth, and buoyed by it, she looked Parker Paul in the eye. "Can you?"

He pushed off from the windowsill and crossed the room to where there was a Keurig machine set up on a table that didn't match his desk. "Coffee?" he asked her.

She shook her head. "Florie did work for the festival that afternoon. She handed out brochures on Public Square. That was before she went to Tremont, where her body was found."

"Yeah, lucky for us, huh? Otherwise she wouldn't have been wearing her costume. Hey. Hey!" When Jazz stepped forward, her arms at her sides and the brochure in her right hand crumbled in her fist, Paul automatically took a step back. "I don't mean to sound callous."

"But you do. You are."

"I'm just trying to make some good out of a bad situation, you know?"

"Tell that to Florie's parents."

He rubbed a finger alongside his nose. "I guess . . ." His coffee was ready, and he grabbed his mug and took it back to his desk and sat down. Maybe he felt more comfortable with the width of the desk between him and Jazz, because while he sipped the coffee, he raised his brown eyes to hers.

"I never thought of it that way," he admitted. "I mean, I never thought about how there are people like Florentine's parents, people like you who —"

"Care?"

"It's not like I don't," he insisted. "But you've got to see it from my point of view.

154

I've got people depending on me. Laverne —"

"The woman downstairs?"

He nodded. "And Billy DeSantos. You might have met him. He likes to hang around out back when we're not busy." Just thinking about Billy made Jazz feel uneasy. She lectured herself. About tolerance. About not judging people by their looks. But even that wasn't enough to make her skin stop crawling.

"They're all I've got in the way of staff right now," Paul explained. "At least until I hire somebody else to do what Florentine was doing. They're handling a lot of the grunt work, and heck, if it wasn't for me, if it wasn't for the festival, Laverne, she wouldn't be paying her rent, and Billy . . ." Maybe Jazz wasn't the only one unsettled by Billy's black leather and studs. Paul jiggled his shoulders. "That guy loves horror like no one I've ever met."

"Great makeup."

"Oh, that's not makeup. That's how he always looks. But hey, what can I say? He's my go-to guy. You know, when I have questions about anything to do with blood and gore."

"So Florie's reputation and talent, her memory, they get sacrificed on the altar of making Laverne's rent and Billy's . . . what?"

"It's not just them." Paul slugged down another mouthful of coffee. "We've got investors who've sunk a whole bunch of money into the festival. We can't let them down. I can't let them down. We show our first movie two weeks from tonight and we haven't sold nearly enough tickets."

"And you're hoping the more you hype Florie's murder, the more people will notice what you're up to, feel all creepy and horrible, and buy tickets."

His shrug was as pathetic as his plan. "Hey, you work with what you've got."

"And Florie's work?"

He yanked open the top drawer of his desk. "You know, the cop who came to talk to me asked me all these same questions. Don't cops talk to the family of the person who got killed?" He pulled out a manila folder and plopped it on his desk.

Jazzed leaned forward and saw *Florentine Allen* on the folder tab.

She leaned forward a little more when Paul pulled a slim stack of papers from the folder and paged through them.

"She was here for . . ." He looked at the printout of a spreadsheet. "A couple months. She gave us maybe . . ." He counted low under his breath. "Sometimes fifteen, sometimes twenty hours a week."

"That's a lot of time for a kid who's in school."

"Was she?"

The question was too casual.

Jazz stepped closer to the desk. "How well did you know her?"

"Florentine?" Paul's laugh was forced. "Now you do sound like that cop. Maybe you're going to be like him and ask where I was the night Florentine died."

It wasn't like she was investigating, she reminded herself. But she was invested. In Florie's years at St. Catherine's and now in her death. She pinned Paul with a look.

"Where were you?"

He tapped the papers in front of him into a neat pile, tucked them back in the folder, and shoved the folder in the drawer before he folded his hands on the desk in front of him. Paul's fingers were short and fat, like pork sausages. He wore a simple gold-band wedding ring.

"Atlanta," he said, his voice locked as tight as his fingers. "My wife's nephew got married. And no . . ." He rose to his feet. "Don't you dare ask to see hotel receipts. The cop, he did that, and I had to show him. But you're just a friend of the girl's family. You have no right."

"Her family has the right to know about her life."

"There's nothing I can tell you."

"Did you ever see her outside of work?"

His jaw twitched. His lips pressed into a tight line.

She stepped back. Reconsidered. Decided *what the hell.*

"Florie needed money. Did she try to get it from you?"

A muscle bunched at the base of his jaw. "She wasn't the nice kid you think she was."

"I never said I thought she was."

He dropped back in his chair. "I'm sorry the kid is dead. Really. And believe it or not, I do understand how her family wants to gather all the memories they can and hold on to them. I've got daughters. Three of them. I'd want to do the same thing. But those people, they don't have to know that Florentine and I had a little fling."

The news stung like a slap.

"It didn't last long," Paul told her. "A couple weeks. A couple drinks together. A couple . . . well, you get the picture."

"I do."

"Then you should also get this . . . after we were together a couple times, after . . ." A color like blood rushed up his neck and into his doughy cheeks. "After I was stupid enough to think she actually enjoyed being with me, that's when she told me she was going to tell my wife what was going on between us."

"Did she?"

"No. But only because I paid what she asked."

Jazz sucked in a breath and swallowed down the sudden sour taste that filled her mouth. She'd known Florie was desperate for money, she'd just never imagined . . .

She shook her head to clear it.

"Did you tell the cop?" she asked him.

"You think I'm stupid? That makes me look like a suspect, doesn't it?"

"Except you were in Atlanta."

"I was."

"And there's a whole wedding full of people who can vouch for you."

"They can."

It was warm in the office. That must have been why Jazz felt suddenly as if she were an ice cube in the sunlight, melting by the moment, getting smaller and smaller.

"I appreciate your honesty," she told Paul.

"And will you . . ." There was a pad of paper and a pen on his desk, and he straightened them even though they didn't need it.

"Will you tell her parents what I just told you?"

Finally, they were back on solid ground; she didn't need to lie. "No. There doesn't seem to be anything to be gained from them knowing. I think it would be best if we kept this our secret."

The word reverberated in her head as she made her way downstairs.

Secrets.

Florie had secrets.

And now Jazz did, too.

She was so preoccupied, she'd already pushed out of the back door when she remembered Billy DeSantos. As luck would have it, he was nowhere to be seen, and Jazz scuttled out of the alley, grateful to be away from the monster on the poster and the ugly truth of Florie's past.

It wasn't until she crossed the street and was headed back to St. Catherine's that she felt a chill skate across her shoulder blades.

Like someone was watching her.

CHAPTER 10

As the daughter of a firefighter, Jazz had experiences kids with parents with nine-to-five jobs could never imagine.

She had played in and around fire trucks for as long as she could remember. Early on, she discovered the comfiest recliner in the firehouse TV room, and she raced Hal and Owen to it when they visited and she won every time.

By the age of six, she knew holidays weren't dates on a calendar, but the time spent with family. Often, her dad — and now, her brothers — had shifts on holidays. Sure, when she was a kid, she had been envious when her friends talked about how they tore open their gifts on Christmas morning. Jazz and Hal and Owen sometimes had to wait a full twenty-four hours after Santa brought them to open their gifts, but if anything, that only made the holiday more delicious.

She treasured the times her dad would call from the station to ask if her homework was done and wish her sweet dreams, and the times he came home smelling like soap and aftershave and the ashy aroma of smoke.

She knew time spent together was a rare and wonderful thing.

Which was why she was caught off guard that Saturday night when her doorbell rang and Luther shot off the couch and to the front door.

Both Hal and Owen were on her front porch.

"Hey, guys!" When they stepped into the living room she gave each of them a quick hug, no easy thing since Luther was so excited to see them, he ran in circles and demanded attention.

"You didn't tell me you got a dog!"

Hal should have known better. At least that's what the look Jazz gave him said. "It's Luther. Greg's dog. His mother had a stroke in Florida."

"Jazz is babysitting," Owen added and scratched the dog's ears. "Haven't you talked to Mom? Mom knows everything."

She did. She always did. Though she either didn't know or didn't bother to mention to Jazz that both her brothers had the night off and were planning on stopping over.

Jazz closed the door and glanced from one brother to the other.

Hal was the oldest and looked so much like their father, a catch of emotion hitched Jazz's breath every time she saw him. He was over six feet tall, just like Michael had been, and he had the same dark hair, the same blue eyes, the same square-cut jaw that made him look fierce and determined even when he was doing something like Hal was now, wrestling on the floor with Luther, laughing like a kid.

Owen, three years older than Jazz, took after their mother's Polish side of the family. He was shorter than Hal and bulky, like Grandpa Kurcz, with gray eyes and a round face and honey-colored hair that, growing up, Jazz had always wished she'd gotten instead of her ordinary brown.

She stepped around the dog and Hal, still on the floor, and toward the kitchen. "You want beers?"

"Oh, no." Owen grabbed her arm. "We're taking you out."

"Out? As in —"

"Out." Hal jumped to his feet and ruffled a hand over Luther's head. "You know, it's what people do. Well, some people who

163

aren't you, anyway. They go to places where there are other people. They sometimes even talk to those other people."

"And they drink beer there," Owen told her.

She was wearing her oldest jeans and because it was a chilly night, a blue sweatshirt with a red block *C* on it, the symbol of the city's baseball team. "I'm not exactly dressed to go out."

"We're not exactly going anyplace that you have to get dressed up for," Owen told her.

"And Luther —"

Hal cut off her protest. The dog's leash was nearby and in a flash, he hooked it on Luther's collar. "We'll take him for a walk while you do . . ." He waved a hand at Jazz. "While you do whatever it is girls need to do before they go out."

"And speaking of girls . . ." Instead of heading upstairs to get ready, she tipped her head and crossed her arms over her chest. It wasn't that she was sorry to see her brothers. She loved them to the moon and back. But on a Saturday night?

"Where's Kaitlyn?" Jazz asked Hal. Kaitlyn, an RN who worked in the burn unit of a local hospital, was Hal's girlfriend. The family hoped she'd soon be his fiancée. "You can't leave her alone on a Saturday night, not when you're actually off."

"Bachelorette party," he informed her. To prove he was footloose and fancy-free, Hal threw his arms out at his sides. "That means I can do whatever I want tonight."

"And you want to spend time with me?"

"Go get ready." Owen gave her a nudge toward the stairs. "We'll walk the dog and be back in five."

She switched the sweatshirt for a gray sweater and put on a pair of jeans that were less threadbare. "We're walking?" she asked them when they returned with the dog and she got a treat for him from the bag on the kitchen counter.

"Is there anywhere to park in this whole neighborhood?" Hal's question was rhetorical.

"Looks like you found a spot." When they locked up the house and stepped onto the porch, she eyed up his black Jeep, squeezed close enough to kiss her SUV in the driveway.

Hal went to the car, opened the back door, and took out a brown paper shopping bag, then joined Jazz and Owen on the sidewalk, the bag tucked under his arm. He ignored the questioning look Jazz gave him, looping his free arm over her shoulders instead. "Let's go."

They walked up Jefferson, not toward La Bodega, Jazz's favorite sandwich spot, which was a shame, because for the first time in the week since she'd walked these same streets with Luther to test his HRD abilities, her stomach rumbled with hunger.

If she had to guess, she'd say they were headed for Pulaski Post 30, home of the Polish Legion American Vets and dollar draft beers, where they'd play pool and buy bags of potato chips that hung behind the bar, but they walked right by.

"Prosperity?" Jazz couldn't help but be surprised when they stopped outside the Prosperity Social Club, another hipster oasis in a neighborhood that was all about cool. "What?" She looked from brother to brother. "Did you two win the lottery or something?"

"Don't be such a stick in the mud." Owen opened the door and stood back so she could go inside. "And since we didn't win the lottery, don't order anything top-shelf!"

As she expected for a Saturday night, the place was hopping. Still, they were seated quickly in a relatively quiet corner — Hal and Owen on one side of the table with that shopping bag tucked on the floor between them, and Jazz on the other — and had beers in front of them in a matter of minutes. Nothing made Hal and Owen happier than the fact that Cleveland was the center of a craft-beer renaissance, and they each ordered the latest and what their waiter assured them was the greatest. When it came to beer, a can of Labatt was just fine with Jazz.

She popped the top on the beer can and emptied it into the frosty glass the waiter had provided. "What are you two up to?"

"Working mostly." Owen sipped, nodded his approval of the IPA he'd ordered, and passed his glass to Hal, who'd just sipped his lager, nodded his approval, and did the same thing. Done sampling and with his IPA back in front of him, Owen looked over the appetizer menu while Hal braced his elbows on the table and leaned forward.

"We haven't seen you in a while."

It was true, and it was a shame. They were best friends, all three of them, and there was a time growing up when they never would have imagined spending days, and even weeks, without communicating.

Best friends did not need to ease into conversations. They didn't need to lie, either, or to talk their way around subjects that others might find too sensitive, too personal.

She looked from Owen to Hal, then back

167

again to Owen, because when it came to things like this, he was always the first to cave and tell the truth. "You think I'm depressed."

"Are you?" he asked.

"You mean about finding Florie?" She took a sip of the icy beer. "No."

"Are you depressed about anything else?"

Owen could be her strongest ally. He could also be as dense as one of those black holes they're always encountering on *Star Trek*. If he wasn't, he never would have had the sense to ask.

"Why would I be?" Jazz countered.

This time, it was Hal who spoke up. After he gave her a shrug. "It's not every day you find a body."

"You guys do. Well, maybe not every day, but you know what I mean."

"Yeah, but it's our job." Owen ran a finger through the ring of condensation left on the table by his beer glass. "We know what we're getting into."

"Just like I do when I take out a dog to search for human remains."

"Yeah, but . . ." As the oldest, Hal refused to let down his guard, but Jazz knew better — of the three of them, he was the most sensitive. She'd seen him go to pieces the night he'd worked a fire that took the lives of three elderly people. She'd seen him cry openly after coming to the aid of a family at the mall and trying, unsuccessfully, to dislodge a grape Tootsie Pop from a kid's throat. "It's never easy," he admitted.

"I'm not saying it was." In an effort to convince herself that maybe she was wrong, that maybe finding Florie's body wasn't all that different from training a dog to search for the bits and pieces of people who donated their bodies to science, she sat up and sat back and did her best to look and sound confident. "I accept it as part of my volunteer work."

"Which you weren't doing at the time, not officially." Owen wagged a finger in her direction. Back in the day — and she wasn't proud of it even though at the time she felt she was completely justified — he'd pulled that move on her one too many times and she'd grabbed his finger and bitten it so hard, she left teeth marks. "When you and your team are called out on a search, yeah, then you know there's a possibility of finding a body. But getting blindsided like that . . ."

"It was a shock." She would admit that much. "I've told myself that if I just figure out what Florie was up to, just understand

what she was doing and how it happened
—"

"Oh!" Hal's howl was half disbelief, half laugher. He crumpled in his chair. "So now you're what, Jessica Fletcher? Or is it Sherlock Holmes? Out solving murders!"

"I'm not." She crossed her arms over her chest. "I have no intention of solving anything. I'm just asking questions."

Owen poked Hal in the ribs with one elbow. "She's just asking questions. Must have learned that from Nick."

If she didn't have more than half of her beer left to drink, she would have gotten up and walked out. Hal and Owen had always been on Team Nick. While she and Nick were dating, that was great; it was nice to have their support, great to have them include Nick as part of the family at parties and holidays. But after what she had of a relationship with Nick fell apart, they should have known better than to even mention his name.

There was something about being with her older brothers that made it only logical for Jazz to cross her eyes and stick out her tongue.

"Very mature." Owen flagged down the waiter and ordered appetizers — potato pierogies and pita nachos.

"Does that mean you haven't talked to Nick?" Hal wanted to know.

Before she could stop herself, Jazz slapped the table with one hand. "Why is everyone so concerned about who I talk to? I haven't talked to him. I don't want to talk to him."

"That's not what he told me." Smugness did not become Hal. "I saw him downtown. He said he stopped by your place the other evening and —"

"And I told him to get lost. Did he happen to mention that?"

It would take longer for the pierogi to sauté along with the onion, but the waiter brought the nachos over. Then again, maybe he, like Jazz, felt the electric current that buzzed around the table, sibling to sibling, and hoped that a plate of food might help discharge it.

Hal handed around small plates. Owen dug right in. Jazz wasn't sure she was hungry anymore. Then again, she was a sucker for feta and Kalamata olives.

Making sure she got her share of the roasted red pepper aioli drizzled over them, she grabbed a few pita chips along with the cheese and olives.

"Please tell me you didn't drag me over here to lecture me about my love life."

"We didn't drag you," Hal insisted.

"And since you don't have a love life, that doesn't count."

"Look who's talking." Her steady gaze on Owen, she crunched a pita chip. While Hal and Kaitlyn had dated for three years, the women in Owen's life came and went like leaves blowing down the street in a crisp fall breeze. "Who is it this week?" she asked him.

He answered with his mouth full, but Jazz knew exactly what he'd said.

"Lori Simms? The girl I went to high school with? The one with the buckteeth?"

"Not anymore," Owen told her. "She's a hottie now. She works as a bartender over at Great Lakes in Ohio City."

"Really?" Jazz didn't have to pretend to be interested. She remembered that Sister Eileen had told her about the knockdown, drag-out fight between Florie and Grace Greenwald at that pub. Her smile was genuine. "I'll have to stop and see her sometime."

The pierogi arrived, and they waited until they'd eaten it all until they finally settled on dinner. Owen ordered a cheeseburger. Jazz knew he would. Hal went for the Italian sausage meatloaf and swore her to secrecy when he said he knew it would be "better than Mom's." Jazz opted for the shrimp and grits, consoling herself for the indulgence with the fact that after the pierogi and the nachos, she was certain she'd end up taking at least half of it home.

They talked about work, about the slow days at Hal's station and the late-night runs at Owen's and the fact that for Jazz, another school year was ending and wasn't it funny how fast time went. They looked at their calendars and came up with a Sunday when they'd all be available and agreed they'd take food over to their mom's and have a cookout and let Mom put her feet up and do absolutely nothing. They asked about Luther.

"I don't know how long I'll have him. It depends on how long Greg is in Florida."

Owen had ordered another — different — craft beer, and he sipped, wrinkled his nose, sipped again, then decided it wasn't half-bad. "You going to train with him?"

Jazz had just taken a bite of shrimp, so she nodded, chewed, swallowed. "I'm meeting the team tomorrow out at the old Geauga Lake."

"Oh, abandoned amusement park!" Hal hooted. "It's like something out of a bad book."

"It's a great place to train. Lots of buildings so we can practice urban searches. And

173

lots of overgrown fields, too, for a more rural environment. And speaking of that . . ." She touched a finger to her phone, checking the time. "I should get moving. We start training at nine."

"You can't leave. Not yet." Hal put a hand on her arm. "You can't walk home alone."

"Really?" The question dripped sarcasm, and that should have been enough for Hal to let go. He didn't. "Come on." She shook him off. "I walk around the neighborhood by myself all the time. It's perfectly safe."

"On a Saturday night? Too many strangers around." To emphasize the danger, Owen gave an exaggerated shiver. "Besides . . ." He waved over their waiter. "We're going to walk you home. But not until we have another beer."

They had another beer, and as long as Jazz was their prisoner, she had another one, too. It wasn't until they were nearly finished and the bill had been paid by Owen, who insisted on treating (which was plenty fishy in and of itself), that Hal reached down and picked up the brown paper shopping bag he'd brought along.

"I suppose you're wondering why I've asked you all here today." He was going for funny. It actually might have worked if there wasn't a little catch of nervousness in his words.

Jazz sat up like a shot. "You finally asked Kaitlyn to marry you?"

"Really?" It was Hal's turn to sound just as skeptical as Jazz had when she asked the question. "You don't think I'd announce that at some sort of family party?"

"Well, you'd want us to know first," she insisted, and she knew she was right. "You'd want to make sure we were okay with it."

"Are you okay with it?"

"Is Kaitlyn going to want you to move?" Jazz asked him, because Kaitlyn was always talking about a home in the far western suburbs, and Jazz didn't like the thought of Hal living farther away than he already did, in a neighborhood called Kamm's Corners near their parents' house, about a twenty-minute ride in good traffic.

"I'm not moving," he assured her.

"That's what they always say." Owen spoke in a stage whisper directed at Jazz, but meant for Hal. "Once Kaitlyn gets that ring on her finger —"

"She's not getting a ring," Hal insisted. "Not anytime soon, anyway."

Jazz's gaze traveled to the bag in her brother's hand. "Then what . . ."

"What, you thought I brought an engage-

175

ment ring in this big ol' bag so I could show it off to you?" He laughed. "You've got an overactive imagination."

"And you're stalling," she shot back. "Otherwise you wouldn't be hanging on to that bag like there's a bomb inside it. Give it to me!" She made a grab for the bag, but Hal was faster and held on tight.

"Patience," he advised. "There's a story."

"It's about Dad's softball team," Owen added.

Her hand on her beer glass, Jazz froze and swallowed down the sudden lump in her throat. "What about it?"

"Well, you know Dad loved softball!" Owen did his best to lighten the mood with a laugh.

"He was a damn good catcher." She didn't need to remind them, but she did, anyway. "But what does the team have to do with . . ." Again her gaze traveled to the brown bag.

Hal sucked in a breath and let it out slowly. "It's like this," he explained. "Last year, well, Dad's team, they were pretty broken up by what happened."

He didn't need to explain that particular what. The memory hung over all their gatherings, its terrifying reality still painful after a year.

"They dedicated last season to Dad and they filled in game by game with any catcher they could find." With a shake of his shoulders, Owen did his best to dispel the shadow that settled over them. "And this year, they've got a new catcher."

"Ramirez," Hal told her. "From Station Thirty-one. He's a good man."

"And a decent catcher," Owen said.

"And they needed a place for Ramirez to put his things."

"And they hadn't bothered to clean out Dad's locker at the field last year because they felt funny about it and —"

When Jazz gave the brown bag another look, her heart beat double time and her mouth went dry. "And now they did."

"Yeah." Hal reached inside the bag and came out holding a slim stack of papers. "Score sheets mostly." He put them on the table. "And there's a grocery list, too. I don't know if he was buying for Mom or buying so he could cook at the station."

Jazz shuffled through the papers until she found what he was talking about. "Twelve pounds of ground beef? I think he was making his world-famous chili for the station."

"Man, I wish he would have left the recipe for that!" Owen licked his lips. "If I could make chili like that, I'd be the most popular guy in the department!"

"He also left this." Once again Hal reached into the bag, and this time, he brought out a present wrapped in birthday paper decorated with red, yellow, and blue balloons. There was a card taped to the front of it *Snazzy Jazzy.*

Her dad's silly nickname for her.

Her dad's distinctive, unadorned, no-nonsense handwriting.

The lump in Jazz's throat got bigger.

Hal set the gift on the table. "He must have bought it for you early," he said. "He put it in his locker and was waiting for your birthday in May."

But he died at the end of March.

Jazz stared at the cheery paper, at the card, for she didn't know how long. She only knew that when she shook herself back to reality, they all had shots of Jameson on the table in front of them.

"We gotta toast," Owen explained.

They did.

"To Michael Patrick Ramsey, best dad, best firefighter," Hal said.

"Best catcher," Owen added.

Jazz bobbled her shot glass, recovered. "Best dog trainer on the planet," she said, smiled, and knocked back the shot.

The whiskey hit the back of her throat,

and heat exploded all the way down to her stomach, and once it hit in a splash of fire, she said the only thing she could say.

"Wow."

At least the pain helped her forget the gift on the table.

For a few seconds, anyway.

Owen nudged the package nearer. "You gonna open it?"

She was tempted to say "No." Instead, she slid the present nearer. It had sat in a locker for a year in a building that was used spring and summer and locked up tight in the winter, and the tape that held the card on the package was yellow and brittle. One second it sat amidst those cheery balloons on the wrapping paper, and the next it was clutched in her fingers. She pulled in a breath.

"You need another shot?" Owen asked.

"Absolutely not." She turned the card over. "Does Mom know about this?"

"I didn't tell her." Hal put up one hand, fingers folded, Boy Scout–style.

"I sure never said a word," Owen insisted. "We figured you could tell her."

She gave them a sour look. "Thanks."

She slid her finger under the flap of the card and pulled it from the envelope. There was a drawing of a slobbering, smiling dog on it.

DON'T WORRY ABOUT YOUR BIRTHDAY. Jazz read the text above the drawing before she flipped open the card. IN DOG YEARS YOU'RE JUST A PUP.

It was signed *Love, Dad.*

"Here's to that!" Owen raised his empty shot glass and pretended to take another drink.

"You gotta open the present now," Hal told her.

One more breath for courage, and she did, picking at the tape and ripping away the paper.

Inside was a framed eight-by-ten photograph — Dad with Big George, Jazz with Manny — taken the day Manny had passed the final test that made him a certified human remains detection dog.

"It's —" Her voice clogged, and Owen took the opportunity to butt in.

"That was a few years ago. You look like a baby. Maybe you're not so much of a pup after all." He poked a finger at Jazz's face in the picture. "I don't know, little sister, I don't think you're aging well."

Just as he expected, she gave him a sour look. Right before she laughed.

"This is . . ." She gathered the card and

picture and held them close. "It's great. Thank you both."

"Hey, take the shopping bag," Hal said, and passed it across the table to her.

"And you might as well take this other stuff, too." Owen shoved the papers, scorecards, and grocery lists at her. Among them was the business card printed on heavy white stock.

"SEAN INNIS." She read the name embossed on it. "REAL ESTATE DEVELOPER."

"You think Dad was going to do some investing?" Owen asked.

"Or maybe he was finally going to build that summer home by the lake he always talked about," Hal said.

Jazz didn't know. She only knew that when she put the card in the bag with the rest of Michael Ramsey's things and the gift he had given her from beyond the grave, she saw something written on the back of it.

The handwriting was unadorned, no-nonsense.

Ask Darren Marsh, it said.

CHAPTER 11

The good news was that Jazz was able to call Greg late on Sunday and tell him how well Luther had done at training. The shepherd had found a vial of blood hidden inside a storage building in no time flat. It took a little longer for him to locate a scapula that one of her fellow trainers had tucked into an overgrown flower bed, but it was a breezy day, and a few of the younger dogs had trouble with scents. With a little encouragement, Luther eventually succeeded. The bad news was that Greg's mom was still in an iffy state, healthwise, and Greg wasn't sure when he'd be home.

But maybe that wasn't such bad news, after all.

The next morning, just about to straighten the birthday-present photo on the shelf in the living room where she'd given it a place of honor, Jazz paused when the thought hit, and a wave of guilt washed over her.

Of course it was bad news about Greg's mom. But with Greg still in Florida, she got to keep Luther a little while longer, and having Luther around . . .

Automatically, she looked to where the dog was settled on a nest of blankets next to the couch. Luther thumped his tail.

It was nice to have a dog in the house again, she admitted, even when that dog would never be the dog of her heart like Manny was. It was good to walk morning and evening with a dog padding along at her side. It was great to train on Sunday and be among friends, some of them working on their human remains finding skills, others, like Matt Duffey, concentrating on search and rescue.

Naturally, thinking about Matt made her think about Darren Marsh, the firefighter who had killed himself at the station and whose life Matt had fought like hell to save, the one whose name was written on that business card she'd found in with her dad's things. Whatever Sean Innis, the real estate developer, and her dad were working on, whatever her dad was going to ask Darren about it, it didn't matter anymore. Not to either one of them.

It was the way of things.

She knew it.

That didn't mean she had to like it.

One more look at the photo, one more bittersweet smile, and Jazz left for work.

Like all Mondays, this one walked the fine line between frantic and crazy. After a weekend, there were parents calling in for girls who were sick, and Jazz made note of every one of them and entered the information in each girl's file. There were girls who didn't have the right clothes for gym, girls who forgot it was the last day to put down their deposits on prom and were as dramatic about it as only teenage girls could be, girls who lost their bus fare to get home, felt queasy after lunch, couldn't find their English lit books. She handled it all.

Jazz couldn't wait for the bell to ring so she could take a breath and catch up on the administrative work she'd never had time to finish.

As it turned out, she didn't have the chance. The bell sounded and girls hurried past her door, a blur of navy-and-gray plaid. One of them was Dinah Greenwald.

"Dinah!" When Jazz called out to her, Dinah stopped dead in her tracks, and her cheeks flushed. But then, that was the kind of kid Dinah was. Studious, meticulous, shy. Dinah was everything her older sister, Grace, was not.

Jazz walked into the hallway. "How do you get home?" she asked the girl. She suspected she knew the answer. She hoped she was right.

Grace was elegant. Dinah was short, squat, and plain. She had a broad face that looked even rounder thanks to her black-rimmed glasses. She pushed them up on the bridge of her nose, and when she ran her tongue over her lips, her braces flashed. "Sometimes . . . uh . . . my mom picks me up."

"Every day?"

"Not on . . . uh, Mondays. Mom has yoga on Mondays. On Mondays, Grace comes for me."

Jazz bit back a smile. It was what she remembered from earlier in the year when she'd helped with pickup. Meghan Greenwald's black Audi on Tuesdays, Wednesdays, Thursdays, Fridays. But another car on Mondays, a red Mustang.

Grace's car.

"Thanks, Dinah. You can go to your locker now."

When the girl did, Jazz hurried to the back door of the school and scooted around the long line of girls waiting for their rides. When Tremont was first established, its streets marked off and its homes and stores and churches jammed one up against the other, no one had imagined modern traffic. Space was limited. Streets were narrow. Pickups and drop-offs at St. Catherine's were carefully controlled, with cars coming past the school from one direction and one direction only, going through the parking lot in one direction and one direction only. Girls lined up to watch for their rides and had orders to move quickly. The whole process had been choreographed by Eileen and was supervised by teachers who took turns at the assignment, and already looked frazzled when Jazz stepped outside, even though the first cars had yet to be allowed through.

Two steps led down from the back door to the main parking lot, and Jazz paused at the top of them, thinking maybe her eyes were playing tricks on her.

But then, Billy DeSantos was hard to miss.

All black leather and tattoos, he stuck out like an ugly duckling at a swan party in a place where the most unconventional thing they usually saw was a girl who'd neglected her laundry — and the school's strict dress code — and showed up in a white blouse instead of a blue one. But even the fact that he didn't belong wasn't as mind-numbing as the reality that intruded on Jazz's consciousness.

He knew where she worked.

He'd followed her from the film festival.

For the space of a dozen heartbeats, the thought froze her in place. She liked to think she was cool enough, strong enough, confident enough to walk over to where De-Santos leaned against a tree and ask him what the hell his problem was, but before she had a chance, Jerry Tomascewski, the local beat cop who made it a point to keep an eye on the girls every day at dismissal time, hurried DeSantos on his way. He disappeared in a streak of black leather at the same time Jazz saw a red Mustang pull into the drive, and she took off in that direction.

Grace was behind the wheel, texting, her gaze glued to her keyboard.

Jazz opened the door and slipped into the passenger seat.

Grace didn't bother to look over. "What, the geek is actually breaking the rules for once? I said you could get away with it, didn't I? I told you to get out of line and into the car and Eileen would never know. She's not going to bite your head off, loser."

"That's not exactly something I'm worried about," Jazz told her.

At least Jazz had the satisfaction of watching Grace suck in a breath. The next second, though, the girl hid her surprise behind a monumental eye roll. The car in front of them inched forward and Grace did, too. "I'm waiting for my sister."

"And I need to talk to you. I know you'd hate to slow the line for everyone else, so maybe you should pull over into that parking space over there." She pointed.

"Take a reserved parking space? That would be breaking the rules." Grace's protest was as overblown as her wide-eyed look. "I might get a detention."

"It's my parking place and I walked to school today so nobody's going to care. Go ahead." Jazz's words were mellow. Her tone told Grace she wasn't messing around. "Park."

Grumbling, Grace pulled into the space at the back of the building and turned off the car. She pivoted in her seat, the better to give Jazz what she thought was a fierce look. Poor Grace; she was too young to know that the blond hair and the blue eyes, the golden eyeliner stylishly smudged, the peach blush, and the lipstick applied to appropriately plumped lips pretty much negated the fierce.

Besides, Jazz didn't intimidate easily.

"What do you want?"

"Well, for one thing, an apology. You were

188

supposed to meet me at North Coast last Tuesday. I hear you went out for linguini and clam sauce instead."

Grace had the kind of smile that can only be achieved through years of expensive orthodontia. She did her best to dazzle Jazz with it, and when Jazz didn't fall under her spell like so many countless others had, she huffed out a breath. "I forgot."

Jazz settled herself against the leather seat. "Then it's a good thing we've got this chance to talk now."

Grace slid her a look. "About what?"

"Come on, Grace. What else would I want to talk to you about? About Florie, of course."

Grace flipped down the visor, peered in the mirror there, and skimmed one finger over her bottom lip. "What about her?"

"She's dead. You do remember that, don't you?"

She flicked the visor back up. "I'm not stupid."

"You're not sorry, either."

"Why should I be? It's not like we were friends."

"Really? Not even for a couple years when you were here at St. Catherine's?"

Out of the corner of her eye, Jazz saw Dinah approach. When the kid saw Jazz in the car, she instantly backed off, plastering herself to the building, looking faded and fidgety against the old sandstone.

Grace saw her, too. "I really need to get my sister home," she insisted.

"Then we'll just finish up. You were saying . . . about you and Florie being friends here at St. Catherine's . . . ?"

Grace shot Jazz a look. "I wasn't saying that. Because she wasn't my friend."

"That's not how other people remember it. They say she was. Before you two turned on each other."

Grace pouted. "It was years ago, what difference does it make? And why would I want to be friends with a scholarship girl, anyway?"

"Florie told you she was on scholarship?" It didn't line up with what Jazz knew about Florie, about how she hid her poverty, her need.

"She didn't have to tell me. God, the clothes that girl had! And did you ever smell her? She ladled on perfume every day. Cheap perfume. It was disgusting. You'd have to be dumb not to know Florie was trash."

"Do you think all the scholarship girls are trash?"

"I didn't say that."

"You said Florie was."

"She was."

"Why?"

"What difference does it make? It's ancient history."

"Apparently not. I heard about what happened over in Ohio City not long ago."

Grace's back went rigid.

"What were you fighting about?" Jazz wanted to know.

Grace's smile was as thin as the blade of a stiletto. "She bumped into me and spilled my coffee."

"You should have let her buy you another one."

"I wasn't in the mood."

"I hear you were asked to leave."

"The bartender should have handled it the minute Florie got out of line." Grace pouted. "Isn't that what people like that are paid for? She should have tossed Florie's skinny ass out of there, but instead, she didn't do a thing. I had to put Florie in her place."

"By causing a scene."

"Is that what it was?" Grace whooped out a laugh. "I kind of like the idea of causing a scene."

"Is that why you and Florie fought while you were filming the commercial for the

191

horror film festival? To cause a scene?"

"You have been busy, haven't you?" Grace made it sound almost like a compliment. "Believe me, it wasn't my idea. Brody put Florie on the team."

"Why?"

The look she gave Jazz was pointed. "Word was she needed extra credit."

"Her grades were down."

"Yeah, most of them."

"But not all of them?"

Grace let go a long, impatient breath. "I don't know why you care about all this."

"Because I care about Florie."

"Do you? Did anybody? Don't you remember, her parents didn't even show up at graduation."

Jazz had never noticed and a curl of ice formed in her stomach. She should have paid more attention. "Maybe that's all the more reason we should care about her," she suggested.

Grace bit her lower lip. "Maybe," she conceded. "But what difference does it make now?"

"Some. None. I don't know." The frustration — the helplessness — built, and Jazz rubbed her hands over her face. "I'm just trying to get a clear picture of what happened. Like it or not, Grace, you're part of that picture."

"Look . . ." Grace sat back, her shoulders sinking into the leather upholstery. "All I can tell you is we were friends for a while here at Cat's. But then I found out what trash she was and so we weren't friends anymore. You know that. But you should also know I barely saw her at North Coast. I keep plenty busy with my work and I have lots of friends to hang with. Florie . . . well, she'd disappear after classes and no one would see her again until the next day. Besides, she was in photography. I'm in video. And yeah, the photo kids have to do a video project. And the video students have to do a photo project, and so yeah, early this semester I sometimes saw her around when she was working on her video, but it's not like we were best buds or anything."

"Tate Brody never mentioned that Florie made a video."

"He wouldn't, would he?"

Grace let the question hang in the air so Jazz had no choice but to ask, "What do you mean?"

"You want to know the truth? Are you sure? Then listen to this. That video Florie shot, that was the only A she got this semester."

"Good for her."

Grace shook her head, a sure sign that Jazz was too dense to see the truth, even if it was staring her right in the face. "Don't you get it? She tanked all her other classes. Florie was not the brightest bulb in the box. Sure, if all she had to do was take pictures, she was pretty good. But if she actually had to think . . . if she actually had to learn something new . . . That's what the video project was. Something new. And she wasn't happy about it."

"But she obviously got through it with flying colors. An A, that says a lot about her talent and her hard work."

"You think so?" It wasn't so much a chuckle as a laugh of derision. Grace glided one finger over the steering wheel. "I happened to bump into Florie the night before the project was due. It was not a pretty picture."

"You mean her video."

"I mean Florie. She was a mess. Frantic. Panicking. She didn't usually give me the time of day, but that evening . . ." Jazz didn't like the smile that crossed Grace's face. It was way too self-satisfied. "She just about gushed the minute she saw me. Burst into tears. She didn't know what she was going to do. She didn't just not know how to make her video good, she wasn't even sure she could finish it on time. She begged for my help."

"And you said —"

"I told her no one helped me with my photo project."

"So you left her to hang out to dry. Not exactly what we teach the St. Catherine's girls."

"I'm not a St. Catherine's girl. Not anymore. And neither was Florie. Don't you get it?" She slapped the steering wheel. "The night before, she's in a panic. The day the project is due, she turns it in. The next thing you know, she's got an A."

It did seem odd. Unless . . .

Jazz remembered what Parker Paul had told her about Florie, about their relationship, and Florie's threats. Like she'd been sucker punched, she sucked in a breath, but she refused to rise to the bait Grace dangled. She needed more information.

"On the night she died, Florie went back to where you filmed the commercial. Tate Brody was shooting B roll and Florie was taking stills."

"I'll just bet that's what they were doing together in that building in the middle of the night."

"You're telling me something else was going on? That they were having an affair?"

"Damn!" As if it truly was a shame, Grace shook her head. "You're not that much older than me, Jazz. You need to get out of this buttoned-down school where everything's all sweetness and light and remember there's a real world out there. Florie and Brody hooking up? It's the only thing that explains how she could turn in crap and get an A from the same guy she's hanging out with on a Saturday night. Shit, I wish I would have thought of it at the beginning of the semester. Brody's not half-bad to look at and I bet he's plenty lively in bed."

"But Florie . . ."

But what, Jazz wasn't sure. In fact, the only thing she was sure about was that what Grace suggested was a definite possibility, especially in light of what she'd learned about Florie from Parker Paul. But how any of it fit in with Florie's murder, she didn't know.

"Are we done now?" Grace tapped a hand against the console between the two front seats. "Because I think I've pretty much told you all I'm going to tell you."

"You haven't told me where you were on Saturday night at the time Florie died."

Even Jazz couldn't believe she'd had the nerve to bring it up.

Apparently, Grace couldn't, either. She

opened and closed her mouth, sucked in a breath, sputtered out a curse. "You think I'm the one who killed Florie? Why? About some crazy shit that happened in high school? I'll tell you what, lady, you've got plenty of nerve, and if I hear you've been flapping your jaws and mention this half-assed theory of yours to anyone else, you can be sure I'll tell my parents. I hope you're ready to look for a new job."

Jazz popped open the passenger door, but she didn't get out of the car. Not just yet. "Crazy shit that happened in high school, huh? What, exactly, was the crazy shit that turned you and Florie against each other?"

"None of your business."

"And where were you the night she was killed?"

"You've got it all wrong," Grace shot back. "You think because I didn't like the girl, I could have killed her? For one thing, I was out at a club that night, and the fifteen friends from school I was with can vouch for me. For another . . . well, me killing someone, even someone I thought was trash? That would never happen. I would never take the chance. Just for the record, I look lousy in orange."

That Monday evening, Jazz tried to console

herself about the way she'd bungled things with Grace by getting a turkey, double tomato, and pesto sandwich from La Bodega, and ended up picking at it, giving part of the turkey to Luther, and putting the rest in the fridge.

Why did she have the feeling that if only she'd handled things with more finesse, Grace might have told her something useful?

"Then again, she's still Grace."

Luther did not seem especially impressed with this information. He gave Jazz exactly one moment of attention before he went back to chewing a tennis ball.

She flopped down on her couch. "Grace, in case you don't know," she informed Luther, "was never one of the nicest girls at school. That's what happens when a family has more money than they know what to do with. The kids are spoiled."

Luther offered his opinion by way of a yawn.

"Well, Dinah isn't," she said, rubbing a hand over the dog's head. "Dinah's a nice kid. I wonder if she'll always be a nice kid, or if one of these days she'll realize she's a Greenwald and she lives in the stratosphere above us common humans and —"

Luther was up on his feet and standing at

attention before Jazz ever had a chance to finish being philosophical. The dog's ears pricked. The hair on his back stood on end. He let out a low, throaty growl before he raced to the front door and barked.

Startled, Jazz sat up. Ice prickled over her spine.

At least until she came to her senses.

"Damn it, Nick." She got to her feet nearly as quickly as Luther had and went to the front door. "I can't believe a man who's supposed to be professional and mature can have mush for brains," she mumbled and yanked open the door, yelling now. "Nick Kolesov, if I see you around here one more time —"

When all the air rushed out of her lungs, her words dissolved. Her hand tightened on the doorknob.

It wasn't Nick she saw racing shadow to shadow away from the house.

She'd recognize the pierced face and the black leather anywhere.

Billy DeSantos.

CHAPTER 12

If Jazz thought about it — really thought about it — she was sure the panic would eat her whole and she wouldn't be able to stop shaking, not to mention picturing every horrible thing that could have happened if Luther didn't alert her to the hulking presence of Billy DeSantos.

So she refused to think about it.

The hell with fear. She decided instead to be royally pissed.

Pissed that he'd obviously followed her from school to her house, and pissed that she'd never noticed.

Pissed that he thought he could . . .

What?

It was the *what* that ate at the edges of Jazz's composure, so she shoved it aside. Still, it was all she could do to get through the next morning at work.

Even before the lunch bell finished ringing, she was out the door, and a few minutes later, she was glaring at the poster of the monster man with the claw fingers. She didn't bother trying the front door of the building the horror film festival called home. She went right around to the back.

It was the kind of dull, gray afternoon that is a Cleveland specialty in the spring. The alley between the festival building and the bar next door was pocked with puddles, and she zipped around them and into the small backyard. There was a maple tree in one corner, its branches still bare but the catkins on it just bursting to life, vivid green stems topped with fuzzy blooms that looked too bright and cheery against the slate sky.

She paused where building met backyard and realized she was in luck — at least if she could hang on to her adrenaline and her anger — and push aside her fear.

Billy DeSantos had pulled a red plastic milk crate onto the pitted sidewalk outside the back door and sat on it, hunched over his phone, his back to her.

She dared a few steps closer.

From there, she could just make out what he was looking at, blurs of color on the phone screen that he scrolled through with one finger.

Pictures.

Two more steps, and the smudges came

into focus.

Florie in her short black skirt and high black boots.

A close-up of Florie, her eyes rimmed with kohl.

Florie handing around brochures in a crowd that included more than a couple people who looked like they didn't have the nerve to get too near her.

Florie in the office sorting papers.

Florie here in the backyard, a camera slung over one shoulder.

Florie sitting in the office in the chair that belonged to Laverne, her elbows propped on the desk, her eyes focused on the computer screen in front of her, that monster looking over her shoulder.

Jazz was pretty sure she didn't make a sound. It would have been hard, considering the fact that she was convinced her heart had stopped and her breaths were suspended. Still, DeSantos knew she was there.

He spun around.

One look at the metal studs in his cheeks, one instant of remembering how the streetlights had gleamed against them the night before, and every last little morsel of fear, every little bit of hesitation, went up in flames.

"What the hell were you doing outside my

house last night?" she demanded.

DeSantos rose to his feet. Her brief encounter with him a few days earlier and the glimpse of him she'd had at school had left her shaken. Now she remembered why. He towered over her, all bulk and black leather.

"I thought —"

Jazz stepped forward, invading his personal space. She was more than a little gratified when he swallowed his words and took a step back. She set her jaw and raised her chin.

"I don't care what you think," she told him. "I do know that if I ever see you anywhere near my house again, I'm letting the dog out, and if he comes home with his mouth full of leather and your blood on his teeth, just remember, I told you so."

She didn't give him a chance to respond. She turned on her heels and, keeping her head high and her arms tight to her sides, she left the yard.

It wasn't until she was back at St. Catherine's that she allowed herself to collapse into her chair and brace her hands on the desk. She wasn't the least bit surprised they were shaking.

When it came to the bar scene, Tuesday nights were not exactly hopping.

Jazz supposed that was why there was a skeleton crew behind the bar at Great Lakes Brewing when she stopped in.

Lori Simms was not one of them.

She was there on Wednesday night, though, when Jazz returned, and eyeing her, Jazz slipped around a group of middle-aged guys tasting beers and praising them to the high heavens, and climbed up onto the barstool nearest where Lori was washing glasses.

She had never been close friends with Lori. Back in high school (it seemed more like a million years ago rather than ten), Jazz and Lori traveled in different circles. Jazz was a jock — cross-country, track, swimming in the winter to keep in shape. Lori ran with the drama-club crowd, and in spite of those buckteeth of hers — Owen was right, Lori had definitely had major dental work since last Jazz saw her — she'd even starred in a couple of the plays at St. Joseph Academy, the all-girls school they attended. Though they hadn't been close, they had been friendly; their lockers were next to each other senior year, and Jazz remembered that Lori had dreams of hitting the stage in New York.

She was pretty enough.

Lori had clear skin, intense blue eyes, and

light hair streaked with metallic emerald green. She had a small nose turned up slightly at the end and obviously the kind of upbeat personality that was an asset to bartenders far and wide. When she swung around to see what the newest customer at the bar wanted, Lori was already smiling, even before she realized that customer was Jazz.

Then that smile of hers sagged around the edges.

"Hey, Lori!" Jazz leaned forward, her elbows on the bar. "What's up?"

Lori swiped a bar rag over the space in front of Jazz. "What can I get you?"

The bar took up an entire wall of the pub. It was made of gleaming dark wood, and there was a beer list artfully chalked onto the blackboard above Lori's head. Jazz was not a connoisseur like her brothers. She passed on exotic things like sour blueberry porter and went for the tried-and-true. "Dortmunder Gold."

Lori poured from the tap and set the glass in front of Jazz. "You're not here to bust my chops, are you?"

"Why would I —" Jazz sat back, honestly surprised. "You think I'm here to talk to you about Owen?"

"Yeah, well . . ." One corner of Lori's

mouth pulled tight. "Everybody knows about the Ramsey family. You're as fierce about each other as you all are about the damn fire department."

"Maybe, but that doesn't mean I'd try to interfere in your relationship. Even if I didn't like you, it's none of my business. And I do like you. I always have. As far as I'm concerned, you and Owen can date all you want."

Lori didn't even try to control her grin. "We're doing a whole lot more than dating. And yeah, we do it all we want."

This was more information than a younger sister should know about her brother.

Jazz washed the realization down with a sip of beer. "His work schedule is a bitch."

"Tell me about it." Lori took an order for a vodka and tonic and expertly mixed and delivered it. "I haven't seen Owen in a week," she told Jazz when she was done.

Jazz didn't mention she had been out with her brothers just a few days earlier. There is such a thing as too much sharing.

"I hear . . ." Lori paused, obviously trying to decide if this was a subject she should even bring up. Finally, she lifted one shoulder in a what-the-hell sort of shrug. "He's had a lot of girlfriends."

"Owen's a handsome guy." He was,

though that hardly explained his serial dating.

"Should I be worried?"

Jazz couldn't make any promises. "I know he likes you."

"I bet he liked all those other girls, too. He did tell me he's going to be off on Easter. He said he's going to your mom's and he asked me to come along."

"Well, there you have it." Absolute truth, and Jazz was grateful she didn't have to sidestep any more uncomfortable questions. "He's never invited any of his other girlfriends over for Easter."

Lori grinned. "I'll see you there?"

If only Lori knew! Missing a holiday with family was a mortal sin. "I'm bringing the deviled eggs. They're Owen's favorite."

"So why are you here?" Lori asked, more relaxed now that they'd gotten the family stuff out of the way. "I heard from some of the other girls from Joe's that you're living in Tremont. Not enough bars there for you?"

"Plenty of bars. But actually, I wanted to talk to you about —"

Someone at the end of the bar waved Lori down, and Jazz knew better than to try and delay her. A bartender counted on tips, and fast service was part of the deal. She waited until Lori was finished and when she was, she scooted back over.

"I've got a break," Lori told her. She tipped her head toward the front of the pub and the windows that looked out at the stone patio there. "Meet me outside?"

The patio was surrounded by a low decorative iron fence, and in nice weather, it was filled with tables and chairs. This time of year, it was still chilly and there weren't many people outside. There were just a few chairs set here and there to accommodate the smokers. By the time Jazz grabbed her beer and got out there, Lori was already in one of those chairs, lighting up.

"Not something you're going to want to do on Easter. My mom is a fanatic about the evils of smoking."

Lori paled, and as if Claire Ramsey was lurking somewhere in the shadows, watching and judging, she waved a hand in front of her face, dispersing the smoke.

"You won't tell?"

"Not my business. I'm sure Owen will warn you." Jazz dragged over a chair and sat down. "You like it here?"

Lori nodded. "I love it! The customers are friendly, the people I work with are great, and the money's not half-bad. Way more than I was making waiting tables at the last place I worked."

"You dreamed of being on Broadway."

"You always said you were going to join the fire department."

Touché.

Jazz smiled to let Lori know she didn't take it personally. "I heard there was a confrontation here a while ago. Two young women?"

Lori pressed her lips together, thinking. "Maybe I wasn't here."

"I was hoping you were. One of them was the girl who got murdered over in Tremont. You probably saw it on TV."

"That girl?" She sat back, took a drag on her cigarette, studied Jazz carefully. "Owen says she went to St. Catherine's where you work. And it's funny you should mention her. He's working, and he called from the station a little while ago, and he said he needed to talk to you. He told me that he remembered bumping into that dead girl —"

"Florie?"

"Yeah, Florie. He said he forgot all about it. He bumped into her somewhere or another and he remembered her from your cross-country meets. She told him she lived on Murray Hill, right next door to where there was a fire a couple months ago. Owen, he said it was no big deal that he talked to her and he forgot all about it. That's why he didn't mention it to you the last time he saw you, but he said he was going to give you a call and tell you."

He hadn't, but then, like Owen said, it really was no big deal. Florie and Grace's fight at the bar was.

"Think about it." Jazz hoped to get Lori back on track. "Were you here the night Florie stopped in?"

Another drag, and when Lori exhaled, the smoke floated out to the sidewalk and from there, over the redbrick pavers of Market Street. Like Tremont, Ohio City was an old part of town, and on this short block, there was a coffee shop, a wine bar, and an upscale eatery across the way along with a building on the corner that housed a barber college that had been there for as long as anyone could remember. This side of the street had been completely swallowed by Great Lakes years before, much to the delight of the neighborhood. Ohio City home and business owners were dedicated to their urban neighborhood and determined to keep it vital. They welcomed and supported its shops and restaurants and, like the suburbanites who came from all around and made it an institution, they shopped at the massive West Side Market across the way, a landmark that included indoor market vendors and outdoor stalls that sold everything from fruits and vegetables to seafood and meat.

"I'm trying to remember. But like I said, maybe I wasn't here." Lori dragged her cigarette butt across the stone patio to put it out.

Jazz did her best to be patient. She'd brought her beer outside, and she took another drink.

"One of the girls who was here is blond and pretty," Jazz told her, hoping to jog her memory. "Probably stylishly dressed." Since Jazz didn't give a damn about style, she wasn't exactly sure what that meant, but she knew Lori would figure it out. "Her name is Grace. Grace, she told me that the other girl, the one who got killed, she told me that girl, Florie, knocked over whatever she was drinking."

"That's the fight you're talking about?"

It wasn't so much the question as the way Lori said it that caused a shiver to zip up Jazz's back like a current of electricity. "You do remember."

"When you said two young women, that's what threw me off." Thinking, she squeezed her eyes shut.

Intrigued and anxious to hear more, Jazz

ignored the guy from behind the bar trying to get Lori's attention, waving through the window for her to come back inside.

"They are young. They only graduated from St. Catherine's a couple years ago."

"Oh, the blonde was young, all right. And like you said, she was all dressed up. She came into the pub with friends. Four, five other girls. They were waiting for a booth to open up and while they did, they came over to the bar to order drinks. Not that I served them alcohol. None of them was old enough to drink, I could tell from just looking at them."

"One of the girls with Grace wasn't Florie, was it? The girl whose picture you probably saw on TV?"

Jazz was so far off base, Lori waved away the questions.

"No, no. That other girl . . . if she's the one you're talking about . . . she was already sitting at the bar. I mean, that's the person this other girl, this blonde, got into a fight with. It was a corker! No way I was going to get between the two of them. My manager finally came over and handled it. But the way the other girl looked . . ." Lori paused to think and this time, her fellow bartender knocked on the window.

"Got to go!" Lori popped out of her chair.

"Don't worry about the beer. I've got it!"

"Thanks," Jazz told her. "Only you didn't explain. Why did you think the other woman wasn't young? Was she dressed weird? Black leather? Streaks in her hair? Scary makeup?"

Her hand on the door, Lori stopped and turned. "No. Nothing like that. She was really frumpy. And I wasn't working that end of the bar, so I never paid a whole lot of attention to her face. I guess I saw the clothes and just assumed she was one of the old batty women from the neighborhood. She was wearing this ratty raincoat and big black boots. Not like fashion boots. Like granny galoshes. You know, the kind that have those funny metal fasteners on the front. And her hair . . ." Lori made a face.

Jazz got up from her chair and closed in on Lori. "What about her hair?"

"I couldn't see it really well. I wasn't paying a whole lot of attention and she had this hat on, anyway. A knitted hat with earflaps that tied under her chin. I do remember walking by and wondering what the heck was sticking out of her hat. It took me a minute to realize it was actually hair. It was gray and it gleamed in the light like it was made out of plastic. That's how shiny it was."

Jazz thanked her and told her she looked

forward to seeing her again on Easter, and she meant it.

She only hoped Lori wouldn't have the bad sense to light up in front of Mom.

It seemed like the more information Jazz found out about Florie, the more confused she got.

First it was goth clothes and makeup, then the news delivered by Grace (and therefore suspect) that Florie was sleeping with Tate Brody.

Florie was borrowing a neighbor's child.

She was dressed in rags and obviously wearing a wig.

She was looking for a divorce attorney even though she wasn't married.

Jazz's head was in a spin. And it wasn't from the beer.

She parked in her driveway, locked the car, and headed for the back door. She already had her key out, so when she froze, her hand in the air and the key pointed to where the lock should have been, she supposed she must have looked as stunned as she felt.

But then she could hardly help it.

Her back door was wide open.

CHAPTER 13

It was dark outside and in, and from where she stood on the back porch, it was impossible to see anything except the eerie blue glow of the time on her microwave.

"Luther!" Jazz got no response, and it was that more than anything that made her pulse thump and her heart race and her mouth go dry.

If the door had somehow swung open and Luther ran off . . .

If someone had broken into the house and hurt the dog . . .

If Billy DeSantos was stupid enough to come back when she'd clearly warned him away . . .

"Luther!" She tried again, and this time heard the faint scrambling of claws on the floor.

If something terrible happened to Luther, she'd not only have to break the news to Greg, she'd never forgive herself.

She poked her keys up through her fingers like a weapon, took her phone out of her pocket in case she needed to make a quick call for help, and stepped into her kitchen.

The moment she did, the lights flicked on to reveal Luther sitting like a good dog in the doorway between the kitchen and the dining room. He was wearing a headband with pink-and-white bunny ears on it, and he had a green Easter basket in his mouth.

"Surprise!"

When Claire Ramsey stepped around the corner, Jazz wasn't sure if she should give her a hug or read her the riot act.

She decided to pass on the riot act when she saw her mom was grinning. It was an expression that had been all too painfully absent in the year since her husband died.

"Mom!" Jazz pressed a hand to her heart, and the moment her mom let go of Luther's leash, she called the dog over. He deposited the Easter basket at her feet. "What's this?"

"It's just a little something from me and Big George." Claire came over and gave Jazz a peck on the cheek.

Jazz made sure she was smiling when she said, "So you let yourself into my house and scared me half to death?"

"Did I scare you?" The blood drained from Claire's face and she looped an arm around Jazz's shoulders and pulled her into a quick hug. "I'm sorry, Jasmine. You're so smart, I thought you'd figure it out. Who else has a key but me? Unless . . ." The kitchen was far smaller than Jazz's office back at St. Catherine's — stove, refrigerator, sink, a table for two next to the back window. When Grandma and Grandpa Kurcz owned the house, the room was a mishmash of dark wood, red linoleum, and corny signs that said things like KISS THE POLISH COOK. It was the first room Jazz had remodeled when she bought the house from them three years earlier, and she was still in love with the white cabinets and black granite countertops she was able to afford only because Hal knew a firefighter who spent his days off working with a kitchen remodeler.

There wasn't anyplace in the kitchen for someone to hide.

Not unless that someone happened to have superpowers and a cloak of invisibility.

That didn't stop Claire from peering into every corner.

"Nick's not back, is he?"

Jazz groaned. "No, Nick's not back."

"Well, he had a key." Claire defended her jump to conclusions. "If you're not sure who could have let themselves in, it's only natural to assume that Nick —"

"No." Jazz dumped her purse and her keys and her phone on the kitchen table, and while she was at it, she closed the back door and plucked the bunny ears from Luther's head. It was that or he'd end up eating them. "How long have you been here lurking in the dark?"

"I wasn't lurking." Claire went over to the strip of counter between the stove and the refrigerator, and Jazz saw that she'd been there at least long enough to boil water and pour herself a cup of tea. She grabbed a spoon from the drawer, fished the tea bag out of her cup, and tossed it in the trash can under the sink. "I turned the lights off and opened the back door as soon as I saw your car coming down the street. Luther and I wanted to surprise you."

"Well, you surprised me, all right." Jazz picked up the Easter basket and peered into it.

"You're never too old for Easter candy," her mom said. "There's Reese's cups and Cadbury eggs!"

When it came to Cadbury eggs, Jazz was an addict. Years before she had sworn she'd never buy them, because when she did, caloric disaster ensued.

"Thanks, Mom."

Her mother poured milk into her cup and sat down at the table. She was five-foot-two, the same height as Jazz, and had the same brown hair, though Claire's was cut short and, Jazz noticed, recently highlighted with a warm red that made her mom look younger than fifty-two. Her hips were rounder and her face was fuller than Jazz's, but her hands were small and dainty. Her fingers were slim and always busy.

Claire sipped her tea. "Have you had dinner?" she asked.

"No." And now that she thought about it, she was starving. Jazz dug through the fridge, found a tub of hummus, and took it over to the table along with a bag of pita chips. She got two plates out of the cupboard. Though Claire would surely say she wasn't hungry, she was a sucker for hummus.

"Oh, I'm not hungry." Claire reached into the bag for a handful of chips. "But I guess hummus can't hurt."

"Good for what ails you." Jazz dragged a pita through the hummus and chowed it down and watched her mom do the same. "It's Wednesday. Why aren't you at Grandma Kurcz's for dinner?"

Claire always went to her parents' house on Wednesdays for dinner, just like they always came to the Ramsey house on Sunday. "I was there. Grandma made breaded pork chops. She wants to know why you don't stop by more often."

"I'll go next Wednesday." Jazz made a mental note. "Maybe she'll make beet soup."

"If you call and tell her you're coming, I'll bet anything Grandma will whip up a batch."

Jazz would be sure to call Grandma Kurcz the next day.

"That still doesn't explain what you're doing all the way over here." Jazz polished off another hummus-coated cracker. Her Ramsey grandparents were retired and living in Florida, but Grandma and Grandpa Kurcz — Doris and Stanley — lived in Independence, a suburb to the south of the city. Tremont was not on Claire's way home.

Her mom's smile was quick. She picked up her mug, set it back down. "Like I said, Easter candy. I didn't want to wait until Easter to give you your basket."

"Owen's bringing his latest girlfriend, you know."

This was news to Claire. She took another sip of tea, and over the rim of the cup, Jazz saw her cheeks flush with color. "I hope she's not like that last one. That girl could drink a sailor under the table."

"This one's nice. I went to high school with her." Jazz did not mention the cigarettes. There was no use prejudicing Claire. "You could have given me my Easter basket then."

"I could have." Claire set down her mug so she could dip her cracker in hummus. She paused, cracker nearly to mouth. "I saw the picture. The one in your living room."

"Owen and Hal —"

"Yeah, Hal stopped by on Sunday and told me about it. It's a great picture."

It was just as well Jazz had a mouth full of hummus — she didn't have to answer.

"It's kind of nice, don't you think?" Claire tipped her head. "You know he's always thinking about you."

"And you."

"Well, if he's thinking about me, he's thinking about that Honey Do list he never got done!" Claire finished her chip and washed it down with the rest of her tea. "It's a mile long."

"You know I'll help with anything you need to do. Just let me know and —"

"And really, that's not what I came over here to talk to you about." Claire reached across the table and covered Jazz's hand with hers. "It's been a long year," she said.

Jazz sighed. "You got that right."

"And last year at this time, I never even would have believed I could be sitting here telling you this, but . . ." A short, uncomfortable laugh bubbled up from her. "Life is full of surprises."

Jazz wasn't sure where the conversation was going, she only knew that wherever it was, she wasn't going to like it. She flipped her hand so she could wind her fingers through her mom's. "What's up?"

Claire pulled her hand away and popped out of her chair. She walked as far as the doorway that led into Jazz's tiny dining room, then whirled around again. "It's like this," she said. "The boys don't even know, Jasmine. I wasn't sure how to tell them. I wanted to tell you first. You know, to see how you'd react. I figured if you understood, then maybe when I bring it up with them I can be a little more . . . I don't know . . . a little more confident, I guess."

Jazz's stomach soured. "You're sick."

"Oh my gosh, no!" Claire sat back down. She leaned over the table and looked Jazz in the eye. She pulled in a breath, swallowed hard. "I've got a date."

It took a minute for Jazz to process the information, and even after that minute, the only thing she could manage to blurt out was "What?"

"Yeah, I know. I'm surprised, too. Like I said, a year ago I couldn't have imagined it. Heck, a couple months ago it would have seemed impossible. But . . ." She was wearing a gray sweatshirt with the red Cleveland Division of Fire logo on it, and when she shrugged, it pulled across her chest.

"His name is Peter Nestico. We've been working the Friday-night fish fries together at Our Lady of Angels and we got to talking and —"

"You can't just go out with some random guy you met at church!" Jazz couldn't believe her own ears. Was she lecturing her mother? Well, maybe she was. Maybe she had to. Maybe she needed to talk some sense into her. "How do you know who he really is? He could be looking to steal your identity or he could be some sort of crazy person or —"

Her preaching might have been far more effective if Claire didn't burst out laughing.

"I've known Peter for years," her mother told her. "Through church. His wife died of cancer three or four years ago."

"And now he's out trolling for a new woman so he can —"

"Jasmine." It was not so much her mother's tone of voice that stopped Jazz cold as it was the look that flew at her from across the table. Oh, she remembered that look, all right. Claire Ramsey was laid-back and quiet. She could afford to be. When she brought out *that look,* it was far more potent than any amount of yelling could ever be.

"We are not going to run off to Vegas and get married." Claire's voice was level. Jazz remembered that tone from the old days, too. It clearly told her the subject was not open for discussion. "We are going for coffee. Tomorrow evening. Maybe we'll do something crazy after like grab a burger or something. I am not making a lifelong commitment, and Jasmine . . ." This time when her mother reached for her hand, Jazz felt the frisson of emotion that passed between them. "It doesn't mean I've forgotten Dad. That's never going to happen. It just means that Peter is nice, and he's fun to be around, and that sometimes, I'd like to have someone I can talk to. Someone who isn't Big George."

Jazz bit her lower lip. "Is he coming for Easter?" She wasn't sure why it was important; she only knew it was, and she held her breath, waiting for her mother's reply.

"No. He's going to his daughter's because he wants to spend the day with his grandchildren."

"He has grandchildren? How old is this guy?"

"He's just a little older than me. And I'd have grandchildren, too, if my children could ever get their acts together and decide to settle down."

Jazz was in no mood for a lecture she'd heard more than a few times, sometimes with Hal as the subject, sometimes with Owen. More often featuring her. She steered the conversation back where it started. "You're going to meet him at the coffee place, right? You're not going to let him pick you up at home? That way you've got a car there if you need to make a quick escape."

"I promise."

"And you're going to text me when you get home. I mean, the minute you get home."

"Cross my heart," her mother told her.

"Well, all right then."

"Don't tell the boys. I want to do that."

It was Jazz's turn to promise, and once she had, Claire patted Luther, hugged Jazz, and left for home.

In a matter of minutes, Jazz was on her computer, Googling Peter Nestico.

Except for things like his address and the fact that he owned a small company that did some sort of metal-fabricating work, Peter Nestico was pretty much a nonentity in the world of cyberspace. Jazz finally gave up the fruitless search for the juicy information she'd hoped to find, the damning facts that would make her mother change her mind about having coffee with the man.

By then it was late, but Jazz was too keyed up for bed. Since she couldn't make sense of what her mother was doing — and because she desperately needed something in her world to make sense — she switched tactics and did a little more digging into the mystery that was Florie Allen.

Thanks to Owen mentioning that he'd talked to Florie, and Florie telling him that she lived on Murray Hill right next door to where there had been a recent fire, she had new information. On Thursday — the day of her mother's date — she drove to school, and as soon as her day was done, she hopped in the car and headed for Little Italy.

Like the city's other ethnic enclaves, Little Italy was once home to the immigrants who flooded the city in the late nineteenth century. Most of the neighborhood's earliest settlers were stonecutters who left their native Italy to work at the grandiose Lake View Cemetery just up the hill. These days, like in Tremont and Ohio City, the streets of Little Italy were filled with restaurants and art galleries, coffeehouses and bars. But here, every one of them had an Italian accent.

Parking was at a premium and Jazz considered herself lucky when she found a spot on the street not far from the house where she was headed. It was typical of the neighborhood, tall and skinny and painted a dull green that at one time must have looked good with its white shutters and trim. These days the colors were faded and pocked. Like so many of the houses around it (like the one next door where the windows were still boarded and the siding was streaked with smoky gray trails), this one was built at the top of a small rise. Jazz needed to climb four cement steps, walk a short path, then go up the wooden porch steps to get to the front door. There were three mailboxes there — first, second, and third floors. Under each was a single sheet of paper listing the names of the tenants. BRONSON, KRAKOWSKI, and ALLEN lived on the second floor.

She rang the bell and got to the top of the stairway just as a tall young man with hair that stuck up around his head in a curly auburn halo opened the door to the second-floor apartment a crack.

"Yeah, Florie. Sure, she lived here," he

said in answer to Jazz's question. He was dressed in gray flannel sleep pants with the Batman logo all over them and a white V-neck undershirt. His feet were bare. He didn't invite her in. "The cops have been by to talk to us. If you're a cop —"

"I'm not." She wanted to make that perfectly clear. "I'm an old friend. I thought maybe you'd be able to tell me more about what Florie's been up to lately. You lived here with her."

"Not for long!" The voice — it belonged to a woman — floated out from behind the half-closed door.

Jazz peered around the boy with the red hair, and he got the message. He moved back and opened the door wider, and Jazz stepped into the apartment.

It was pretty much what she expected from a students' rental on Murray Hill, a bare-bones living room with one beat-up easy chair, a couch that had a red-and-blue tie-dyed blanket thrown over it, books, and the faint smell of old beer and laundry that needed to be washed.

The owner of the second voice was in the kitchen. Jazz heard dishes clatter.

"What do you mean, not for long?" She raised her voice, but when she didn't get an answer, she turned again to the boy. "What

228

did she mean?"

"Florie." With the way the light flowed in from the front window, Jazz could see that the young man's cheeks were dotted with freckles — hundreds of freckles — that danced this way and that when he made a face. "She wasn't sticking around much longer."

"Really?"

"Yeah, well, she was —"

The woman Jazz heard rambling around in the kitchen walked into the room, a dishcloth in one hand. She wasn't much younger than Jazz, and she, too, looked like she'd just gotten out of bed. Her long dark hair was tangled, her outfit was nearly a match for the man's except that her sleep pants were decorated with the grinning face of Hello Kitty, and her T-shirt was pink.

"Meg Bronson." She stuck out a hand and Jazz shook it. "The guy with the big mouth is Jeff Krakowski but you can call him Croc. Everyone does."

"I'm Jazz," she told them. "And I just wondered —"

"Yeah. Pretty much everyone is wondering about Florie," Meg told her.

"Not over at North Coast. The students there act like they hardly knew her."

Meg draped the dish towel over the back

of the couch. "She hated those asshats."

"Do you know why?"

Meg's phone pinged. She took it out of her pocket, checked the text message, and didn't answer it. "I know she wasn't staying there after this semester."

"Her grades were bad."

"And her finances were even worse." Croc strolled over to the other side of the couch and flopped down.

"Is that what you meant . . ." Jazz looked at Meg. "When you said she wasn't going to be living here much longer?"

"Look . . ." Meg scooped her hair out of her eyes. "We weren't best friends or anything. Me and Croc, we roomed together last year and we lost the med student who was living with us. He went back to Uruguay or Colombia or —"

"Costa Rica," Croc provided the details.

"Yeah. Costa Rica. Whatever." Meg got back on track. "Once he left, we advertised for a roommate and we got Florie. And she was an okay person, but there was only so long the two of us could keep fronting her money. She finally paid January rent in February."

"And she never did pay February and March," Croc added.

"We're not jerks, but it wasn't fair to us,"

Meg said. "We told her she had to be out by the end of the month. Now . . . well . . ." Her eyes welled and she looked away, composing herself. "I guess she really is out for good."

"And you're out the money she owes you," Jazz pointed out.

Meg brushed the thought aside. "We'll get by. Croc's been working extra at the place he bartends, and I'll call and give my dad a sob story. That usually works. But it's the principle of the thing, you know? Florie owed us, and she never paid."

"And she was weird," Croc put in.

Since Croc had already settled in with a game of Call of Duty, Jazz turned to Meg for the answer. "Was she?"

She laughed. "Hey, I'm a theater major over at Case. I see weird all the time! I wouldn't exactly call Florie weird, I'd say she was . . . strange."

"In what way?" Jazz wanted to know.

"Come on." With Meg leading the way, Jazz walked through the dining room (there was a card table in the center of the room with two backpacks on it, and a case of Bud Lite over in the corner) and to a short hallway where there was a bathroom and three bedrooms. Meg opened the door of the room at the end of the hall and stepped back to allow Jazz inside.

"Florie's room?" Jazz asked, but she didn't really need Meg to answer. The first thing she saw was a print of the same photograph she'd seen Tate Brody take out of Florie's studio at school, the computer-manipulated picture that was a swirl of colors and images.

It was the only touch of color in a room that was otherwise a study in monochrome — white bedspread, black fuzzy throw rug, a wooden desk painted white. There were no clothes lying across the single white wooden chair in the corner, no papers on the desk, no signs of life.

The thought was especially poignant, and Jazz got rid of it with a shake of her shoulders. "The cops looked around?"

"I guess they didn't find much of anything."

"Was it always . . ." Jazz took a couple steps further into the room and glided one finger over the surface of the pristine desk. "Was Florie always this neat?"

"I think that's part of the reason Croc thinks she was weird," Meg confessed. "But hey, to each his own, you know? She was the same way when it came to the kitchen. Didn't like things on the counter, cleaned up the table as soon as she stood up." It reminded Jazz of what Loretta at St. Catherine's had said about how Florie liked nothing better than cleaning up the cafeteria kitchen.

"Sounds like Florie should have been the ideal roommate," Jazz ventured. "If it wasn't for the fact that she never had money for rent."

"You got that right. Rent money, and . . ." There was a single closet in the room, and Meg went over to it, opened the door, and stepped back.

Jazz leaned forward and, as much as she tried, she couldn't help herself. She stared wide-eyed at the item of clothing that was front and center, an ankle-length black robe with long sleeves. There was a black veil attached to the hanger, a rosary long enough to wear as a belt looped over it. Odd? This definitely qualified. "Don't tell me, let me guess. This is what Croc meant when he said she was weird."

Meg fingered the nun's habit. "It's not like she went out and bought it or had it specially made or anything. I mean, if she did, then that would be really strange. But she borrowed . . ." The way she emphasized the word told Jazz it was true only in the broadest sense of the word. "She borrowed stuff from our theater department. Stuff like this. Well, really, I borrowed it for her once in a while." Meg scooped the habit off the hanger and hung it over her arm. "I'm glad I showed you this, I would have forgotten about it otherwise. I'll take it back to the theater with me tonight."

"Did she say why she needed it?" Jazz asked.

Meg laughed. "I never asked. What that girl didn't do with clothes! Sometimes she'd go to Goodwill and come back with the strangest stuff."

"Like an old raincoat and galoshes?" Jazz asked.

Meg eyed her with new interest. "Yeah, she did buy that stuff once. And once she bought an old bridesmaid's dress. Pink satin. Hellish! But every once in a while . . ." The habit slipped on her arm and she hoisted it back into place. "Every once in a while Florie would ask me if I could get something special for her. Like this outfit. Or one time it was a pair of those really old lady shoes, the kind that tie up the front and have chunky heels."

"Stuff she couldn't find even at the thrift store."

Jazz was talking to herself, but Meg's eyes lit. "You're right. I never thought about it that way."

"Did you ever ask her why she wanted clothes like that?"

"I didn't much care. She paid me a little something every time I got an outfit out of the costume room for her. But don't tell anyone." Meg looked at her hard, waiting for Jazz to promise she wouldn't.

"Where did she wear this stuff?" she asked instead.

Meg shrugged. "Sometimes she'd dress up in the morning and head out. Sometimes she'd go out late in one outfit or another. I dunno. I pretty much don't care, except I wondered if maybe she and that guy of hers were into some kind of kinky sex. You know, role-playing and all."

As far as Jazz could remember, no one else had mentioned that Florie had a boyfriend. Unless . . .

She told herself not to give in to the tingle of excitement that told her she might be onto something, and instead kept her voice even. "Any idea who that guy was?"

"I never saw him." Meg led the way out of the room. On her way through the dining room, she dumped the habit on the table. "Hey, Croc." He was busy shooting Nazis, so she raised her voice and tried again. "Croc!"

"Yo!"

235

"That guy Florie used to go out with once in a while, did you ever meet him?"

He paused the game and peered at them over the back of the couch. "Who'd go out with a chick who wears a nun's habit?"

"Not the question," Jazz reminded him. "Did she ever have a guy come over?"

"Not that I ever saw," he told her. "But a few times when she left here, she'd go downstairs and get into a car."

"What kind of car?"

"That's what that cop asked." As if she was picturing it, Meg went to the windows that looked out over the front yard. "Hard to tell from here. And it was usually dark."

"An Audi. That's what I told the cops because I'm pretty sure that's what it was," Croc said. "And the one time she went out there, the guy, the driver, he was getting something out of the trunk."

"Did you get a look at him?" Jazz closed in on the couch, the better not to miss a single thing Croc said. "What did he look like?"

"Old guy," Croc told her. "I mean, maybe forty. Lots of dark curly hair, a little bit of a beard. Nobody I know."

Maybe not, but Jazz was pretty sure it was someone she knew.

Tate Brody.

CHAPTER 14

There was no use driving all the way back to this side of town on another day. She was already close to North Coast, and Jazz decided to make the best of it.

She went back to the building where the students had their studios, and when there was no sign of Tate Brody there, she went in search of his office.

He'd just gotten in — at least if the light jacket he was wearing and the Starbucks cup he set on the desk meant anything. The office door was open, and he thought he was alone. Even as she watched, he flicked on the vintage banker's lamp on his Hepplewhite desk. The lamp had an amber shade, and the light illuminated the seashell marquetry on the desk and the laptop on it and cast the rest of the room in soft shadows that made Brody's face into a study of planes and angles. The entire wall to the left of his desk was taken up with bookshelves, the books on them neatly and carefully tucked away. There was no sign of that photograph of Florie's, the one he'd taken from her studio.

Jazz rapped on the doorjamb.

When Brody's head snapped up, his eyes lit with recognition. Even if he wasn't exactly sure who she was. "Miss . . ."

"Ramsey. Jazz Ramsey. I was here last week. About Florie Allen."

"Of course." He slipped off his Eddie Bauer fleece and draped it over the back of his desk chair. Like the last time she'd seen him, he was dressed casually. Charcoal pants and a long-sleeved rusty shirt, the color intense in the amber light, the shirt cut slim to make the most of his runner's build. Either Brody had a flair for fashion, or someone who shopped for him did.

"What can I do for you?"

Jazz stepped into the office. "You can tell me why the last time we talked, you didn't bother to mention that you'd been with Florie the night she was murdered."

He was just about to sit down and he froze, his spine suddenly rigid. He gripped the back of his desk chair, and though he tried to make it look like the most natural thing in the world, she couldn't help but notice that his knuckles were white. "Since

I had nothing to do with what happened to Florie, I can't see how it matters when I saw her last."

"If you had nothing to do with what happened to Florie, it seems odd you'd keep something like being with her the night she died a secret."

"Explain this to me again." The moment of surprise evaporated, and a half smile tickled the corners of his mouth. He was handsome and accomplished, the idol of his students. He knew it. "You work where Florie went to school a couple years ago, and you think this is your business because . . ."

"Call me nosy." It wasn't either an excuse or a reason, but it was all Jazz had, and her smile told him as much. "I can't believe something that important slipped your mind."

"I can't believe you'd have the nerve to come here and ask me about it. There's really no reason for me to talk to you. I've already talked to the police."

"Did you tell them what you didn't tell me?"

In the glow from the desk lamp, his eyes were the color of Lake Erie in November. Gray and stormy. "I'm sure what I told them went into their official report. Since

I'm still here . . ." He threw his hands in the air. "They obviously haven't locked me up so I think you'll have to agree they don't share in your taste for drama. I'm not some lunatic murderer. I was with Florie that evening because we were shooting B roll."

"For the commercial."

"Yes, for the commercial. We did what we needed to do and then we left. I went my way and she went hers."

"Did the two of you walk outside the building together?"

"Again, you're asking questions, and I don't understand why."

"It just seems weird, that's all." Though she clearly hadn't been invited, she sat in the chair in front of his desk and settled back, hoping to look casual so he wouldn't catch on to the fact that her insides twisted and flipped. She had never been very good at minding other people's business. That was Sarah Carrington's job. Jazz was all about keeping things on an even keel.

Except murder didn't qualify, did it?

She crossed her ankles, her nonchalance a mirror of his. She wondered if he was faking it, too. "That B-roll project, you were giving Florie the opportunity to earn some extra credit."

"I told you she needed it. I hoped it might

help her maintain her grades and keep her scholarship."

"No luck, huh? I mean, she only got one A all semester, and that lonely A came from you."

He slipped into his desk chair and twined his fingers together, his hands on the gleaming mahogany surface in front of him. Not standard issue from the school, Jazz would guess. This desk was old, elegant. "What's that supposed to mean?"

Jazz leaned forward, her elbows on her knees. "The night before the video project was due, Florie was in a panic. She didn't have a clue what she was doing. Then she turns in her video and . . . voilà! She gets an A. I'm just wondering, that's all. I'm just wondering if that has anything to do with the fact that you were sleeping with her."

He went as still as a statue. One minute melted into two and Jazz swore he never even breathed. She held her breath, too, and when he yanked open the top drawer of his desk, the sudden noise cracked through her like a rifle shot. She expected him to pull out a cell phone and call security to haul her sorry ass out of there. Instead, he held up a flash drive.

He popped open the laptop in front of him and inserted the drive. His fingers flew over the keyboard and when he was good and ready — only when he was good and ready — did he aim a laser look across the desk at her.

"Come over here."

In the silence of the office, his voice was clipped. In the weird half shadows, his expression was unreadable.

Jazz braced herself against a sudden apprehension.

If she hesitated, he'd read right through her and know she was scared out of her wits.

If she made up an excuse, he'd realize she was winging it, just like she'd been winging the last two weeks of her life.

If she walked out, he'd make sure she never got the chance to talk to him again.

Her knees rubbery, Jazz got up and went to stand next to him.

"What is it?"

"Just watch."

The screen flashed with an image that was either a sunrise or a sunset, a bright blaze of orange, a blink of yellow, a slash of pink.

Sunrise, she decided. It must have been, because the next thing she saw was a shot of downtown Cleveland taken from high up in one of the office buildings that ringed Public Square, where just two weeks before, alive and well, Florie had handed out brochures for the horror festival. The camera zeroed in on a group of people rushing to their jobs, the morning sun on their faces, backpacks slung behind them, their hands filled with tote bags and coffee cups like the one on Brody's desk, where a tiny wisp of steam rose from the top, ghostly in the light.

The camera zoomed in a little more, and soon, one person was singled out in the crowd, a single face flashed on the screen. Then another. Then another.

The next four minutes were a dizzying whirl of features and faces, people from all walks of life, short and tall, black and white and Asian, young and old. The background scenes changed, too, from Public Square, to the West Side Market Jazz had looked at from outside the brewery pub only the night before, to a park, to the lakefront. People coming and going, each frame of the video revealing personalities and moods, histories in the blink of each eye. Throughout, the lighting was perfect, filled with mood and shadow one minute, bright and promising the next. The background music was upbeat and not intrusive; the transitions from scene to scene were smooth and easy on the eye.

When it was finally over, Jazz felt as if she'd met the entire population of Cleveland, up close and personal. She was impressed. And incredibly moved. Especially when the final credit came on the screen.

Cleveland, it said.

By Florie Allen.

"That was . . ." Jazz struggled for the words. It would have been easier if there wasn't a lump in her throat. "It was —"

"Remarkable? That was the one word that occurred to me the first time I watched it," Brody said. He stared at that last screen — the credits, Florie's name — before he shook himself away from the spell of the video. "The assignment was simple enough — create a video that could be used by local government to tell the story of the city. Some students talked history. Some of them focused on industry. Florie is the only one who concentrated on the people. So . . ." His chair swiveled and he turned it slightly so his knees brushed Jazz's. "You don't think that deserved an A?"

"It did," Jazz admitted. "Florie did. But just the night before she turned it in, she told Grace she was desperate, that she didn't know what she was doing."

"And you believe Grace? As much as I admire the girl's talent, I know better than to take anything she says about Florie at face value. You should, too. You claim to know them both."

It was a sobering thought. Had she gotten so caught up in the fire of what she'd come to think of as her mission to learn the truth that she'd made assumptions? Had she cobbled together the bits and pieces of information she'd come across into some sort of story that made sense in her mind, but not in the real world? Had she . . . had she really . . . gotten so carried away that she had the balls to accuse an admired teacher of sleeping with one of his students?

Jazz swallowed down her mortification, but she knew there was no way she could keep the heat from her cheeks.

Brody noticed.

Of course he noticed.

That made her embarrassment — and the heat — even worse.

Jazz cleared her throat, scrambling for some subject — any subject — that would ease the knot in her windpipe. "What about Florie's other classes?" she asked.

"You mean the ones she was failing? What about them?"

"If she could do such excellent work . . ." She glanced again at the computer screen. *By Florie Allen.* "How could she do so well in one class and so poorly in all the rest of them?"

"I can't speak for any of those instructors.

I know Joyce Wildemere, who teaches screenwriting, said working with Florie was a losing cause. And Joyce never gives up on any student."

Brody stood. He was taller than Jazz, and standing too close. "Now Ms. Ramsey, you've seen the quality work Florie turned in. Do you still think the only reason she got an A was because I was sleeping with her?"

"But you went to her house to pick her up on more than one occasion."

"Did I?"

"Her roommates told me, they said it was a man with curly hair and a bit of a beard."

He brushed a hand over whiskers the color of oak leaves in autumn. "I doubt I'm the only guy in Cleveland with a beard."

Jazz refused to let it go. Yes, Florie's video was spectacular. Yes, she deserved an A. Yes, certainly, he was right, it could have been anyone there outside the house on Murray Hill.

But if all that was true, then she knew no more than she did the night Luther signaled his find in the abandoned building.

And that wasn't good enough.

"You were with her the night she died."

"I never denied it, though I did fail to mention it to a woman who had no business asking about it in the first place."

He was being gracious, and Jazz was pretty certain she didn't deserve it. Not after she marched into his office and threw out accusations and demanded answers.

"You're right." She dipped her head, fighting for composure and the words that might explain her actions. Before she could find them, a woman breezed through the office doorway.

She wasn't expecting Brody to have company. She came to a stop just inside the door, and a flash of surprise froze her delicate features. To her credit, she recovered in a heartbeat, and by the time she strolled over to the desk, Brody had already stepped away from Jazz.

"Hey!" He kissed her cheek. "I didn't know you were planning to stop by."

"Obviously." Her eyes were dark, but her coloring was porcelain. The combination was striking. Her smile was sleek, and she put a hand on Brody's arm and left it there, and in that moment, Jazz knew who did his shopping.

"I had a meeting over at the natural history museum about the fundraiser next month," she told him. "And now I'm headed to dinner at Club Isabella with Blaire and Tommi and the rest of the board, but I couldn't be this close and not stop to say hello." She swung her gaze to Jazz, and her voice changed ever so slightly. Warm and fuzzy to passionless, aloof. "Hello."

"Hi." Jazz had nothing to feel guilty about, but still, she felt as if she owed the woman an explanation. She stepped back, putting a little more distance between herself and Brody. "I'm not a student."

"I'm not, either." The woman stuck out a hand. "Sloane Brody," she said.

Of all the things Jazz cared about in the world, what went on in so-called "society" was way at the bottom of the list. But even she recognized the name. Sloane Brody's photograph routinely appeared in the paper and online along with articles about the orchestra, museums, and charitable work of all sorts.

Sloane tightened her hold on Brody's arm. "Tate is my husband."

Jazz wondered how many other women she'd had to remind of that not-unimportant fact.

Sloane wore a jacket that cost as much as Jazz made in a month. Her makeup was perfect, her lipstick glossy. The diamond in her wedding band sparked like lightning.

Jazz didn't give a damn. At least not as much of a damn as she did about Florie. "I just stopped in to talk about —"

"The student who was killed," Brody finished the sentence.

Sloane's smile withered. "That poor girl. And they were together that night, you know. Tate and that . . ."

"Florie." When Sloane couldn't come up with it, Jazz supplied the name.

"Yes, Tate and Florie. They were working on a commercial together. Did he tell you that?"

"He did." Jazz lied because there didn't seem much use in pointing out that the first time she'd talked to him, Brody had conveniently edited out that part of the story. "And then when they were done, he must have gone home."

"Oh, no. Didn't you tell her?" Sloane dropped her Marc Jacobs bag on the chair that had recently been Jazz's. "He left the shoot and met me over at the Bourbon Street Barrel Room." It wasn't far from where Jazz found Florie's body. "Isn't that right, Tate? I was waiting there for you."

It was his turn to smile. "I'm a lucky man. Yes, my wife was waiting there for me."

Jazz was sure Nick had asked all these same questions. If he had any doubts about the time line or Brody's alibi, she knew Nick would be all over him.

249

"But you did walk outside the building with Florie." It seemed like a lifetime ago that Jazz had originally asked the question — before the incredible video and the beaming wife. "Didn't you?"

"My students had filmed in the building just days before and we were just finishing up. So you see, Ms. Ramsey, everything is under control." His look wasn't as pleading as it was simply conspiratorial. Jazz owed him. For the conclusion-jumping. For the accusations. He wasn't admitting to any of it, not the grade-fixing or the sex. He was just reminding her that she had no right to ask about any of it, and his wife had no need to worry. "Just like you thought it was when you came by to confirm the facts."

"You're absolutely right." There was nothing else Jazz could say, and besides, there was no disputing the truth. She wished them both a good night.

Outside the office, she listened to the low hum of their conversation. But only long enough so she wasn't eavesdropping. In those few seconds, she decided not to go to her car.

If the instructor who gave Florie her one and only A couldn't help, what about the others, the ones who'd watched Florie's academic career go up in smoke?

It didn't take her long to find Joyce Wildemere's office. She was grading papers, her head bent over her desk, and the overhead fluorescent lights glinted against gray hair that looked as if it had been chopped by a toddler. She stood when Jazz walked in, maybe because she was polite, maybe because she wasn't sure who Jazz was and if she'd have to make a quick getaway. She was wearing a black skirt that brushed her ankles, boots that looked as if they'd be more at home on the back forty than in a classroom, and a blue-and-white top with buttons down the front that gaped over her large and drooping breasts.

"Can't tell you much of anything," she said in answer to Jazz's questions about Florie. "I gave her plenty of opportunities to turn in her work and she never did. I had no choice but to fail her."

And that was that.

Or at least it would have been if Jazz hadn't noticed one thing. When she walked into the office, when she mentioned Florie's name, Joyce Wildemere had casually reached a hand across her desk and slid an envelope beneath a stack of books. It was a Pepto Bismol–pink envelope decorated with white polka dots the size of half dollars.

At the same time she thanked Joyce Wildemere for taking the time to talk to her, Jazz reminded herself that she didn't believe in coincidences.

She made a quick stop at Florie's school studio.

And found it completely bare.

The sign that said FLORIE'S PLACE was gone. So were the photographs on the wall — the champagne bottle popping, the wise old woman, the tabby cat.

All gone.

So was the stack of pink envelopes.

"You just missed them."

Just walking out of the studio, Jazz turned in time to see Khari walking into one of the other studios, his long dreadlocks swaying around his shoulders and brushing the extra-large pizza box he carried.

"Florie's parents came by earlier," he told her. "They cleaned out her studio."

Jazz thanked him and raced to her car. She couldn't say why it mattered; she only knew it did, and she was disappointed when she got to Murray Hill and heard the same thing from Meg and Croc in the second-floor apartment.

Florie's parents had been and gone and her room was bare.

There wasn't a trace of Florie Allen left anywhere.

CHAPTER 15

Spring can be ugly in Cleveland, and the next Sunday proved it.

There was a bone-chilling rain falling when Jazz took Luther for his morning walk, an icy spray too persistent to call a mist that turned into a steady downpour by the time they got home, had breakfast, and she loaded him into the car to go to the derelict amusement park to meet her fellow trainers.

Once there, Jazz parked her SUV up against a maintenance shed with peeling green paint and a roof with missing shingles, and watched raindrops patter on the windshield.

"Doesn't it figure?" she asked Luther, though she couldn't say if he was listening or not since he was in his crate, all the way in the back of the vehicle. "I think the universe is trying to tell me something."

That would certainly explain why the

weather matched her mood.

Gathering the enthusiasm for heading out into the elements, she couldn't help but think about what she'd spent every waking hour since Thursday thinking about. Well, when she wasn't thinking about her mom's text (*Home, honey, and reporting in as ordered. One more glass of wine and we'll call it a night*) and what it meant, and if the mysterious Peter Nestico was destined to become more of a presence in their lives than Jazz was ready for.

When she wasn't worrying about her mom, she'd been giving herself a figurative kick in the pants.

What was she thinking, accusing Tate Brody?

How on earth did she imagine that embarrassing herself and chasing shadows was going to help Florie?

In that one moment, with the rain pinging against the car like buckshot and her fellow handlers hunched under a nearby overhang and looking like wraiths thanks to the fogged car windows, Jazz decided she was done.

There was nothing she could do for Florie, no peace she could bring to the girl's family. There was nothing to discover that she didn't already know.

And what she already knew was that she was wasting her time and making herself look like a horse's ass.

Determined to get on with her life the way it had been before she found Florie's body, ran into Nick, inconvenienced half of Cleveland with her questions and her innuendos, and even heard the name Peter Nestico, much less imagined what he and her mom were up to, she pushed open the car door and hopped out.

Cathy Greztman had obviously been waiting for exactly that, because in a matter of seconds, she splashed her way over. As the newest member of the training team, Cathy was still in her probationary period — that time when both the team and the prospective member size each other up and decide if they're a good fit — and Jazz knew she'd never make it.

Cathy was a habitual complainer, a retired accountant who had a head of silvery hair and a frown like a shriveled jack-o'-lantern. She peered at Jazz from beneath the hood of her navy-blue rain jacket. "Really? We're really going to spend a few hours out here in this weather?"

"You don't have to." Jazz had left Luther in his soft-sided portable crate in the SUV. There was no use both of them being miserable. Without a leash to hold, she poked both her hands into the pockets of her yellow slicker. "But it is good for the dogs to work in all sorts of weather. Scents spread differently in the rain, remember, and you don't want Arnold . . ." Cathy's dog sat at her side, and when he heard his name, the pitty mix looked up, his tongue darting out of his mouth to capture a raindrop. "You don't want him to be skittish in rain."

"He's not skittish. I'm skittish," Cathy harrumphed, but she set her jaw and went to stand with the rest of the team, waiting beneath the minimum protection provided by the building's overhanging roof. The others — there were six who'd come out in spite of the weather — had left their dogs in their cars, and Cathy finally got the message and kenneled Arnold.

One less animal to worry about.

Jazz closed in on her fellow handlers, stepping into a small dry spot outside the door of the maintenance shed. "Matt ought to be here by now," she said.

"He better get his ass in gear." Donny Folbrook was a longtime member of the group, a registered nurse who lived and breathed human remains detection and was an excellent handler. His Australian cattle dog, Sheik, had won competitions around the country. Donny lit a cigarette. "Matt's in charge today. He said he had the training all planned out."

"I hope nothing happened to him." Remembering her own white-knuckle drive, Jazz glanced beyond the chain-link fence that ringed the property. The streets were slick with standing water, and too many drivers were unconscious idiots. She'd seen more than one near accident on the ride from home, and what should have been a forty-minute trip had taken an hour. "I'll call him."

Before she could, Matt's SUV wheeled up to the main gate. He leaned out the window, poked in the security code, and a minute later, he was parked nearby.

When he sauntered over, his smile was not in keeping with the weather.

"We were worried," Jazz told him.

Matt hadn't bothered to pull up the hood of his slicker. Raindrops plopped on his head, rolled across his forehead, snaked along his cheeks.

He clapped a hand on Jazz's shoulder. "No problemo! What are we waiting for?" he asked no one in particular, and they got to work.

Jazz and Luther were up first, and she was just as glad. She was more than willing to stand out in the rain and watch the other dogs work, offer advice, learn a thing or two, but once his training time was done, Luther could go back into the car and snuggle into the blankets she'd put in his crate.

Considering the rain and the stiff breeze that kicked up out of the north, the shepherd did great. He found the ulna Matt hid behind the maintenance shed, and a metacarpal Matt had taken a real chance with, dropping it into a two-inch-deep puddle. Detecting the scent of decomp through water was a specialty not even Manny had ever mastered, and Jazz couldn't wait to call Greg that evening and let him know that they'd discovered new depths (literally) to Luther's talents.

Once he was finished working, Jazz gave Luther a treat and put him back in the car. By the time she rejoined the group where they stood in a cluster on top of a rise at the end of a pitted asphalt drive, the rain had let up a little, but they still had their hoods up, their shoulders hunched, their hands in their pockets. Matt had just sent Cathy out to hide behind an old hot-dog stand so one of the search-and-rescue dogs could get some work in, and Jazz came up behind him.

"I know why I'm in a good mood," she

told him. "Luther did great today. I can't wait to tell Greg."

"I can tell you've been working with him."

Jazz swiped a raindrop from the tip of her nose. "That doesn't explain why you've been smiling the whole time you've been here."

Like every other member of the team, Matt watched the golden who belonged to Bob Harris do sweeping figure eights between rows of dilapidated buildings where parkgoers had once bought food, played games of chance, had their names etched into flattened pennies. From there Scooter raced across the drive to the waist-tall vegetation that grew in an empty lot. Oblivious of the rain, the dog pelted along, back and forth, his nose in the air, waiting to catch Cathy's scent, and when he did, he took off toward the old hot-dog stand to be sure, then came back to sit down next to Bob, signaling that he'd found what he was looking for.

"Show me," Bob said, and handler and dog took off. A minute later, they came back with Cathy, who looked more miserable than ever, and the team called out praise for the dog.

"Good boy, Scooter!"

"Way to go, Scoot!"

While Scooter went from person to person so they could play with him and the tug toy Bob had given him as a reward, Matt slipped an arm around Jazz's shoulders.

"Thanks," he said.

"Thanks for . . ." She glanced at Matt. "What did I do?"

"You introduced me to Sarah."

"I did. But I didn't —" Jazz groaned. "Damn! I'm sorry, Matt, you asked for Sarah's number and I told you I'd ask her if it was okay. It completely slipped my mind. But —" She gave him a careful look. Nonchalance was not Matt's strong suit and he didn't even try to disguise the smile that lit his face. "If that's true, why are you grinning like that?"

"You didn't ask her if it was okay. You didn't give me her number. As it turned out, you didn't need to. Sarah found me all on her own."

"How —"

"Don't ask me!" Just the way she'd seen her brothers do when they were particularly pleased with themselves, Matt rocked back on his heels. "I think she called every fire station in town until she tracked me down. Some woman, huh? Just proves how anxious she was to see me again. We went out last night."

"Went out as in had dinner and saw a movie and said good night at the door, or — ?"

"Oh, definitely the *or.*" Matt winked. "Her kids were with their dad, the lights were low, the champagne was flowing, and —"

"I don't need to hear this!" As if it could stop the images that automatically danced through her brain, Jazz covered her ears and pulled away from Matt. She'd always thought of him as another brother, and she did not need specifics from a brother. Besides, she was sure she'd hear it all — in detail — from Sarah. "I'm glad you two are —"

It was just as well Matt's phone rang, because Jazz wasn't exactly sure what she was going to say.

I'm glad you two are getting along seemed pretty lame, considering.

I'm glad you two had wild, passionate sex and you're still smiling about it was a little too personal.

"Hey, people!" Matt finished his call and tucked his phone in his pocket. He raised his voice and waved to the team. "We just got a call, a missing kid in Cleveland. Anybody want to put their dogs through the paces?"

Except for Donny, who said he'd hang

back with Sheik, the ulna, and the metacarpal, and Cathy, who used the excuse of an oncoming cold — and would obviously never be back now that she'd gotten a taste of how uncomfortable training could be — they all did, and a few minutes later they were in a caravan, following Matt and driving toward the city. Training was over. It was time for the dogs to get down to real work.

The recreation center where ten-year-old Samantha Luckey was last seen was separated from a freeway by a playground and a baseball field. Half the team went in that direction, the dogs sweeping back and forth, noses in the air, alert and anxious to do their jobs.

Jazz hung back. Luther had picked right up on the scents of the other dogs, who'd headed across the ball diamond, and he knew he was missing out on the action. In his crate, he panted and whined, antsy to join them, but he wasn't trained in search and rescue and — thank goodness — no one coordinating the search had even said the words *human remains.* Once Matt got his final instructions from the uniformed police officers he talked to outside the rec center, she'd tag along with him and Buddy.

It would be a treat, really, to join in the search for a living person and not worry about the dead.

Jazz held onto the thought — at least until she saw Nick step out of the building.

At least until he caught sight of her and closed in.

He was dressed casually, in jeans and a green sweatshirt from Cleveland State University, and since it had stopped raining, his jacket was unzipped and his hood was down.

"Did you bring Luther?" he asked, a strip of blacktop between them like a gulf.

Her throat clutched. "They think the little girl is dead. You wouldn't be here otherwise."

"Oh, God, no!" He closed the distance between them, and she had the feeling he would have pulled her into a comforting hug if he had the nerve. She was glad he didn't. "I heard the commotion and came out to see what was going on. I told Santiago and Tom . . ." His look at the black-and-white patrol car with its rollbar flashing told her those were the two uniformed cops talking to Matt. "I offered to help out if I could. I'm really just here for a meeting about this year's baseball season."

He didn't have to explain. Nick had

263

coached baseball there at the rec center for years, and if he was asked, he would no doubt say what he always said — he loved the game. Jazz knew better. An only child, he'd grown up just around the corner with no dad and a mom who, even though it was just a bit past noon and a Sunday to boot, was probably already getting hammered at one of the local bars. Nick wanted to give neighborhood kids the attention he'd never had.

The attention he'd never given their relationship because he was always too busy with his work and other people's children.

Jazz brushed away the thought. Right now all that mattered was that one of those children was missing.

"When I saw you, I thought you knew something had happened to the girl."

"As far as we know, Samantha just wandered away."

"You know her?"

"I know the face." He twitched his shoulders. "I work with the boys, but Samantha, she's here a lot so I've seen her around. She loves Beyoncé and jump rope. Nice kid, though I hear her mother is a real piece of work."

Jazz did not point out the obvious. She didn't ask about Kim, either, because if she did, he'd tell her what he always used to tell her when she asked about his mother — Kim was fine.

Even though she never was.

Nick poked a thumb over his shoulder. "I thought I'd walk the neighborhood and see what I can see. As long as you're here, you could bring the dog and come along."

She could. If she was certifiable.

"Luther's not a search-and-rescue dog," she said.

Nick closed the distance between them and leaned close enough to peer into the back window of the car, and Luther barked. "I hear you were out at Geauga Lake. That's a long drive. I bet he'd like to stretch his legs."

She took her car keys out of her pocket. "We're not far from home. I'll walk him there."

"I get it." He backed away from the car and the conversation. "I understand you probably don't want to risk it. I mean, I don't think anything happened to Samantha, but if it did, if there was a chance you might find another body, I can see how you'd be feeling a little gun-shy."

She bristled. "Are you questioning my professionalism, Detective?"

Nick was quick to defend himself. "Hey,

nobody could blame you if that's how you feel. Finding Florie Allen like you did, then going out looking for another possible victim so soon after, that would make anybody hesitant."

"Except I'm not hesitant."

"But you are hesitating."

She hit the release button on the back of the tailgate, hooked Luther's leash to his collar so he could jump down, and locked the car.

"Let's go," she said.

She felt a rush of gratification when Nick had to scramble to catch up to her.

Unfortunately, it didn't last long.

Jazz locked her knees and shot him a look. "You did that purposely."

"Did what?"

"Said that about how I was afraid to go out and do a search. You did that purposely because you knew you'd piss me off. You knew I'd come with you."

He had the nerve to smile. "It worked, didn't it?" When she stepped back toward the car, he darted to the side, blocking her way. "Come on, what can it hurt? A walk will be good for both of us. And for Luther."

He was right about the dog. And maybe he was right about himself, too. Jazz wasn't so sure how right he was about her.

She waved to Matt, a signal that she was heading out.

"Matt's looking well." Nick carefully avoided a puddle. But then, he didn't know he'd be out in the elements that day. She was wearing waterproof boots. He had on sneakers. "I haven't seen him in a while."

They had known each other well back when Nick and Jazz dated. Nick, Matt, Hal, Owen. Her dad liked to call them the Four Stooges, only when he did, it was always with a smile.

Jazz knew it was dangerous to get too personal, yet it didn't feel right not sharing news so monumental about people they both knew. "Matt and Sarah are dating."

Nick whistled low under his breath. "No offense, I mean, I know she's your friend and everything, but —"

"Sarah's high maintenance." It wasn't news to Jazz. "And Matt's no prize, either. He's got a reputation when it comes to women."

"And it never ends well."

Jazz shrugged. "Not my problem." She knew it would be. When whatever it was that Matt and Sarah had of a relationship fell apart, she'd hear about it from both of them and be expected to take sides.

She couldn't worry about it. "The two of

them will figure it out for themselves," she told Nick, and reminded herself. "Right now . . ." She remembered what Matt had told her back at the amusement park. Low lights, champagne, and —

This was not the time and place to think about it.

This was really not the person to think about it with.

Jazz shrugged. "I guess it's going pretty well."

"I hear dating can be really nice sometimes. I mean, the right kinds of dates with the right kind of person." They were at the street and they waited for a bus to rumble by, then crossed to the sidewalk in front of a funeral home. "I mean, sometimes two people can actually spend time together and get along. In fact, I remember —"

She remembered, too. Exactly why she cut him off. "Are we searching, or what?"

He knew a brick wall when he saw one. "Lead the way."

Jazz looked up and down the street. In one direction was a hardware store with a wide-open parking lot and beyond that, a white-frame house and a car dealership. In the other direction, an abandoned building that might at one time have been a bank, an Asian grocery store, a bar.

"What does your experience tell you?" she asked Nick, because she realized when she looked over the area it was through the eyes of a trainer and the dog at her side. Where would the scent be the strongest? Where were they most likely to lose it? Nick's take on the scene was completely different. Like all police officers, Nick had started his career in uniform and on patrol. These days working in homicide, he saw the aftermath of life's tragedies and he worked to right its wrongs. But when he was on the streets, he'd seen those disasters unfold. He fought to stop them.

"If I was a ten-year-old girl and I didn't want anyone to find me . . ." He scanned the area. "I'd go where it's easiest to hide. And if I was someone who hurt a ten-year-old girl, or wanted to, I'd do the same thing." He eyed the parking lot of the hardware store. "Too much empty space over there. Let's head in the other direction."

Together, they turned toward the bank building next to the funeral home. It had once been an imposing presence in the neighborhood. These days it was simply sad. The building's two-story stone facade had been whitewashed. The front door was painted green and scrawled with graffiti.

The windows were boarded.

Because they were in the city and Jazz didn't want to take a chance with traffic and Luther running loose, she'd hooked him to a long leash. She unreeled it, swept a hand at her side. "Find Henry!"

Luther thought he was just being taken for a walk. Hearing it was time to get down to work, his ears pricked, his eyes flashed. In an instant, he took off down the alley between the abandoned building and the Asian grocery store.

Jazz kept her distance, allowing the dog to make his own decisions. He skirted three garbage cans stacked near the back door of the grocery store, sniffed a door stoop and turned away, jogged through what had once been a backyard where now there were waist-high weeds, discarded beer bottles, old tires.

"I don't want him to find anything."

Jazz didn't even realize she'd said the words out loud until Nick looked her way.

"I don't want him to find anything, either, but I'm glad he's here. It doesn't hurt to cover all the bases."

Finished with the yard, the dog made a U-turn and came back up the alley. He sniffed his way around to the front of the building, with Jazz and Nick hanging ten feet back.

"So what do you say?"

Since Jazz wasn't sure what Nick was talking about, she could be forgiven for wrinkling her nose and looking up at him as if he'd started speaking the exotic and indecipherable language on the sign in the front window of the building. "What do I say about what?"

"About dating."

She'd always been a sucker for his blue eyes, for his lopsided smile. Jazz had to remind herself to keep her eyes on Luther. It was the only way she could control the sudden erratic beat of her heart. "Dating you?"

"Well, yeah. I'm not exactly going to fix you up with someone else. Though there are plenty of guys who are interested. Remember O'Halloran?"

"The big guy with the beard?"

"He asks about you all the time."

She watched the dog disappear around the corner into the alley between the grocery store and the bar. "What do you tell him when he does?"

"That you're spoken for."

"Even though I'm not."

"A man can dream."

It was a mistake to ask, but she couldn't

help herself. "And what is it you're dreaming about?"

They turned to the right to follow Luther, and she was just in time to see that old, familiar smile flash across Nick's face. "At this point, just a date."

"Just a date." It wasn't a question. It was more confirmation. More assurance. More verification that they weren't talking about him having her house key and her having his.

"I was thinking . . ." At the back of the building, they watched Luther pick his way around the area where people came out of the back door of the bar to smoke, and Nick went on, "Well, see, the way I figure it, we moved too fast last time."

That was putting it mildly.

He must have remembered. It would explain why he dipped his chin and looked her in the eye. "See, I was thinking we could start over. If we just had . . . I dunno . . . one date a week?"

"You mean like real people on Saturday nights?"

"Hard to say. I mean, about Saturday nights." They stood and watched Luther nose around a dumpster, and when the dog slipped around to the back of it, too interested in something, Jazz held her breath.

Nick must have done the same, because when Luther finally emerged without barking, he sighed. "I don't exactly have a real people job. Not one with dependable hours, anyway."

"And Saturdays during the day are out because you're here coaching baseball."

"And Sundays are out because you're training the dogs."

It was the same old stalemate, and now, like always, the reality of it settled somewhere deep inside Jazz, cold and uncomfortable.

Avoidance seemed the only appropriate response.

"Have you found out anything?" she asked. "About Florie?"

Maybe he was just as relieved as she was that the subject had changed. Maybe that explained why some of the stiffness went out of his shoulders.

"It's a tough case."

"There was something going on with her."

When Luther darted up the alley and back to the sidewalk, Nick and Jazz followed, and Nick said, "How would you —"

"I've talked to a couple people, that's all. Florie was flunking out of school."

This was not a surprise to Nick.

Jazz knew she should just leave it at that,

but something deep down inside her just wouldn't let go. The way she figured it, she was still stinging from the embarrassment of accusing Tate Brody, still trying to make sense of everything she'd heard from him. About him. That was the only reason she went on. "She only got one good grade this semester. An A from Tate Brody."

Far be it from Nick to ever give too much away. Still, his eyebrows rose just a fraction of an inch. "Tate? What, you two are BFFs now?"

She rolled her eyes. "He's married. I met his wife."

"Looks like you've talked to the good instructor."

It was the way he said *good* that made her take notice.

"You think there's something fishy going on with Brody, too."

It wasn't a question, but she hoped he'd answer.

"I think . . ." Nick kept his eyes on Luther. Whatever he was going to say, he brushed aside the thought. "I wonder if you're hearing what I'm hearing. All that bad stuff about Brody. I wonder if you're hearing it from the same person I'm hearing it from."

"Grace Greenwald."

"Consider the source. And maybe . . ."

He hesitated, but Nick had never been one to keep his opinions to himself. The details of his job, absolutely. The way his mother had spent the last thirty-three years cutting his heart to pieces, sure.

But an opinion?

Never.

It was one of the things Jazz loved about him. One of the things that drove her crazy.

"Maybe you should just mind your own business," he said.

Outside the front door of the bar, she locked her legs. "I am minding my own business. I knew Florie. Hell, I'm the one who . . ." The words caught in her throat. "I'm the one who found her."

"And I know that's not easy, but —"

"But nothing! It's not like I'm stepping on your investigation, Nick. You didn't even know I was asking around."

"And what have you found out?"

It was on the tip of her tongue to tell him she'd pretty much determined only that she was a horse's ass, but since she was afraid he might agree with her, she said, "She was desperate for money."

"Because she was desperate to stay in school."

"Except her grades stunk. Which is why she was desperate to bring them up out of the gutter. Which is why I figured she was sleeping with Brody."

There. She'd said it.

And Nick didn't laugh at the absurdity of it all.

In fact, he twitched his shoulders. "I thought the same thing."

Encouraged, she stepped closer to him. "And they were together the night of the murder."

He slanted her a look. "You know that, too, huh?"

"He says he met his wife for dinner right after. She confirms it."

"She does, and so do the people at the restaurant where they had dinner. They sat together at a table near the window. And yet . . ." As if searching for the truth, he scanned the street, his shoulders set, his expression so intent, she found it hard to believe he didn't bust every perp in the city all by himself through utter willpower.

"I wish we could find Florie's phone," he grumbled.

"I wish I understood why Florie and Grace hated each other so much."

"I wish I had answers to what Florie was doing in that building. If Brody really did leave right after they were done filming, why did she hang back?"

"I wish I could understand what she was up to with the costumes and the clothes changes and the kid next door."

"I wish —"

Nick's phone rang. When he answered, Jazz tensed. *Please, please don't let it be about Samantha.*

But it was.

He jammed the phone back in his pocket. "They found her," Nick said. "Samantha's fine. She told Santiago she was mad at her grandmother and she hid when Grandma showed up to get her so that Grandma would get worried. She's been inside the equipment room in the rec center the whole time. Matt and Buddy tracked her down."

Jazz let go a breath that felt as if it had been trapped behind her heart. Her shoulders relaxed. She reeled in the dog.

"Good boy, Luther! Come!" And when he did, she got a treat out of her pocket for him. "You did good work."

"He did." Nick squatted down to play with the dog. "There's nothing I like better than a happy ending. I couldn't take another bad one today."

The comment was so offhand, Jazz's blood turned to ice. "Another one what?"

His hand stilled over the dog's ears. "It's nothing."

"It's something."

With a sigh, he stood.

"You said you wanted to start over," she reminded him. "All right, start over. Last time, we didn't share."

"You mean you never shared, not even about the old man you found dead in the snow."

"And you never shared, either. Not about . . ." As if it explained it all, she waved an arm toward the neighborhood around them. "Not about anything."

He studied the sidewalk, then raised his chin, his jaw tensed, his mouth set in a thin line. "I had to visit a mom not far from here early this morning to tell her that her fourteen-year-old son was shot dead on a playground last night."

She didn't know how it happened, she didn't mean to do it, but she wound her fingers through his, offering what little comfort she could in a situation that was beyond reason to a man who thought it was his responsibility to keep the world safe. "I'm sorry."

"Senseless." The lines deepened at the corners of his eyes. "Senseless, senseless violence." Because he had no choice, he shook away the thought. "But we've got a happy ending here. That's something at least." He started across the street.

Jazz held back and when she pulled on his hand, he stopped.

"Just once a week?" she asked.

His mind was other places, but she knew when it came back to their earlier conversation. That would be when he smiled.

"Like Tuesdays. How do Tuesdays sound?"

"Coffee?" she suggested.

He nodded. "Coffee on Tuesdays."

Jazz couldn't believe the words that came out of her mouth. But then, she couldn't believe the warmth that gathered inside her when she said them, either.

"It's a date."

CHAPTER 16

Thirty hours and seventeen minutes.

Not that Jazz was counting or anything, but she glanced at the clock. Again.

In thirty hours and seventeen minutes, she was meeting Nick for coffee at a nice little place out of her neighborhood and nowhere near his.

Neutral territory.

They would drive separately. They would leave separately. There would be no exchange of intimacies.

She had it all worked out.

"You've been avoiding me."

When Sarah Carrington zoomed into her office, Jazz flinched. If she'd been paying more attention she would have seen Sarah coming and avoided her the way she'd been avoiding her all that Monday. Not avoiding the detailed retelling (in full living color) of Sarah and Matt's date. That was bound to happen no matter what.

Avoiding spilling the beans about Nick.

"I haven't been avoiding you," she told her friend.

Uninvited, Sarah plunked down in the guest chair in front of Jazz's desk. She was on lunch hour and she'd brought along a plate of lentil-and-quinoa stew. She lifted a forkful of it to her mouth. "You weren't here before the first bell this morning."

"Gretchen Turk called in sick and they needed help out in the parking lot with drop-offs." Gretchen was the chemistry teacher and it was the first time in years she'd taken a sick day. It had been the perfect excuse for Jazz to make herself scarce.

Jazz looked at her friend. She wasn't sure if it was the blue-and-yellow madras plaid of Sarah's skirt and yellow necklace, the smear of green oil paint on her chin, or Sarah's mile-wide smile that shone brightest. "I've got news."

"You went out with Matt."

Sarah's smile wilted. "He told you."

"I'm psychic."

"Aren't you dying for the details?"

Jazz hated to admit it, but she was. Well, maybe not all the details, just the salient parts. And definitely not the details of her own upcoming date. She wasn't ready to share that information.

"Drink after work?" she suggested to Sarah.

"You, girl . . ." Sarah pointed with her fork. ". . . are reading my mind."

They agreed on Grumpy's Café just up the street, because it had a parking lot, and Sarah could drive and leave for home right from there.

Until then . . .

Jazz watched Sarah sail out of the room, and once she was gone, she knew she had to keep herself busy.

The St. Catherine's monthly newsletter was finished. She'd logged in all the girls who'd been called in as sick that day. Tuesday's morning announcements were printed out and already waiting on Jazz's desk.

If she didn't find something else to occupy her time, she was pretty sure she was going to obsess about what was going to happen in . . . she looked at the clock, then grumbled a curse . . . thirty hours and thirteen minutes. If she didn't do something, she was going to lose her mind.

To that end, Jazz logged into the class-scheduling program.

Just as she thought. Dinah Greenwald was at lunch.

Yes, Jazz had told herself she was done poking and prying into Florie Allen's life. But desperate times, desperate measures. And she was desperate to keep her mind off Nick.

The last time Jazz had been in the cafeteria, it was to talk to Loretta Hardinger and it had been late in the day. Then, the lights were low, the cafeteria quiet. Now, when Jazz pushed through the double doors, it was the height of lunch hour, and a Monday. The energy in the room — not to mention the noise level — was off the charts.

At one end of the cafeteria, a group of seniors was programming music into the sound system, jabbing and pushing at each other the way girls in high spirits do. Close to the door, three sophomores chirped about an encounter over the weekend with a group of guys at one of the boys' schools in the area. All around her, girls sat in tight circles, their salad bowls and lunch trays between them, their heads together, their voices sharp and high, pinging around the room, punctuated with laughter.

Dinah Greenwald was at the table farthest from the door. In the seat farthest from the aisle. Alone.

"Hey, Dinah!" When Jazz sat next to her, Dinah flinched and stuck a finger into the book open in front of her. "What's up?"

"Up?" Dinah dragged a bookmark over, put it where her finger had been, and closed the book, then pushed her glasses up the bridge of her nose. There was a carton of yogurt, an apple, and half of a ham sandwich on the tray in front of her, untouched.

"Not hungry?" Jazz asked.

"Oh, well, I am." As if to prove it, Dinah picked up the sandwich and took a bite. "I just forgot, that's all. I'm reading Jane Austen. When I read, I kind of get lost in the story, you know?"

Jazz didn't. Not that she had anything against reading or the people who did it, but she could never sit still long enough to do any reading.

"You always eat alone?" Jazz asked her.

Dinah took another bite of sandwich, chewed, and swallowed. "I usually sit with Stella Glowacki."

Stella had called in sick that day. She was a quiet brainiac like Dinah. Jazz was happy they'd found each other.

"Is that a problem?" Dinah wanted to know.

"You mean sitting with Stella? Or sitting alone when Stella's not here?"

It didn't seem to matter. Either way, if it was a problem, Dinah was ready to apologize for it.

Jazz didn't give her the chance. "I was just wondering . . ." She glanced back at the lunch line, all but nonexistent now that the first rush was over. "What's on the menu today?"

Dinah didn't have to think about it. One look at the menu board and Dinah had the list memorized. She was that kind of kid. "Chicken salad. Ham sandwiches." She glanced at hers. "Veggie burgers."

"Then a veggie burger it is." Jazz popped out of her seat. "Do you mind if I come back here and sit with you to eat it?"

Jazz had the feeling Dinah was still considering the question by the time she returned to the table with her lunch tray.

She saw Dinah slap her book closed. "How's the book?"

"*Sense and Sensibility?* Dreamy. Everybody knows that."

"Sure." Jazz loaded her veggie burger with ketchup. "I just wondered what you thought."

Sometime while Jazz was up at the lunch counter, Dinah had finished her sandwich. She carefully folded the paper it had been wrapped in — in half, in quarters, in eighths — and set it aside before she popped the lid on her raspberry yogurt.

Jazz bit into the burger and chewed, then set it next to the broccoli salad that came with it.

"Sorry I made you wait the other day," she said to Dinah, and when all she got was a blank look, she added, "You know, when Grace came to pick you up and I was talking to Grace in the car."

"Oh, that. It's okay. Really. I'm never exactly in a hurry to get in the car with Grace, anyway."

It was, in fact, a telling point about Grace and Dinah's relationship, but Jazz pretended Dinah was going for funny and smiled. "I get it. Grace can be —"

"She's not exactly spoiled." Dinah came to Grace's defense the way a sister is supposed to. "Our parents treat us the same. Grace is just . . ." She searched for the word. "Entitled."

Trying not to look too eager, Jazz took another bite of burger while she thanked her lucky stars for the perfect opening. "Do you think that's why she didn't get along with Florie Allen?"

Though she hadn't touched her yogurt, Dinah put the lid back on and pushed back her chair. "I don't want to be late for my next class."

"The bell isn't going to ring for twenty-two minutes yet." As if to prove it, Jazz showed the girl the time on her phone. While they were on campus, the girls of St. Catherine's weren't allowed to carry their cell phones. Eileen's school, Eileen's rules, and as far as Jazz could see, this particular one was golden.

They sat side by side in silence.

"I've got a date tomorrow," Jazz said, then wondered what in the world had made her tell the girl. She gave Dinah a sidelong look and saw that clearly, Dinah thought dating was an activity exclusively for the cool girls in school, not for old people like Jazz.

"I'm a little nervous," Jazz admitted. "You know?"

Dinah puckered. "I don't date."

"You will. When you're ready."

"Why aren't you ready?"

"You mean, why am I nervous?"

Now that she was trapped in this new conversation, Dinah opened the yogurt again and spooned up a mouthful. She nodded.

"He's cute," Jazz told her. "And he's really nice. And we used to go out. I mean, a while ago, and we broke up and now —"

"Why?" Dinah wasn't being nosy, she just needed to understand. Dinah needed to understand everything.

"Why did we break up?" Jazz was about to take another bite, and she set down her burger and thought about it. There was no use listing all the ugly details — Nick's drunken mom, Nick's mule-headed dedication to his baseball team, Nick's job with its crazy hours and off-the-charts stress. There was no use hanging out her own shortcomings on the line for the world to see, either — her commitment to spending every Sunday with the dog-training team, her afternoons and evenings working with Manny, walking Manny, playing with Manny. It wasn't fair to tell a kid like Dinah that relationships, even the good ones, are far more complicated than they look from the outside. Then again, maybe a kid like Dinah — maybe especially a kid like Dinah — already knew that. Maybe that's why she told her, "I guess Nick and I forgot that we were supposed to be the most important thing in each other's lives."

From behind her glasses, Dinah's eyes were steady and far wiser than they should have been. "Isn't that a no-brainer?"

It was hard to face the truth when it came from a kid with raspberry yogurt on the tip of her nose. With one finger, Jazz pointed it out, and Dinah wiped her face with a napkin.

Jazz picked at the broccoli salad. "I guess the whole point is, we're all nervous sometimes. About people. About telling the truth. Do you know the truth? Do you know why Grace and Florie didn't get along?"

Dinah's eyes were as round as dinner plates. "Grace would kill me dead if I told."

"She'll never find out. I swear."

Though this was clearly a generous offer, Dinah had to think about it. She studied the apple on her tray. "Can I get in trouble if I don't tell?"

Jazz had no choice but to be perfectly honest. "No."

"But if I do tell, then you'll know I did something . . ." Dinah's cheeks shot through with color. ". . . nefarious."

It was a big word from a little girl, but Jazz didn't dare smile. "Like what?"

Dinah looked down to where she clutched her hands together on her lap. "Like look through Grace's diary."

This time, Jazz did allow herself a smile. "That's no big deal. Sisters always do stuff like that to each other."

"Do they? Really?" Dinah's head came up and relief washed over her expression. "I thought I was the only one. Like a sinner, you know, only worse, because I was a sneak, too."

"No way!" Jazz made light of it. "I used to do stuff like that all the time. Not that I have any sisters," she added quickly, because she was close to getting Dinah to open up and she couldn't afford to let the girl catch her in a lie. "But I have two older brothers. I used to sit outside their bedroom door and listen to them talk to their girlfriends on the phone. If they knew the stuff I heard, they'd go nuts."

Dinah laughed. "Yeah, if Grace knew this, she'd go nuts, too. Especially since I found out she was . . ." She dropped her voice and leaned closer to Jazz. "Grace wasn't exactly being on the up-and-up when she was here at St. Catherine's."

Dinah was so serious, so mortified, it could only mean one thing. "She cheated?"

Dinah didn't dare say the word. "Algebra. Geometry. French. Big time in French. And Florie . . ." There was so much sound bouncing around the cafeteria, there was no way anyone could overhear, but Dinah looked around anyway, just to be sure. "Florie found out."

"How?"

Dinah shook her head. "Grace didn't say. Not in her diary. She only said something about how Florie was a no-good, dirty, rotten . . ." She swallowed the rest of the sentence along with her mortification. "Well, you can guess the rest."

Yes, Jazz could.

Especially since out of the corner of her eye, she just so happened to catch sight of Loretta Hardinger and remembered what the cafeteria manager had told her. Florie of the cast-off clothes.

And what Parker Paul had mentioned.

Florie, who needed to pay rent.

Then and now, Florie was desperate for money.

"Dinah, was Florie . . ." Now Jazz made sure to keep her voice down, too. "Was Florie blackmailing Grace?"

A single nod spoke volumes. "It started sophomore year and kept up the whole rest of the time they were here at St. Catherine's."

Jazz let the truth sink in. No wonder the girls went from friends to enemies in no time flat. No wonder there was still bad blood between them two years after graduation.

"Do you think . . ." It was a lot to ask the kid. Jazz asked anyway. "Do you think maybe she was still doing it? Do you think Florie still had something on Grace?"

"You mean, do I think my sister had a motive to kill Florie?"

Dinah was so matter-of-fact, it took Jazz's breath away.

"I didn't say that," she protested.

"No, but it would take a total moron not to think of it." Dinah tucked the apple into her backpack. "Grace doesn't live at home anymore," she said, and she pushed back her chair and stood. "So I haven't had a chance to look at her diary lately. It's too bad. It sure would be delicious to find out Grace was the killer." She grabbed her tray to deposit it — of course — exactly where it was supposed to go, and while Jazz was still stunned by how much resentment there was between Dinah and her sister, Dinah grinned.

"Good luck on that date," she said.

Blackmail.

For the first few minutes after she heard it, the word pounded through Jazz's brain.

But then her blood pressure ratcheted down, and her thoughts settled. After she had some time to think about it, she realized it was the natural progression of things.

Florie needed money. That's why she slept with Parker Paul, then threatened to tell his wife if he didn't pay up. That's why she was ready to turn in Grace for cheating. Did that also mean Jazz had been right about

Tate Brody all along? When Florie needed an A, did she sleep with her professor?

What else might she have done to get what she wanted?

Back at her desk, long after lunch, Jazz checked the time on her phone. She wasn't scheduled to meet Sarah until five. She had forty-five minutes. She locked up her office and raced home and got her car. Just a couple minutes later, she was in Ohio City.

Florie's parents weren't home.

It wasn't what she expected — not what she wanted. She had hoped to talk to Renee and Larry Allen a little more, to dig a little deeper, and for a minute, Jazz stood on their front porch and stared at their aluminum screen door and considered her options.

The choice became eminently clear the moment she heard a sound from next door like the keening of a banshee.

The woman there answered the door, her eyes bloodshot and rimmed with gray smudges, her dark hair as tangled as a squirrel's nest. The baby propped on her hips had tears streaming from his eyes. He hiccupped and spluttered, his gnome face screwed into an expression that said he was only catching his breath. A second later, he crying started again.

"Hi." Since Jazz wasn't sure the woman

could hear her above the racket, she added a friendly wave. "We met. A couple weeks ago." She pointed back to the sidewalk where they'd talked the day Jazz met Florie's parents. "About Florie Allen."

"Sure, sure. Look . . ." She bounced the baby. It didn't help. "Lalo, he's teething and I haven't slept in like forever. Maybe we could talk another time?"

"It won't take long. It's about the photographs. The ones Florie took of Lalo."

The kid's cheeks flamed. He flailed his arms and kicked his chubby legs and screamed his lungs out.

"Yeah, pictures." The mother backed away from the door.

"I'll pay you for them," Jazz blurted out.

For a couple long seconds, the woman eyed Jazz, considering her words and probably wondering if Jazz was some kind of nutcase. Finally, she held up one finger and walked away.

But she didn't close the door.

The sounds of Lalo's desperate cries faded, and a second later, the woman was back without the baby and with a pink envelope with white polka dots on it. She opened the door, but she hung on to the envelope.

"How much?" she wanted to know.

Calculating how much cash she had with her, Jazz stalled for time. "How many pictures are there?"

The woman opened the envelope and slid out a stack of eight-by-ten photographs, counting silently, holding them close to her chest.

"Ten," she told Jazz.

"And I've got . . ." Jazz riffled through her purse for her wallet. She'd been planning to stop for bread and milk and treats for Luther after she had a drink with Sarah, and just before she left the house, she'd grabbed some cash. Thank goodness. "Fifty bucks. Five bucks a photograph. And I don't even want to keep them. I'll copy them and get the originals back to you."

The woman studied her through bleary eyes. "Fifty?"

Jazz handed over the money.

And left the house with the pink envelope full of pictures.

A few minutes later, she slid into the seat opposite Sarah at a table near the window of the café.

Sarah already had a glass of pinot grigio in front of her, and when she took a sip, she eyed Jazz — and the envelope — over the rim. "What's that?"

"Exactly what I'm dying to find out," Jazz

told her, and slid the photos from the envelope.

Just as Lalo's mom had told her, there were ten of them, all eight-by-tens, all black-and-white.

When the waitress came over, Jazz ordered a beer and got down to business. "Take a look at this one." She slid the top photograph to the center of the table. "What do you see?"

Sarah eyed the picture. Little Lalo was in the foreground, out of focus and off-center. His right ear and right eye, half of his nose and wide-open mouth were there in the frame. The rest of him was lost somewhere beyond the edges of the photograph.

"I thought we were here so I could give you the lowdown on my date with Matt." Sarah had been squinting at the picture, and when she raised her head, she still looked skeptical. "And you're here to talk about really bad photography?"

"I do want to hear about your date with Matt," Jazz told her. "All about it. But . . ." She tapped a finger just to the left of Lalo's ear. Farther from the lens, the scene was in focus, even if it was anything but interesting. A park bench. Two people, a man and a woman sitting next to each other, their heads bent together, their shoulders touching.

One by one, Jazz set the other pictures out on the table between them.

Lalo out of focus on a playground swing.

Lalo out of focus in front of a church.

The back of Lalo's head; the bottoms of Lalo's feet; Lalo's fat fist in the air.

"Florie took these pictures," Jazz said.

Sarah's expression morphed from skeptical to total disbelief.

"Are you telling me that Florie . . . our Florie . . . are you telling me she took these lousy pictures?"

"Exactly."

The enormity of the news sunk in, and Sarah leaned forward, her elbows on the table.

"Impossible. Florie didn't take bad pictures."

"Right."

"Which means . . ."

"She wanted to take bad pictures."

Sarah considered this and arrived at the same place where Jazz found herself. "What does it mean?"

"I'm not sure." Jazz pulled the pictures closer and added, "Not yet!" because she hated for Sarah to think all talk of Matt had been pushed to the back burner for no good reason. Now all she had to do is find out what the good reason was.

Jazz studied the pictures.

In each and every one of them, as Jazz had noticed from the start, Lalo was an afterthought. In one of the pictures, there were two women in the background, laughing. In another she saw a couple coming out of a church, down the front stairs, their fingers touching against the hand railing between them. In another, there were two men in the center of the picture.

And Lalo?

Parts of Lalo — his nose, his arms, his chubby body — were always out of frame, out of focus.

"Out of sight, out of mind." She mumbled the words, and Sarah was apparently thinking the same thing, because she nodded.

"Why pay to rent a kid and then take lousy pictures of him?" Jazz asked Sarah and herself. "Unless —"

The thought was so preposterous, Jazz couldn't find the words to explain. Before she could consider it and dismiss it as ridiculous, she picked up the photos and tapped them into a neat stack.

Then she went through them again, one by one.

By the time she restacked the photos and

dealt them out like cards on the table, her heart beat double time.

"She wasn't taking pictures of Lalo," she told Sarah, pointing from picture to picture to picture. "That's why she didn't care if he was in focus or not. That's why she didn't care what he looked like. And that's why she kept changing clothes!"

This was a new thought, and because Sarah wasn't up to date with the information, Jazz filled her in. "Florie had lots of different clothes. But they weren't really clothes. They were more like costumes. Old raincoats, wigs, even a nun's habit. They were disguises."

Sarah might be an artist, and as such, as right-brained as can be, but she could be logical when the occasion called for it. Her eyes lit. "She was trying to blend in."

"So no one would notice her." Jazz gripped the edges of the table with both hands, and when her beer arrived, frosty and foamy, she ignored it. "Florie needed the kid as a sort of decoy because it made perfect sense for a woman with a kid to be at a playground or a park or walking down the street as church let out. It made sense for her to be taking pictures of the kid, too. No one would even blink an eye if they saw that. There were other times when she obviously didn't need the kid, but she still had to make sure she'd blend in. That's when she'd dress as a homeless person."

"Or a nun," Sarah said.

Jazz nodded and glanced at the couples in the center of every picture. "She was watching them."

Sarah gulped. "Like a stalker."

"Not stalking. Not exactly." Jazz studied the photo of the man and the woman on the park bench and wondered who they were. "But she was watching them all, all right. Watching them all. Florie was photographing their secrets."

CHAPTER 17

The next day after school, Jazz zipped over to the Allen house.

"You cleaned out Florie's studio at school and her apartment on Murray Hill," she said to Larry when he came to the door and after she reintroduced herself. "There was an ad? For a divorce attorney?"

Larry wasn't so sure and Jazz supposed she couldn't blame him. His daughter's life had been cut short — brutally, senselessly — and he and his wife had been left to gather up the flotsam and jetsam of everything that had once been Florie. One ad cut from a newspaper was small potatoes.

"Maybe I could look through her things?" Jazz suggested.

Larry wasn't sure about that, either. It wasn't until he glanced over his shoulder that Jazz realized Renee was behind him in the shadows. Her blue fuzzy slippers flapping, she stepped forward and squeezed into

301

the space in the doorway beside her husband.

"Why would Florie need a divorce attorney?" Renee wanted to know.

"I don't think she did. But I think . . ." Okay, so she didn't know for sure, but it was the only theory Jazz had been able to cobble together after studying the photographs she got from Lalo's mother. "I think it might have something to do with her murder."

Renee and Larry exchanged looks, hers clearly saying he was in charge.

"Sounds crazy to me," he grumbled. "How —"

"I don't know yet. I'm not sure." Jazz let go a shaky breath. "I saw the ad in Florie's studio, but I wasn't paying a whole lot of attention. If I could just look at it and get the phone number, I could talk to the attorney. Unless . . ." She didn't want it to get to this, but she didn't want Larry to shut the door in her face, either. "Unless you'd like to find the ad and call me with the information?"

When he stepped to the side, the floorboards inside the front door moaned in protest. "I guess it wouldn't hurt," he said.

Jazz wasn't sure if it wouldn't hurt for him to find the ad on his own, or it wouldn't hurt for her to come in and take a look for herself. Since the second scenario fit better with her plans, she grabbed the door handle and yanked open the aluminum screen door.

She was met with a gust of air so musty and stale, it caught in her throat.

Jazz swallowed down the sour taste in her stomach, and when she stepped into the house, Larry and Renee had no choice but to each step to one side.

"Thank you," Jazz managed to stammer. It was just as well she got the words out before she looked around. After that, it was anyone's bet if she could have said anything if she tried.

Instead, she stared at the piles that towered around her. Newspapers on top of boxes on top of chairs. Clothes bundled into loose, lumpy wads, tossed atop one, two, three, four old TVs. Two green hair dryers from some long-ago beauty salon, their seats stacked with knickknacks and books and a trombone and cans of tomato soup; the goosenecks that traveled from the chairs to the domes that rested against customers' heads were draped with towels and blankets and more clothes.

"Oh." Jazz gave herself a kick in the pants. It was the wrong way to react. "Where . . ." She glanced at one particularly precarious-looking pile and wondered how the rumble of a passing truck didn't topple it. "Where are Florie's things?"

She managed to step further into the living room down a pathway that was maybe eighteen inches wide between the piles. Larry followed her into the maze. Renee kept her place at the door and scraped her palms along the legs of her jeans. "You really don't want to . . . we really can't let you . . ."

"I get it," Jazz said. Even though she didn't. Even though she didn't want to. "Maybe you could point me in the right direction?"

Of course they couldn't. With Jazz standing where she was, there was no way for either Larry or Renee to get past her.

Because of the piles, the windows were blocked, and Larry motioned somewhere into the gloom. "That way," he said.

With no clear way back to the door, Jazz turned and followed the path. Halfway through the living room, it branched off in two directions. One led into the kitchen, where she could see dozens of blue plastic grocery bags stuffed with other blue plastic grocery bags. More boxes. More cans of soup. A metal container with a lid.

Florie's ashes?

Her stomach flipped, and when Larry

poked her shoulder, Jazz flinched.

"Over there," he said, pointing to the right.

Here the path was narrower. Magazines. Board games. Empty milk cartons.

Jazz sidled through it all and headed up a stairway where each step was heaped with newspapers and every movement she made caused the stale, heavy air to rise up and assault her nose.

There was more of the same on the second floor, and when Larry directed her to a room at the end of the hallway, she could barely squeeze through the half-opened door. Behind it was —

Jazz didn't know what was hidden behind the plastic milk crates that loomed over her. She only knew that whatever it was, it smelled like old socks and older food. And fish.

Another couple steps, and she found a two-foot-square patch of floor where there was nothing but stained and faded maroon carpet. She would have taken a deep breath if the air — thick and dusty — didn't stick in her throat, and while she struggled not to cough or gag, a thought overtook her repulsion.

No wonder Florie liked to clean the stainless-steel counters in the St. Catherine's cafeteria.

No wonder she liked to help with washing the pots and pans and lining them up in neat, shiny order.

"Might be in here."

Larry's comment snapped her back to reality.

"Might be . . ." Jazz looked at the stacks of junk piled around her. "You just brought it home," she said, and then because it sounded too judgmental, she added, "but I can see how you'd get confused. I'm sure you have a lot on your mind."

Larry squeezed by her, closer to the nearest pile, flannel blankets that jiggled when he put a hand on them. Jazz jumped when an orange cat popped out from between the layers, came at her, then disappeared into the hallway.

"There's that picture." From her place in the doorway, Renee pointed a finger. Across the room, beyond a pile of books and what looked to be a lifetime's worth of old birthday cards, was the dizzying photograph Jazz had seen first at Florie's office, then in her apartment, the trippy colors standing out against the cardboard and dust of the room.

"Tate Brody has one just like it," Jazz mentioned, and she wasn't sure what she expected them to say in return. That they hadn't told Brody he could have the picture? That he'd scooped it up before they got to the studio and they had no idea another one existed?

Instead, they said nothing at all.

Larry poked through the pile nearest the photograph, and when Jazz came up alongside him and made to move a stack of magazines, he shot her a look. "You better not," he said.

She stepped back to the small bare spot, her hands tucked behind her, her breath hanging suspended, her gaze darting back and forth between the piles and the stacks, the heaps and the gobs.

"Wait!" When Larry moved a cardboard box filled with cans of cat food, Renee stepped up and squeezed herself into the space in back of Jazz. "You shouldn't touch that, Larry." Her voice trembled and her hands shook. "We should just go downstairs. We should all just go downstairs. We should just leave . . . leave everything alone."

"We will," Jazz promised. "As soon as we find the ad. I know we're close." She perked up when she saw a stack of pink envelopes. "There!" She pointed to direct Larry's attention to a spot between a coil of Christmas lights and a dresser with its drawers open and crammed with paper shopping bags. "I saw those envelopes in Florie's studio. I bet the ad is right there." The ad was small and looked like junk, and Jazz's shoulders slumped and her mood plummeted when she told herself there was no way Larry was going to find it. At the same time, she looked around, and for the first time since she walked into the house, she was encouraged by what she saw. They didn't throw anything away. The ad would be there. It had to be.

"This?" When Larry spun to face her, he had a scrap of paper in his hands.

"Yes!" Jazz plucked it away before he could stop her, and when she heard Renee suck in a breath, she struggled for a compromise. "I'll just take a picture of it," she said, and as if to prove her intentions were honorable, she took her phone out of her pocket. "Just a picture. You can keep the ad. Is that all right?" she asked Renee.

Her eyes were wide and uncertain, but the barest of nods from Renee gave Jazz the go-ahead, and once she had it, and the picture, she thanked the Allens and told them she'd let them know what she found out from the attorney — Howard Moritz — whose name was on the ad in bold letters.

They trudged back through the maze and were already at the front door when Larry asked, "And if you do find something out from that lawyer guy, you'll tell that cop. Right?"

Jazz assured them she'd take care of it and congratulated herself; she waited to groan until she was back in her car.

She hadn't planned on spending so much time at the Allens'.

That cop was waiting for her at the coffee shop.

And she was late for their date.

He was sitting at the table next to the window and farthest from the door.

Their table.

It wasn't like Glen and Abby, the nice folks who ran the coffee shop, ever said as much. But it seemed like every time they showed up — back in the days when they'd stop there before a concert or a movie or after they went to her mom's for Sunday dinner when Jazz was done training with Manny and Nick wasn't chasing down bad guys — it was the table where they always ended up.

Since the place was relatively empty and Nick had his choice of tables, she wondered if he remembered. What did it mean if he did?

And what did it mean if he didn't?

"I'm late." The words rushed out of her even before she sat down. "I got busy and time got away from me, and —" Her feeble smile was all she could offer by way of an apology.

He was wearing a navy-blue suit and the Jerry Garcia tie she'd given him for Christmas once upon a time, green and blue swirls of color with splashes of yellow and purple. The colors reminded her of the psychedelic photograph back at the Allens'. Of the photograph Tate Brody had taken from Florie's studio.

"I had some stuff to do," she said, and she sat down. "I'm sorry."

He wrinkled his nose. "You smell like a sewer."

She sniffed the air and realized he was right. "Sorry," she said again. "I had to stop and see the parents of one of the girls from school and . . ."

It wasn't much of an explanation, but it was just penitent enough. Most other guys would have been satisfied.

Nick wasn't most other guys.

He studied her, his expression not exactly accepting but not accusatory, either. "Not Florie's family, I hope."

She wondered if lying on a first date was a sin and consoled herself with the fact that technically, this wasn't a first date. Still not willing to take a chance, she skirted the subject. "They . . . the family of the girl I visited . . . they're pack rats."

"Yeah, hoarders. Been there, seen that." He sat back, one arm draped over the empty chair next to him

She told herself to shut up, not to push it, to change the subject, but she couldn't seem to help herself. He'd waited. At their table.

"It took longer than I thought," she told him. "I shouldn't have made you wait."

He didn't have a chance to respond. The waitress came over carrying a tray, and before Jazz could order the coffee of the day like she always did, the woman set a mug in front of her.

"Coffee of the day for you," the waitress said. "And double espresso with the coffee of the day." She set that cup in front of Nick, who explained his menu choice with a grimace and "I've got to work late tonight."

The waitress left and was back in a flash. "Two forks." She set them on the table. "And one chocolate truffle tartlet in a salted shortbread crust."

Jazz's favorite dessert, the one they'd always shared on special occasions.

"I . . ." The words stuck in Jazz's throat

and she coughed them away. Maybe she was going to thank him. Maybe she was going to remind him that this really wasn't a special occasion. That it couldn't be. That it was just a date.

Rather than think about it, she concentrated on the dessert in all its glorious decadence. "It looks fabulous."

"And I didn't have lunch. I'm starving." Nick grabbed his fork.

"This is your dinner?" She watched him take a bite and give her a wink that said the tartlet was as good as ever. "It's not exactly healthy."

"I'll grab something later." He pushed the plate a little closer to her and, with one finger, indicated that she should pick up her fork and dig in. "It's still early."

She dutifully took a bite. He was right. The best was still the best.

"So what did Florie's parents have to say?" he asked.

It was a good thing she was chewing, Jazz had time to stall. She washed down the tartlet with a gulp of coffee. "Who says I was with —"

He leaned forward, his elbows on the table. "You always were a lousy liar."

"Except I never lied. Not to you. Not ever once."

"Until now."

He looked entirely too self-satisfied, and it made Jazz's blood boil. Or maybe that was just the heat she felt from taking a chance, getting too close.

"What, you can read minds now?"

"I could always read your mind."

She might have gone right on being annoyed if the last of the late-afternoon sun didn't slant through the front window and turn his hair golden. In all the time they were together, they'd gone on exactly one getaway, two days (it was all either of them could manage to cobble together) at a bed-and-breakfast on the lake. It was May and the weather was glorious, and when they sat and watched the sun slip into the water in the evening, the light reflected off the lake and brought out the honey highlights in his hair. She remembered thinking he was the handsomest man on the planet.

Back then, there were fewer lines at the corners of his eyes.

"How's Kim?" she asked.

He made sure he took another bite of the dessert before he answered, and though Jazz was pretty sure there wasn't anything interesting happening out on the street, he watched something there intently. "Same old same old."

313

"I'm sorry."

His gaze flickered to hers. "You're sorry about a lot today."

"I'm sorry I smell like a sewer."

"You see, that's exactly how I knew you were lying." He took one more bite, then pushed the plate to her side of the table. "You think I made detective for nothing? I've been to the Allens', remember. I'd recognize that smell anywhere."

There was no use explaining. With a sigh, she dug out her phone and showed him the picture she'd taken upstairs in the fishy-smelling room.

Nick didn't say a word, just raised his eyebrows.

"It was on the bulletin board in Florie's studio."

"I saw it. I'm surprised you did."

She tapped a finger against the photo instead. "And this didn't strike you as odd?"

"It struck me as plenty odd." He sat back and eyed her, not the way he used to when they were together, when they were alone. Then there was a spark of heat in his eyes. Now, they were lit with nothing more than curiosity. "What do you make of it?"

"I'm not sure," Jazz admitted. "But I've got an idea. Florie was renting the kid next door."

She was moving too fast, and he held up a hand. "Renting —"

"The kid who lives next door to her parents. Sure." She nodded. "And she had a collection of odd clothes. Clothes that made her look old and homeless. Or clothes that a mom would wear to the park. You know, for when she went there with the kid."

"Because . . . ?"

"Because she was following people. She was taking their pictures. And I think she was doing it because she was working for this Howard guy, the divorce attorney." As if he might have forgotten, she waggled her phone at him. "If one of those people caught on, if Florie saw something she shouldn't have seen . . . or if Florie was freelancing . . ."

This was a new thought, and it fell out of her mouth before she had time to even think it through. There was no better way to see where it was headed than to think out loud. "Florie had these big pink envelopes."

Nick nodded. He'd seen them in the studio, too.

"And the photos I got from the neighbor, the ones Florie supposedly took of the woman's kid, were in a pink envelope. And that What's-Her-Name . . ." Jazz came up short on the memory. "Anyway, one of the

315

teachers at Florie's school had one of those envelopes on her desk, and she didn't want me to see it. When I walked into her office she slipped it under some books. The way I see it, scenario number one is that Florie saw something she shouldn't have seen when she was working for the divorce attorney. That she took a picture she shouldn't have taken. If the subject of that picture found out, that would be a motive for murder, right?" Before he could tell her that she — or her theory — was half-baked, she went right on.

"And Florie was desperate for money, you know. She was working as hard as she could just to pay her rent, working so hard that her grades suffered and she lost her scholarship. What if she went off the reservation? What if she was working for that attorney, following people and taking pictures, and what if she kept some of those pictures for herself? What if she was blackmailing somebody? It wouldn't be the first time, Nick. Florie blackmailed a girl back at St. Catherine's. Blackmail would be a motive for murder, too, right?"

"You've been watching too much TV."

"Yeah, and hanging around too much with a cop."

A smile flickered across his face. "Not yet,

but I'm hoping you will be hanging around with a cop too much very soon."

She could not be so easily put off. Not even by that old, familiar glint in his eyes.

Too keyed up to sit still, she finished off the tartlet. "You'll look into it?"

He sat back, raised his chin. "Already have."

Just like that, her excitement dissolved. "You mean you already knew all that stuff?"

"Not about the kid," he admitted. "That was pretty clever of Florie and it explains all the weird clothes in her closet. Good work on your part finding it out."

"But . . ." She couldn't help but stammer. He'd pulled the rug out from under all her theories, all her work. "But . . ."

"You're right," he said, and apparently, that was supposed to make her feel better, because he allowed himself a quick grin. "Florie worked part-time for Moritz. And yes, she was following people. As for her scooping up business for herself . . . If he knew about it, Moritz never told me."

She slapped both hands, palms down, on the table. "You talked to him?"

"And every single one of his clients who Florie was following."

"And . . . ?"

"And they've all got credible alibis, including Moritz. Thanks to a gallbladder attack, he was in the ER the night Florie was killed."

"You could have told me."

He controlled a grumble of frustration, but just barely. "I didn't need to tell you. I don't need to tell you."

He was right.

Which didn't mean Jazz was going to give up. "Then what about Grace Greenwald?" she asked. "Grace and Florie were always at each other's throats. Grace might have killed her. And then there's Parker Paul over at the film festival. He says he was in Atlanta at the time of Florie's murder, but —"

"He was in Atlanta at the time of Florie's murder."

"Then what about Billy DeSantos at the film festival? He's —"

Nick sat up, his jaw tight, his eyes narrowed. "Stay away from Billy DeSantos. He's got a record."

It wasn't often that he went caveman on her, but every time he did, she reacted the same way.

Jazz inched back her shoulders, and maybe the tartlet wasn't sweet enough, because her voice was suddenly edgy.

"All I did was talk to him."

"All you have to do from now on is stay

away from him."

"Why? Do you think he's the murderer?"

"If I thought he was the murderer, I would have arrested him by now."

"Not if you didn't have evidence."

"Evidence." Maybe the tart wasn't sweet enough for Nick, either. His mouth twisted. "It would be great to have some evidence."

Before he was even done grumbling the words, his phone rang. He swiped the screen. "Kolesov," he said, and listened. "Really? Where?"

Just like that, Jazz felt the weight of all their yesterdays settle on her shoulders. It was always the same, always the job.

Nick was already out of his chair when he told the caller, "I'll be right there," and when he ended the call, regret softened his eyes, rounded his shoulders. "I gotta go."

She didn't mean to snap. Blame it on the sugar rush. Or the fact that he'd ignored the suspects she'd mentioned. Well, except for the ones he'd already eliminated. And the one he'd ordered her to avoid. "Of course you do."

"If you hadn't been so late, we would have had more time together." His frown told her he hadn't meant to snap, either, but there it was.

Nick dug out the money to pay for their

coffee and dessert and more than enough to cover a tip and stacked it in the center of the table. "How about . . ." He took a deep breath and let it out slowly, then, like a kid making a wish in front of a birthday cake, he lowered his voice. "Next Tuesday? Right here?"

"Will it ever be any different?"

"I dunno," he admitted. "But I think it's worth trying to find out, no matter how many Tuesdays it takes."

With that, he was gone, and Jazz was left with nothing but the question of what she'd do next Tuesday. That, and a half a cup of cold coffee and the thought of pink envelopes with white polka dots on them.

CHAPTER 18

Joyce Wildemere was no more a fashion plate that evening than she had been the first time Jazz stopped to see her. Last time, it had been a long black skirt and a pair of dirty boots. The evening of Jazz's date with Nick, the screenwriting instructor was decked out in a pair of farmer overalls and wore a long-sleeve gray T-shirt underneath that was sprinkled with stars that matched the silvery color of her hair.

For a moment, all Jazz could do was stare.

"Yes?" Wildemere looked up from her computer and over to the doorway. "Do I know you?"

"Jazz Ramsey." She offered a smile that wasn't returned. "I stopped in a few days ago to talk to you about Florie Allen. You told me she failed your class."

Wildemere was holding a pen, and disgusted, she tossed it down on the desk and sat back. "What, you're going to argue with me about the girl's grade?"

"No. Not at all." Jazz took a few steps into the office. Unlike Tate Brody's, with its antique banker's lamp and wooden bookcases, Wildemere's office was bare-bones basic, standard issue from the school, no doubt — a gray metal desk, a couple chairs, a metal bookcase against one wall where books were piled one on top of the other.

"Actually . . ." Jazz tried for another smile. "I was going to ask if Florie was blackmailing you."

Whatever Wildemere had expected, it wasn't this. What little color was in her face washed away completely, then returned again in blotches that dotted her doughy cheeks and nose. The left corner of her mouth twitched. "What the hell are you talking about?" she demanded.

"I think I'm talking about a motive for murder," Jazz confessed. "Not that I think you killed Florie or anything." This she was not sure about at all, but it seemed the safest way to continue the conversation. "I'm just trying to confirm a theory to myself. You see, Florie was working for a divorce attorney, following people and taking photographs. Only I think maybe she decided to get a little cut of the action on her own, to cut out the middleman and see if she could turn a profit. If you know what I mean."

When she spoke, Wildemere's voice was tight. Her fingers curled into her palms. "No, I don't know what you mean. I do know you need to leave. Now."

"I will," Jazz promised. "I just want to know if —"

"Get the hell out of here." Like a glacier inching toward the ocean, Wildemere stood. She leaned forward, her palms pressed to her desk. "How dare you accuse me."

"I'm not. I'm not accusing anyone. I just thought if Florie was involved in something she shouldn't be involved in, if she took some pictures of you —"

"What makes you think she did?"

Jazz looked at the desktop where only days before, she'd seen the proof. "Pink envelope," she said. "White polka dots."

Wildemere looked where Jazz was looking, exactly where the envelope had been the first time Jazz visited. For Jazz, that pretty much confirmed her theory.

The instructor shrugged. "Whatever you're talking about, I don't see any pink envelope here, do you?"

She didn't. Jazz swallowed down the familiar taste of regret. First she'd accused Tate Brody. Now she'd nearly come right out and called Joyce Wildemere a murderer.

Regrouping, she closed her eyes.

"It's just a theory," she said.

"Maybe you'd better get your facts straight before you start throwing your theories around." Her fists on her wide hips, Wildemere faced Jazz. "You think I'm hiding something."

"If you are, it only makes you look guilty. At least that's what the cops will think. It makes you look like a suspect."

Wildemere barked out a laugh that pinged against the metal furniture. "Suspect? If that's what you're looking for, you'd be better off talking to Tate Brody."

"I have," Jazz told her. "He says —"

"Oh, I can imagine what he says. Pure as the driven snow, right? That's what he'd like everyone to believe. But let me tell you, I walked in on them once, on Tate and that Allen girl. It was not the usual teacher-and-student meeting, if you get my drift." She added a broad wink so Jazz would, indeed, get it. "That ought to be enough to tell you something isn't right about that guy and if it isn't . . ." There was a window behind her desk, and Wildemere stalked over to it and flicked aside the blinds.

"You didn't notice the cop cars outside?" she asked Jazz.

Of course she'd noticed two police cars

parked out on the street, but Jazz hadn't paid a whole lot of attention. She was used to seeing police cars in the city. Now, she took a step closer to the window and looked at the street, three stories below. There were two patrol cars out in front of the building and there were two more cars parked nearby that she hadn't been able to see when she walked in. Unmarked cars, like the one Nick drove.

"I saw the patrol cars when I came in," she told Wildemere. "I just figured —"

"What?"

Jazz twitched her shoulders. "There are always police in this area of town. I didn't think anything of it."

Jazz took another step toward the window, another look at the cars outside. She gave the teacher a sidelong glance. "What have you heard?"

Wildemere made a noise, half grunt, half raspberries. "Maybe you need to watch the news like everyone else."

"You already know. School grapevine?"

"Grapevine. Text messages. Emails." Wildemere's smile was tight. "We're a small school and when something happens, word travels fast."

"Word about . . . ?"

"What, we're best friends now and you

expect me to pour my heart out to you?" When she laughed, her stomach jiggled beneath the bib of her overalls. "You just walked in here and accused me of being a killer."

"Actually, I just walked in here and asked if you were a victim. If Florie was blackmailing you —"

"She wasn't."

Wildemere's denial was a little too quick. A little too forced.

"If you know if she was blackmailing anyone else —"

"Can't say."

"Which isn't the same as you don't know."

"Which isn't anything since I asked you to leave a few minutes ago."

"I will. Sure." Jazz backstepped toward the door. "But if you could tell me what the police are doing here —"

"Sweet baby Jesus, you are one annoying woman!" Wildemere's eyes bulged, and her already blotchy cheeks got even redder. "They found her phone, all right? They found Florie Allen's cell phone."

This was news, and the enormity of it took Jazz's breath away. "Who —"

"Somebody on the maintenance staff. At least that's what I'm hearing from the text messages that have been buzzing around for the last hour or so. Found it dumped in a trash can, and whoever it was who found it, he was smart enough to turn it in to security. They were the ones who called the cops."

"Do they know how it got there?"

"Now, see . . ." Wildemere wagged a finger at Jazz. "You're thinking like the blockhead kids around here think. I present them with a scenario and they right away jump ahead of themselves. At this point, you shouldn't be asking how it got there, you should be asking where *there* is."

"You said. In a trash can."

Wildemere nodded. "In a trash can, all right. One right outside Tate Brody's office."

Tate Brody's office was in a different wing of the building, on a different floor, and Jazz slowly made her way there. Now she understood why Nick had raced out of the coffee shop. She also understood that, good cop that he was, he'd never let her — or any other civilian — anywhere near the scene.

Jazz took the steps rather than the elevator and pushed out of the stairwell door and into the hallway that intersected the one where Brody worked in the elegant glow of his banker's lamp. There were . . . *one, two, three, four* . . . office doors between her and the L where the hallway cut to the right.

Brody's office was two doors down from there on the left.

And there was yellow crime scene tape between her and there.

She wasn't surprised, but that didn't mean she wasn't aggravated. She grumbled a curse, and when she caught the sound of a familiar voice, she swallowed anything else she might have been tempted to say and stepped around a trash can and toward a nearby drinking fountain.

"Get the ones over this way," she heard Nick say. "Clancy and his team are checking the trash cans on the other floors."

She didn't hear the crime scene technician's response. She didn't have to. Nick was younger than most of the detectives in the department, but he had a reputation for being smart and thorough and for kicking asses when he had to. He was well respected, well thought of, and easy to work with as long as everybody pulled their own weight and didn't drag down either Nick or his investigations.

When a technician rounded the corner carrying a black garbage bag, Jazz took a long drink of water, watching out of the corner of her eye as the man dumped what was in the school trash can into the bag he was holding.

She supposed in the best of all possible worlds, she would have called out to him when he turned to leave and a piece of paper fluttered from the bag and landed on the floor.

Instead, she waited until the technician disappeared again beyond the yellow tape. Then she closed in.

"It can't be," she mumbled, and in the next breath reminded herself to be quiet. She didn't need either Nick or the tech to come around the corner, not until she retrieved the scrap of paper.

There wasn't much to it, a three-inch-by-four-inch sliver of paper, its edges ragged, ripped. She wouldn't have noticed it at all if not for the colors.

Bright psychedelic swirls, and so familiar.

"Good God, Jazz, why do you smell like the lunches my boys leave in their backpacks over the weekend?"

The next day Jazz was so busy studying the photograph propped against the bookcases in her office, she didn't see Sarah sail into the room. She barely spared her a glance, just curled her lip to let Sarah know what she thought of the comment.

"You're not close enough to smell me."

"I don't need to be close." Sarah waved

one hand in front of her face before she went over to the far end of the office and threw open a window. "Honey, you need to go home and take a shower. You can't spend the rest of the day smelling like that."

Jazz knew she was right. But at that moment, she didn't really care.

"I want you to take a look at this picture," she told her friend.

Giving Jazz a wide berth, Sarah came back across the room. She stopped four feet to Jazz's right and cocked her head, studying the photograph. "Nice. What is it?"

"It's Florie's."

Sarah raised her eyebrows.

"I stopped to see Florie's parents yesterday and I went back there this morning. I bought the picture from them just a little while ago. Well, after I unearthed it."

She hadn't had a chance to tell Sarah about her visit to the Allens' the afternoon before, about the house, the mounds of junk, the smell. No wonder Sarah looked skeptical.

"They're hoarders," Jazz explained.

"So the smell —"

"Kind of goes with the territory."

"And the picture —"

"There were two of them. This one was hanging in Florie's bedroom at her apartment." She waved toward the photograph across the room. "This one . . ." She plucked the scrap she'd found outside Brody's office from her desk and waved it in Sarah's direction. "This is all that's left of the other one, the one Tate Brody took out of Florie's office at school because he thought it was the most wonderful work she'd ever done."

"It is magical." Tipping her head from one side to the other, Sarah closed in on the photograph. "So why did he rip it up?"

"That's what I'd like to know."

"And what's it supposed to be?"

Jazz kept her gaze on the photo. "You're the art expert."

"Well yeah, but . . ." A couple more steps, and when Sarah parked herself between Jazz and the photograph, Jazz had no choice but to round her desk so she could stand beside her.

Sarah wrinkled her nose.

"Sorry," Jazz said.

"The kid just died. The picture couldn't have been stored for all that long a time. The smell shouldn't be clinging to it."

"You have no idea. I saw it yesterday in an upstairs bedroom. This morning when I stopped by, the Allens didn't even remember the picture, and let's face it, it's pretty hard to forget. Fortunately, they were cooperative. They let me go up and find it myself. Between yesterday and today . . ." She shivered at the memory. "Less than twenty-four hours and things had already changed. It's like the whole house is alive. It morphs and grows. Like some kind of giant fungus or something." She wrapped her arms around herself. "There was a stack of *Life* magazines that wasn't there yesterday on top of the photograph. And two bags of shredded paper. And the cat's litter box."

Sarah digested this information in silence. "How much did you pay them?"

"All I had, and I only had it because I stopped at an ATM on the way over to their house. It's a good thing Friday is a payday. I wiped out my account. Two hundred bucks. They didn't haggle."

When Sarah tipped her head to the left, her purple dangling earrings brushed her shoulder. "It's worth it."

"You think?"

"It would look great in your living room."

Sarah had long been trying to get Jazz to introduce more color — more style — into her home. It never worked. Jazz liked her world simple. Clean lines and colors that wouldn't jar her senses and that she wouldn't easily tire of. Like gray. And beige. No muss, no fuss.

"I didn't buy it to hang," she told Sarah. "I bought it to try and figure out why Tate Brody bothered to ask the Allens if he could have the picture, take it from Florie's studio, then rip it to pieces."

"What did you decide?"

"Nothing yet. That's why I need your help. I thought if we spent our lunch hour in here doing some brainstorming, we might get somewhere."

"There is no way I'm eating lunch with you in this room!" Leave it to a best friend to be unforgiving. Sarah pinched her nose with two fingers. "I'd gag just trying."

"Then don't eat lunch." Jazz dragged a yellow legal pad off her desk. "But you still have to think. The way I smell won't affect that. You're the artist, tell me what you see."

For a woman who lived and breathed art and style and preached its gospel far and wide, it was an offer Sarah couldn't refuse. She stepped back, stepped forward again, squinted.

"The colors are certainly amazing." She pointed toward the upper left quadrant of the picture. "See the way the oranges and the yellows merge and blend over here? And this blob in the middle. It's out of focus, and normally, our brains would rebel. We want our world to make sense, and if we have to wonder, if we have to think and speculate, it makes the logical parts inside us get all antsy. But that's the beauty of this piece, isn't it? We have to stop. We have to stare. We really do have to think about what everything is and why it's there and what Florie was trying to tell us by what she included in the picture, and what she left out. Like this." She pointed dead center. "Is that a car? Or an animal?"

Jazz had wondered the same thing the first time she saw the picture, and because she was no closer to an answer now than she had been then, she shook away the thought. "How about the rest of it?" she asked. "I mean, some of it's pretty obvious, right? Like here in this corner." She closed in on the photograph so she could point out the image in the upper left-hand corner. "Brass numbers on a red door."

"An address?"

"That's what I thought, too. But see . . ." Jazz leaned closer. "The numbers are blurred, and there are only three of them, and if you look really closely here . . ." She pointed to a narrow strip just to the right of the door. "It doesn't look like paint. Or like siding. Or like stone or brick like you might see near the front door of a house. It looks like —"

"Wallpaper!" Smell or not, Sarah saw what Jazz saw and came to stand beside her. "You're right. There's a bit of a pattern to it."

"I'm thinking hotel room door," Jazz said.

Sarah's mouth fell open. "That's brilliant. It explains the . . ." She narrowed her eyes. "Three thirty-six. Those are the numbers, right? So it's the door to hotel room number three thirty-six. Which hotel?"

Jazz hoped her raised eyebrows were enough to tell Sarah she was asking for the impossible. "Let's make a list," she said instead, and she started one on the legal pad, sketching out a rectangle and then writing *hotel room door* in the spot where the door was on the photograph.

"The blob in the center . . ." It had always been questionable, yet now, Jazz looked at the smears of color with new appreciation. Jazz wasn't at all sure how things like computer graphics and special effects worked, but she imagined Florie had used some special technique on this part of the photograph. "It looks like the back of a car. See, here," she told Sarah.

"But not a license plate."

"No." Jazz chewed over the thought, and the truth of the thing might never have occurred to her if she hadn't visited Florie's apartment on Murray Hill, if she'd never talked to Croc, if she didn't turn on the TV before she left for work and hear the news that had electrified all of Cleveland that morning — that the police were interviewing a person of interest in the Florie Allen murder.

She suspected she knew who that person of interest was.

"Oh my gosh! It's the Audi symbol. Look. One, two, three, four interconnected circles. Only the way Florie manipulated the images, they look more like suns."

"Exploding sun," Sarah commented. "I wonder what that says about the person who owns the Audi."

Jazz wondered, too. Just like she wondered about the other images Florie had memorialized and Tate Brody had thought so much of that he wanted to own a copy of the photograph.

"It's a love letter." The words escaped Jazz on the end of a gasp of amazement. "A love letter to Brody."

"Which means this . . ." Sarah pointed to a patch that beneath bright zigzags of hot pink and molten orange, looked green and leafy. "A favorite spot to meet? I bet it's a park."

"And look here." It was Jazz's turn to poke

a finger at the photograph and trace a shape that was blurred and so distorted it reminded her of the modern and incomprehensible art Sarah had once dragged her to a museum to see.

"I'd bet anything that's Florie," Jazz said. "See, here's her nose, her chin, her shoulders."

"That girl always did have an incredible imagination. And the technical skill to take what she saw in her head and bring it to life in new and interesting ways." Sarah sighed. "But if it's that personal, why would this Brody character rip up his copy of the picture?"

"Maybe because it is personal." Jazz lowered her voice. "I'll bet anything he's the person of interest they arrested last night. Maybe Brody knew they were closing in on him and he didn't want the cops to find the photo and figure out what it was all about, just like we're figuring out what it's all about. Except . . ." Something had been bothering Jazz about the whole Brody connection ever since she visited North Coast the evening before. "They found Florie's phone in a trash can near Brody's office," she told Sarah, because she didn't know if this piece of information had been released to the press. "And you can bet your bottom dollar he's telling the cops he doesn't know how it got there, that anybody could have put it there. You know, to frame him."

"He's right."

Jazz conceded at much with a nod. "And all along he told me that he and Florie were nothing more than student and teacher. But this picture proves there was more going on between them. Or at least it should." Her shoulders sagged.

"He could say the same thing about the picture that he's probably saying about the phone," she told Sarah. "That sure, that might be Florie there in the picture. That there's a hotel room door, a pretty park. And obviously, he's not the only one who owns an Audi. Brody can say that Florie could have made this photo for anyone. Or maybe the whole thing is some sort of fantasy straight out of her imagination."

"But not just anyone ripped it up."

"It didn't have to be Brody who destroyed the picture," Jazz pointed out. "Anybody could have done that and left the pieces so they'd be found, just like the phone, so they'd make Brody look guilty."

Jazz pressed her fingers to her temples. Ever since she'd found the scrap of photograph, she'd been trying to make sense of it, and every time she felt as if she was getting close, she'd run up against a new brick wall.

"I wish we knew what that was." Jazz pointed to the last unidentified part of the picture. This bit was off to the right at the bottom of the photograph. Like the rest of the picture, it was overwashed with acid colors, and this bit was shot through with yellow, like fire.

"Tabletop," Sarah suggested.

"Briefcase. See, here." With one finger, Jazz outlined the shape. "There's a bit of a darker patch right here. It could be the briefcase latch." She was off base and she knew it, but it was worth a try in the name of brainstorming.

"Book?"

"Baloney sandwich." When Sarah made a face at her, Jazz shrugged. "Hey, we're tossing out ideas, right?"

"Ideas about what?"

Eileen swept into the room and came to stand between Jazz and Sarah. She wrinkled her nose but didn't comment on the smell. Instead, she gave the photograph a once-over. "What is it?"

"That's what we're trying to figure out," Jazz told her.

Sarah jumped in. "We think it's a sort of a —"

"Message. Like a letter. A love letter." As if it would somehow prove what she said, Jazz showed Eileen the legal pad. "See, we've got almost all of it figured out, but there's this one patch —"

"Here." Sarah poked one bright-green fingernail against the bottom right-hand corner of the picture. "We can't figure out what this is."

Eileen crossed her arms over her chest and settled her weight back against one foot. "A love letter, huh?" She closed in on the picture and tapped a finger against the darker patch. "That is a birthmark," she said, and glided her finger across the rest of the image that Jazz and Sarah had tagged as a briefcase and a tabletop and a baloney sandwich. "A birthmark on the inside of a man's thigh. I'd say . . ." She touched a hand nearly to her groin. "Right about here."

Eileen backed up and headed to her office, shaking her head as she did. "You girls need to get out more."

CHAPTER 19

Greg called that evening just as Jazz was driving home from dinner at Grandma and Grandpa Kurcz's house.

"Surprise! We just landed in Cleveland," he told Jazz. "You'll be thrilled to know we're on our way to get Luther. I sure have missed him, and I'll bet you'll be glad when he's out of your hair."

Glad.

Sure.

Two hours later, Jazz sank further into the couch cushions and glanced at the place where before Greg and Toni arrived, Luther had been sprawled on top of a pile of blankets, happily snoring.

The spot was empty now. Cold. The house was as quiet as it had been before Luther came to visit. After Manny was gone.

Automatically her gaze traveled to the shelf where she'd set the picture of her dad and Big George, her and Manny. Dad and

Manny had passed, gone on to new adventures. Big George was old and retired.

And Jazz?

A truck racing by outside muffled the sound of her sigh.

Jazz was a dog trainer without a dog. An investigator with no credentials and zero credibility. A girlfriend who wasn't really a girlfriend because the man she'd once thought of as the man of her dreams knew exactly what she knew — coffee once a week was all they were ever likely to share.

"God, could you be any more depressing?" Jazz lambasted herself, and just for good measure, slapped a hand against the empty cushion beside her before she pushed up from the couch. She went into the kitchen and a couple minutes later she was back, a glass of cold milk in one hand and three of Grandma Kurcz's homemade chocolate chip cookies in the other. She set the glass and the cookies on the coffee table along with a DVD in a jewel case that she pulled out of the jacket she'd worn to the Allens' that day, and did her best to settle herself in spite of the harsh reality that intruded — even chocolate wasn't enough to lift her mood.

A glug of milk washed the taste of self-pity out of her mouth. A bite of cookie settled her stomach, which had been doing a pretty good imitation of a Mexican jumping bean ever since she and Sarah discovered the secrets of Florie's mind-bending photograph.

Was it worth calling Nick to tell him what she'd found out?

She glanced at the clock and decided not to bother him. It was late, dark, and if what she'd seen on the six o'clock news meant anything, he'd had a hell of a day. Sure, he had a person of interest he was interviewing, but like she suspected would happen, that person — probably fashionable, handsome, two-timing Tate Brody — had been released from police custody due to lack of evidence.

What might have been a birthmark on what might have been a man's inner thigh on a photograph taken by a student who was later murdered wasn't going to change any of that. Not tonight.

Tired of listening to the sounds of her own rough breathing, bored with the workings of her brain, round and round like a hamster on a wheel, Jazz grabbed the TV remote and hit the On button.

The first thing she saw was the blue-skinned monster from the poster at the film festival.

Think you can stand the terror?

The monster's face faded and the picture blurred. When it came back into focus, her TV screen showed broken wiring, pitted tiles, falling plaster.

The building where she and Luther had trained.

The place where Florie had been killed.

The commercial the kids had cobbled together for the film festival.

Her boredom dissolved in a whoosh of adrenaline, and Jazz sat up.

Three nights of fright.

The narrator's voice was low and gravelly, a whisper from the grave.

Three nights of panic. Three nights of . . .

The picture shuddered violently. The camera panned out of control from pock-marked floor to falling-down ceiling to cobwebbed corner.

Three nights of horror!

A graphic, the letters bloodred, flashed across the screen. Web site, theaters where the movies would be shown, times.

The commercial was short. And surprisingly well done. Jazz was sorry Florie never got to see the finished product. It wasn't anywhere near as impressive as the video project Florie had produced on her own, of course, but that was no big surprise. The commercial involved teamwork. And Grace. The video project, that was all on Florie, and she'd come through with artistry and a big dose of panache.

At the same time she reached for another cookie, Jazz grabbed the jewel case she'd tossed on the table. Since it hardly seemed to matter in the face of the monumental discovery that Florie's photograph was a tribute to a lover who might be Tate Brody, she hadn't mentioned to Sarah that when she was at the Allens', she'd found something else there in the upstairs bedroom between the framed photograph and a pile of hot-pink envelopes.

"Video Project, Florie Allen." She read the words scrawled in purple marker across the case and felt as bad now as she had when she pointed it out to the Allens and told them she'd love to make a copy, and they told her to just take it, that they had no use for it.

Maybe they could show Florie's incredible video project at the memorial service they were planning at the school in her honor.

Suddenly feeling as if there was some purpose for sitting there — more than just feeling sorry for herself — Jazz popped the disc into her DVD player and sat back, ready to be amazed by Florie's talent all over again.

She sat up like a shot when the first scene showed on the screen.

WELCOME TO CLEVELAND.

A sign on the berm of the freeway.

The sounds of traffic whizzing, so loud it nearly drowned out the narrator's voice. Florie's voice.

"Cleveland was founded in 1796 by a man named Moses . . ."

Florie must have turned away from the microphone; her next words were lost beneath the grumble of a passing eighteen-wheeler.

"No, no, no!" Jazz scooted forward on the couch. "This isn't right. This isn't Florie's project. Where's the beautiful sunrise? Where are the people hurrying to their jobs and their schools?"

Instead what she saw was a mishmash of images, many of them out of focus. The narration was clunky. The music was too loud and often drowned out Florie's voice. The scene breaks were abrupt, jarring.

Jazz's insides flipped. Watching the total train wreck that was the video project, she couldn't help but remember what Grace had told her. The night before the project was due, Florie was in a panic.

If what Jazz was watching was all Florie had prepared at the time, Jazz could see why.

By the time it was over and the final screen said *Cleveland, By Florie Allen,* Jazz didn't even bother to shake her head in wonder. She needed answers, and as far as she could see, there was only one person who could give them to her. She picked up the phone and left a voicemail for Eileen. She'd be a little late getting into work the next day.

She had never been to North Coast except in the evening. Then the school had a sort of laid-back vibe. Smooth and easy.

In the early-morning hours, the energy was different. Frenetic. Between the nearby Case Western Reserve University, the massive hospital complex just a block away, and the throngs of people who visited the museums in the area, the neighborhood hummed. Crossing the street, Jazz dodged a driver who was more interested in texting than keeping her eyes on the road. She scurried into the school and zipped up to Brody's office.

He was right where she hoped he would be.

"Good morning."

It was clear from the start that Brody must

have been the person of interest who'd been talked about on the news, and that his run-in with the law had done nothing for him, mentally or physically. Like a man on drugs, his eyes were dull. They were rimmed with gray, sunken, sad. His clothes were as stylish as ever, though this particular morning, his shirt looked too big for him, his shoulders lost in the folds of white cotton. His footsteps when he turned from where he was standing at his bookcase were unsteady.

He'd pulled a book from the shelf and, seeing her, he tossed it over to his desk. "What the hell do you want?"

"Just to talk."

"Every time I see you, you tell me all you want to do is talk. Talking to you hasn't gotten me anywhere but in deep shit."

"Not my fault," she answered automatically, then thought better of sounding too confrontational. Instead, she took a careful step into the room. "The cops, they interviewed you. And they released you."

"Of course they released me. I haven't done anything. And how do you know about it, anyway? My name wasn't mentioned on the news. My wife watched all the stations, she checked all the online stories."

"I was here Tuesday. The grapevine was

already buzzing."

"Which explains why most of my colleagues wouldn't meet my eyes when I saw them on the way into the building this morning." His mouth twisted. "I suppose I have you to thank for that, too."

To distance herself from the accusation, she held up her hands. "I don't have that kind of power. I'm only —"

"Yeah, a friend of Florie's. Concerned about the poor girl's sad fate. Thanks to you, I have a meeting with the dean this afternoon. I'm sure he's going to ask about my relationship with Florie."

"Maybe you should just come right out and tell him the truth."

"That I slept with Florie?"

"I don't have any proof of that and hey, it really doesn't matter to me. Your business is your business. Yours and Florie's. But I do know you helped her out when it came to that one A she received this semester." As if to prove it, Jazz reached into her pocket and pulled out the DVD she'd watched the night before. "Her video project was a disaster."

One corner of Brody's mouth pulled tight. "And I was a sucker."

"That's what she demanded, right? She'd sleep with you. In return, you replaced her video project with a really good one, probably one you filmed yourself."

His breath stuttered over a sigh. "Nobody else fell for her blackmail."

"You mean like Joyce Wildemere? I think Florie tried. I'm pretty sure she had taken some incriminating photos of Ms. Wildemere."

Brody's nod was barely perceptible. "Joyce would have caved eventually. She's not made of strong stuff. Joyce would have paid whatever it was Florie was asking, or changed Florie's grade to make sure she passed. If Florie hadn't died. No way Joyce would want her husband to know she's seeing Margie Teester from the admin office on the side, even though everyone on the staff has known about it for years."

The information proved her theory about the pink polka-dot envelopes, and Jazz should have been happy. Or at least felt vindicated. Instead, a sadness settled over her, pushing on her shoulders, softening her voice as well as her resolve.

"I just . . ." Jazz lifted her shoulders. "I just wanted you to know. That's all. I just wanted you to know that I know about the video project."

"And now you'll tell the cops, give them more ammunition." Like he was moving under water, Brody trudged to his desk.

"I doubt the fact that you did Florie's project for her will make any difference as far as the investigation," Jazz told him. "According to what I heard on the news, the cops don't have any proof that you . . ." She couldn't bring herself to say the words. ". . . that you were involved in her death."

"It's not possible to have proof because there's nothing to prove." He picked up a sheaf of papers on the desk, then slapped them back down. "Why would I want to kill Florie?"

"She threatened to tell your wife what you two were up to?"

Brody barked out a laugh. "It didn't matter anymore! See, the night Florie was killed, the night we went back to Tremont to film that B roll together . . . well, I asked her to come along and take some stills. Truth is, I didn't really care about the stills. We didn't need any more stills. I only asked her to come because I wanted to talk to her. Someplace where no one could interrupt us. I told her it was over between us."

"Seems to me that would make her more determined than ever to make sure your wife found out what was going on. I mean, if Florie was upset."

"Except she wasn't," Brody assured her. "As a matter of fact, she thanked me for finally getting it over with. She admitted she'd only slept with me for the grade."

"Florie always was good at getting what she wanted."

"On the flip side, you should know she didn't mean anything to me." Brody was a little too nonchalant. "She was just a willing kid and I'm just a guy nearing middle-age and looking for a little excitement. So you see . . ." He sat at his desk, his gaze on the closed laptop in front of him. "There was no real passion. There never had been. There was just sex."

"Except she thought enough of you to create that photo montage, right? The one you took out of her studio. And you thought enough of yourself to destroy it."

His jaw tightened and his gaze shot to hers. "Oh, you are thorough."

"Just lucky, really. I asked the right questions and got some answers."

"And screwed me royally in the process." His chest rose and fell. "Do the cops know about the photo?"

"Would it make a difference? If you and Florie broke up —"

"We did."

"And if you claim you have no reason to have killed her —"

"I didn't. All right?" He slapped a hand

against his desk and stood. "She meant nothing to me. And maybe you don't understand, Ms. Ramsey. A relationship — a real relationship — is all about passion. Sometimes that passion turns into love. Sometimes, it explodes into hate. But without it . . ." He mumbled a curse. "I couldn't have killed Florie. I didn't have any passion for Florie. Truth be told, I didn't care if she lived or died."

"Nice speech!"

At the sound of the voice coming from the doorway, Jazz jumped and whirled around. She was just in time to see Nick step into the office.

And just in time to see Tate Brody's jaw go rigid.

"Good morning, Ms. Ramsey." His expression blank, Nick tipped his head in Jazz's direction. "I'd like to say I'm surprised to see you here, but really, I'm not."

Jazz took a step in Nick's direction. "I was just —"

"You were just leaving." Nick's voice simmered with authority. "Officer Franklin!" The uniformed officer Jazz had seen the night Florie was killed stepped up behind Nick. "Escort Ms. Ramsey out of the building."

She didn't argue. Nick was in no mood to

negotiate. Jazz joined Officer Franklin in the hallway. They hadn't gone three steps when she heard Nick's voice echo back at her from the office.

"Tate Brody, you're under arrest for the murder of Florentine Allen."

The dismissal bell had already rung and most of the girls were gone for the day. Jazz finished the last of the paperwork that was waiting for her when she got back from North Coast and checked her phone one more time. Her app for a local TV station still hadn't updated the story. There was no news about Florie Allen's murder, not a word about the arrest of her killer.

"Got a minute?"

The last person she expected to see was Nick, so when he rapped on her door and stepped into her office, she was at a loss for words.

"I can come back," he suggested.

"No." Jazz rose from her chair behind her desk. "Come on in. I figured you'd be knee-deep in wrapping up the case."

"I am. And I need to get right back to the station. I just wanted to let you know what was going on."

"You arrested Tate Brody. It hasn't been on the news yet." As if it proved anything, she lifted her phone, then plunked it back on the desk. "But of course I heard you in Brody's office."

"Because you were there first, already talking to him when I got there." Back when they were a couple, Nick had visited her a time or two at school, and he strolled further into the office without bothering to look around. Nothing at St. Catherine's had changed. Nothing had changed at all except the something between them, the something that wouldn't change again anytime soon because one look — at the way Nick juggled his car keys, at the way he stood in front of her desk with his feet slightly apart, at the way he sized her up with that careful, cagey look that said she wasn't an ex-lover or even a friend, just a source — told her he was there on business.

He confirmed it when he asked, "What were you doing there?"

There was no use pretending. Not anymore. Not with Nick. Jazz rounded the desk and went over to where Florie's psychedelic photograph still leaned against her bookcases. "I wanted to ask him about this photograph," she told Nick. "It's Florie's work, and I think it tells the story of Florie and Brody's relationship." She noted his indifference and found herself feeling both indignant and disappointed. She had hoped it would be as big a deal to him as it had been to her when she made the discovery. "You already know."

"I know they were having an affair. That was one of the first things Brody admitted when we brought him in today. But this picture —"

She pointed out what she and Sarah and Eileen had discovered the day before, ending with the birthmark and the bet they'd find it on Brody.

"Good work," Nick admitted. "But why —"

"Because there are two photographs, Nick. Or at least there were two. Only my guess is that Brody didn't know that. He had the one that used to hang in Florie's studio. This is the one she had her apartment. You probably saw both of them."

He nodded but didn't comment, so Jazz went right on. "Brody destroyed the photograph he had. I think he did it because he knew it was too personal, that someone would eventually figure out that the picture was all about him, all about his relationship with Florie, and he didn't want anyone to know about it."

"And you know this because . . . ?"

There was no use lying, so she admitted

that she'd been at the school when the trash cans were emptied, that one of the techs had dropped a scrap of the photo. As if to prove her sincerity, she took the discarded piece of photograph from her desk and handed it over to Nick.

"You must have found more of it." She ventured the guess.

Nick's gaze snapped from the scrap of photograph to her. "The guys at the lab said they'd found pieces and they were fitting them together. They said they'd call me when they were done, but they were pretty sure the picture was nothing but discarded trash."

"But see, that's how I knew it must be important," she told him. "Because Brody destroyed it."

He chewed over this new piece of information in silence and might have gone right on standing there and thinking if Sarah hadn't breezed into the room.

"Oh!" Her eyes wide, she looked from Jazz to Nick and back to Jazz, then turned around and raced out.

Nick dropped into the chair in front of Jazz's desk. "I guess Sarah's not feeling chatty today."

"Or she doesn't want to intrude."

His look — top lip curled and eyes

squinched — told her *that will be the day,* but it settled soon enough. "You're going to hear it on the news sooner or later so I figured I might as well break the news to you," Nick told her. "We found the murder weapon."

"That's why you arrested Brody!"

He nodded. "It was a lanyard. You know, the kind you wear around your neck to hold a photo ID. Black background, white skulls."

It sounded familiar, and it was no wonder why. "Florie had it on her backpack. I remember it from those pictures you showed of the afternoon she died. She was on Public Square handing out brochures and she had her backpack with her and —" Another thought hit. "It wasn't on her backpack when I found her. Brody . . ." Jazz's stomach soured, and she swallowed hard. "You know, he broke up with her that night. At least that's what he told me. Maybe it was the other way around. Maybe she broke up with him. He got angry. He tore the lanyard off her backpack and . . ." She couldn't put words to the image that flashed through her mind.

Another nod from Nick. "We found the lanyard in the trunk of Brody's car, of all places. It's got blood on it. We don't have a DNA match yet, of course, but the blood type is Florie's."

"And let me guess, Brody's telling you he has no idea how the lanyard got there. That's what he said about Florie's phone, too, right?"

Nick waved away the information as inconsequential. "He was right about the phone. Anyone could have put it in the trash can near his office. Apparently, people aren't very careful with the trash there." It was all he said — all he'd ever say — about the fact that Jazz had walked off with a piece of the photograph. "We checked his phone records. And hers. There were plenty of calls between the two of them, all hours of the day and night."

"He says it doesn't mean anything."

"Maybe it doesn't," Nick admitted. "But it's a fact, and I deal in facts. The phone could have been dumped by Brody; he admits he and Florie were having an affair; he had the murder weapon in his car. Facts. All of them."

"But he's denying it all, right?"

"It's weird." Cocking his head, Nick thought about it. "When I questioned him the first time, he denied having anything to do with Florie's death. But since we found the murder weapon . . . Well, he hasn't declared his innocence lately, but he might just be waiting until he consults his lawyer. Which he's doing . . ." Nick checked the time on his phone. "Right now." He sat up and worked a kink out of his neck. "I've got to get back and wrap this thing up."

Jazz let go a long breath. "That's good. We can all have some closure. And you get to close your case."

It wasn't exactly a smile that lit Nick's face. It was more pained than that, a grim acceptance of the fact that though the case might be closed, even an arrest wouldn't change what had happened. It wouldn't bring Florie back.

CHAPTER 20

"I'm thinking Monday would be good."

After four years of working at Eileen's side, Jazz was used to her mind moving like quicksilver. Most of the time, she was able to keep up.

This wasn't one of those times.

The next morning when Eileen zipped by Jazz's desk and into her office, Jazz left off sorting the day's mail and followed. "Monday would be good for what?" she asked.

Eileen had been at a meeting at the diocesan office downtown. Before she sat at her desk, she kicked off her black pumps and poked her feet into the Toms waiting for her on the carpet in front of the fireplace. Her sigh of relief preceded her words. "The memorial service for Florie. I've been watching the weather. Monday sounds perfect. Midsixties, sunny. We'll take the girls across the street to the park. As much as I love the chapel, on a spring afternoon, the great outdoors seems more fitting. I didn't want to do the memorial sooner. Not until . . ."

This time Jazz knew exactly what she meant. "Until they found the man who killed her." She managed a smile, sure that it wobbled around the edges. But then, thinking about Florie, about Tate Brody and the misery he'd brought to his wife and to his school and his colleagues . . . well, it all had a way of tangling around her heart. "You're right. This seems like a good time."

"And a lot of work for us, I'm afraid. It's already Friday."

Jazz's mind flew through a list of details. "Priest?" she asked.

"I saw Father Donovan from St. Pat's this morning and he owes me a favor. He'll be here Monday at one."

Father Kevin Donovan was a good choice. He was young and enthusiastic, the perfect combination of devout and congenial. He'd conducted a few classes at St. Catherine's and was the girls' favorite. It helped that he was as cute as can be. And leave it to Eileen to come up with the perfect time, too. By one, lunch hours would be finished and Jazz would have the morning to wrap up details.

"Music?" Jazz asked.

"The school choir and orchestra. You'll

talk to Marni?"

Marni Gulick directed both St. Catherine's choir and orchestra, and Jazz made a mental note to contact her as soon as she was done there with Eileen. "The orchestra's been practicing 'Farewell to Stromness' for the spring concert."

"Perfect."

"And the choir?"

Eileen grinned. "Whatever you and Marni decide will be fine. Make it something nice and Catholic!"

"Done!" There would be a million other details, but Jazz would worry about them later, and she'd have the weekend to make arrangements. "Balloons?" she suggested.

Eileen nodded.

"School colors?"

"Of course."

"Flowers?"

Eileen glanced out the window and Jazz did, too. If the weather predictions were true and the weekend was warm, the daffodils along the paths that surrounded the gazebo at the center of Lincoln Park would be in full bloom by Monday.

Eileen's smile was soft. "Let's let God take care of the flowers."

Fine with Jazz. It was one less thing for her to worry about. "Will you speak?" she asked Eileen.

The nun thought about it. "I'd rather not, but I suppose it will look weird if I don't. I'll write something up. Short and sweet. We'll keep the whole thing to under an hour. We can gather at the gazebo."

"I'll check with the city to see if we need a permit. And maybe . . ." Jazz pictured the scene — Eileen and Father Donovan at the front of the crowd, the school's small choir under the roof of the gazebo, the orchestra gathered around them. It was nice. Fitting. "Maybe it will make people forget the bad parts of the story," she suggested, though she knew it was unlikely that would ever happen. The day's news was filled with talk of the instructor who'd been arrested, of his relationship with his young, pretty student. The media was all about sordid details, and they were feasting on everything they knew about Florie and Brody and filling in the blanks with conjecture. It all made Jazz glad that Larry and Renee Allen probably couldn't find a working TV in their house if they wanted to. They didn't have to listen to the ugly story.

They didn't have to see the same picture Jazz had seen, either, the one every local and cable station had picked up to go with the story — Florie in her little black skirt, her tall boots, her over-the-top makeup.

"We need to show the real Florie," Jazz decided right then and there. "I'll get some of her photos blown up and we'll put them on easels, but it would be nice to have her picture, too. Without the makeup and the piercings."

Eileen couldn't have agreed more. "Her yearbook photo will work."

"It will, but something newer would be nice." She knew better than to think she would get a recent photo from Larry and Renee. "North Coast might have Florie's student ID picture," she told Eileen. "Or . . ."

Jazz knew exactly where she could get recent pictures, and plenty of them, but for now, there were a million other things to think about, a million details, a million calls she had to make, and she hurried back to her office to get down to business. Once the school day was over, she knew exactly what she had to do, where she had to go, and who she needed to talk to.

Were her hands shaking when she made up her mind about what she had to do?

She liked to think not, but she wasn't very good about lying to herself.

Like it or not, she needed to track down Billy DeSantos.

The Exorcist was playing at the Capitol Theater that night, the opening volley in the barrage of scary movies that was the Cleveland Horror Film Festival.

By the time Jazz finished up at school and went home to get her car, she was lucky to find a parking place where she could squeeze her SUV between a shiny black Porsche and a red Cooper Mini in the parking lot behind a bank that was closed for the day. She crossed the street and joined the surprisingly large number of people headed toward the theater, doing her best to quiet the voice in her head that sounded remarkably like Nick.

He's got a record. Stay away from that guy.

It might have been easier if she could erase the memory of Billy hanging around outside St. Catherine's. If she could calm the tattoo of fear that started up in her insides when she remembered how she'd found him outside her house.

Nick had never said what Billy DeSantos had done that had earned him a reputation with the CPD. He didn't have to. Jazz was not the type who judged people by what they wore or how many tats they did or didn't have, but she was enough of a realist to know that the way Billy dressed sent a message, loud and clear. Sure, some of the folks in the crowd headed to the movie who were dressed in black or had spiked hair or (like the guy next to her) creepy red contact lenses . . . sure, they were all about the mystique of horror.

But something, something deep down and undeniable that left her with a rock in the pit of her stomach, told her Billy was the real deal.

A cascade of shivers crawled over her arms.

"Hope you brought a sweater, it's always cold in this theater."

Jazz didn't realize she'd run her hands over her arms until the middle-aged woman walking alongside her offered the advice. She assured the woman she'd be fine, and when they turned the corner and met the roadblock of people waiting to get into the theater, she bumped her way from the center of the crowd to its edges, stepped into the street, and did her best to scan the sea of faces.

Black capes. Black jackets. Black dresses and eye shadow. Still, it wasn't all that hard to spot the guy with the shaved head dressed in black leather with an octopus crawling up his neck.

Her heart knocked against her ribs, and when Nick's voice inside her head tried to reinforce his warning about Billy, she told it to shut up. She skirted the edges of the crowd, pushed through the line of people coming up the street from the parking lot at the back of the theater, and stepped up to Billy's side.

He was handing out flyers that listed the times and places of the other movies the film festival would feature — Parker Paul's new brochure bitch — and he passed one to her without even bothering to give her a look.

"We need to talk," she told him.

Billy's head snapped up, his lips pressed so tight that the metal ring stuck through the bottom one looked like a twin to the sliver of moon that rode overhead. "Why? You never wanted to talk before."

"What do you mean —"

He'd been leaning against a tall stool while he worked, and he pushed off and moved from the pool of light thrown by the spots and into the shadows in front of the storefront next door. "You thought I killed Florie."

She'd followed him, and, in the gloom, she nearly bumped into him. She pulled herself up short just before she did and planted her feet, her fists on her hips. The stance might not make her feel any braver, but she hoped it made her look capable of standing up to him.

"I never said you did."

"You wanted it to be me. It made more sense, a guy with piercings instead of the teacher with the ritzy wife."

"It's a terrible thing no matter who did it."

"Like I told you all along. . . ." He lit a cigarette and took a drag. "It wasn't me."

There was no use beating around the bush or trying to convince him that she'd never been a threat. Not much of one. Not really. "We're planning a memorial service on Monday. At the high school Florie attended."

"And you want me to lead the prayers?"

"You have pictures of Florie on your phone. Lots of pictures of Florie."

He'd just taken another puff of his cigarette, and his grunt of protest escaped along with a long trail of smoke that collected in the darkness between them and made him look blurred around the edges, like a figure out of a fever dream.

"You just don't let up, do you, lady? Don't you watch the news? Or are you some kind of idiot? They got . . . they got the guy that killed Florie." His voice broke, and Jazz wished the light was better. She would have loved to see the expression on his face.

Billy took another puff of his cigarette. A second. A third. He tossed the butt on the sidewalk and ground it with his boot heel.

"They got the guy," he said again, his voice level now except for the suffocating sadness that edged his words. "The pictures don't mean a thing. You can leave me alone now. You can let . . ." He coughed. "You can let Florie rest in peace."

The anguish in his voice caught Jazz by surprise and made her breath catch over a realization so astounding, she could barely get the words out.

"You loved her. You . . . you followed me because you —"

"Because you're a nosy bitch. Yeah, that's why." Billy's smile was tight. "When you came around asking questions, I thought . . ." He turned away long enough to compose himself. "I had to know what happened. Do you get that? I couldn't just let Florie go away, let her disappear. Not just like that, not like she was nothing and she never existed. And you were asking questions so I thought . . . I thought maybe you could tell me something. Maybe you could help me make sense of the whole thing."

At the same time Jazz's heart clutched, she put a hand on Billy's leather-clad arm. "I thought —"

This time his smile was wider. "Yeah, I know. Big and scary. I have that effect on a lot of people."

"I shouldn't have assumed —"

"I just wanted to know more and I was thinking —"

"That I could help. I'm sorry. I should have. I didn't realize how much Florie meant to you. I'm sorry about Florie."

"There is no Florie. Not anymore." His voice was as thick as the cloud of smoke that floated between them and so filled with pain, Jazz could only say what she'd already said. "I'm sorry."

He turned away. "Why are you sorry?"

It was the same question she'd been asking herself since the night she found Florie, but suddenly, Jazz knew the answer. "Because Florie was a talented woman and she would have made a difference in the world."

He faced her again. "That's not what they're saying on the news."

"All the media cares about is ratings. You cared about Florie."

"I wasn't stalking her." His words rang

against the stone storefront. "I never would have hurt her, not the way I loved her."

She didn't ask if Florie loved him back. She wasn't sure Florie was capable. She wasn't sure it mattered.

Jazz cleared away the tightness in her throat with a cough. "We need some pictures for her memorial service. You think you could pick out one for me?"

He pulled out his phone. "Let's go . . ." He tilted his chin back toward the theater entrance. "The light is better there."

It was, and in the glow of the spots, Jazz watched Billy scroll through pictures. Hundreds of pictures. He slowed down when he got to the pictures she'd seen before, the ones of Florie handing out brochures on Public Square the day she died.

"I'd rather have one where she isn't in her film festival makeup," Jazz dared to tell him. "Not that I think there's anything wrong with it," she added quickly, "but I'm trying to show another side of Florie, not what they're showing on the news. The girl we knew at St. Catherine's and —"

Her gaze on the screen of Billy's phone, her words dissolved in a burble of disbelief.

"Is that . . ." When she pointed, Jazz's finger shook. "Is that Florie going into the building on Tremont the night she was killed?"

Billy eyes were sad. He nodded.

"Billy . . ." The better to draw him out of whatever he was thinking when he looked at Florie — at the confident tilt of her chin, at the way her backpack was slung over her shoulder, that lanyard that would be the murder weapon swinging from it — Jazz put a hand on his shoulder. "You never told me you were there."

Billy grunted. "Yeah, that's all the cops needed to find out."

"But you have pictures. Evidence. How did you —"

"Know she was going over to Tremont? That's easy. Florie told me. She was all proud of being asked to shoot pictures for that son of a bitch Brody, all excited about it. When we were over at Public Square, she told me he was picking her up and where they were going."

"And you followed them."

"You make it sound creepy."

There was no use arguing the point. Jazz looked at the next picture. "Florie went around to the back of the building. That's how she got in. The cops figured she used the back door. You went around that way, too."

"Yeah, and look who's letting her in that door." He pointed to a picture that was dark and grainy. Billy had taken it from an odd angle in the shadows because he didn't dare get any closer. Still, there was no mistaking the cap of unruly, sexy hair or the stubble of beard on the man who poked his head out of the doorway to greet Florie.

"How long until he came out again?" she asked Billy, because she didn't have a shred of doubt that he'd waited.

"Here." He scrolled to the next picture. The angle was different — Billy must have found a more advantageous place to watch and wait. In the picture, Tate Brody was standing in the doorway looking outside, his lips pressed together, his hands bunched into fists at his sides. Florie was behind him, her mouth opened wide.

Jazz took one look at the desperation in Florie's eyes, the tears streaming down her cheeks. "He wasn't lying about breaking up with her," she said. "He was lying when he said she didn't care."

The next picture showed Tate Brody walking out of the back door of the building with Florie still in the doorway, bent at the waist as if the very act of breathing was excruciating.

"Wait!" Jazz put her hand on Billy's to

stop him from scrolling further. "Are you telling me you actually have proof that Florie was still alive when Brody left?"

Billy's face twisted with disgust. "I got a call from Parker Paul, the fat shit. He needed me over at the festival office. Son of a bitch is too lazy to do any of the real work, and some big-ass posters, a rush job, came over late from the printer. He needed me to unload them. So, yeah, I had to leave. But it's pretty obvious, don't you think? Brody left. Right here." He tapped the picture on the phone screen. "But he must have come back. Don't you think? Otherwise the cops wouldn't have been able to prove he killed Florie."

It made sense in light of the evidence Nick had unearthed.

"So that's it. The last of your pictures?" Jazz asked Billy.

"I got one more before I had to go." He scrolled to it. The picture showed Florie still framed in the darkened doorway, one hand clutched to her backpack as if holding on to it would help keep her world from spinning out of control. Some sound from behind her had startled her, and her head was turned, her free hand braced against the doorway as if she was all set to push off, ready to run.

Jazz stared at the photo, her words caught up against the block of ice that strangled her breathing.

"Someone else was there."

CHAPTER 21

For once, the weather forecasters were right.

Monday was a glorious spring day — sunshine, blue skies, warm temperatures.

Aside from the fact that they had an hour-long break from classes, Jazz couldn't blame the young women of St. Catherine's for being a little too frisky. But she still couldn't allow it.

"Emma!" Jazz whispered the warning as soon as she saw Emma Marsh smack her red balloon against Gia Cartossi's yellow one. Just because they were in the last row of juniors gathered around the gazebo in Lincoln Park didn't mean they could get away with messing around. "Quit it!"

Gia and Emma snapped to attention, though Jazz was enough of a realist to know it had less to do with her than it did with the laser look of death the girls got from Shauna Best, their homeroom teacher and a woman known to take no prisoners. That mini crisis averted, Jazz stepped back and scanned the area, checking — again — to be sure every detail was taken care of, everything was going smoothly, and Doogie, the guy with the Rasta braids who sold weed in the park every afternoon, was far, far away from the ceremony.

Satisfied everything was under control, she moved away from the juniors and walked behind where the youngest girls were gathered, seventh and eighth graders whose teachers had used Florie's passing to teach a hard lesson about life and loss. She deliberately avoided even glancing toward the reporters and TV cameras at the furthest edges of the crowd. As much as she and Eileen had discussed the consequences of their presence all through the weekend, as much as they would have liked to ban the media altogether, they were both pragmatic enough to know it would never happen, not in a public place and not when the memorial service was designed to honor the victim of a sensational murder. The extra uniformed police officers the local commander had sent down to the park to control the crowd helped keep the reporters in their place.

"Police."

Far enough away from anyone to be overheard, she grumbled the word and slipped her phone from her pocket.

Still no callback from Nick.

"Nothing?" Sarah must have been watching her, because when she looked up, Jazz saw her mouth the word from the far side of a group of sophomores. Jazz had told Sarah about her theory that someone else besides Florie and Brody was in the building where she'd found Florie's body, and naturally, Sarah was as anxious to hear what Nick would have to say about it as Jazz was.

Jazz shook her head, stashed her phone, and did her best to control emotions that bounced between disappointment and annoyance.

She'd called Nick any number of times since she saw Billy's pictures over at the Capitol Theater.

She'd told him in her first voicemail that she had information pertaining to Florie's case and she knew he'd want to hear it.

She'd told him in subsequent voicemails — at least a dozen of them — that she really needed to talk to him.

And Nick?

Jazz wasn't sure if the irony of the situation was funny or just plain pathetic.

Even the details of Florie's murder, Florie's relationship with Brody, and the video instructor's fall from grace (and society) had taken a backseat to the weekend's news, a hotter-than-Hades story about a city council member, a love nest complete with mirrors, a hot tub, and a heart-shaped bed, and a dead hooker.

Nick had his hands full.

Swallowing down her disappointment, Jazz listened to the orchestra perform flawlessly. The choir sang, their sweet young-girl voices flying up to the heavens like birdsong. Father Donovan said the opening prayer. Now — right on time with the schedule Jazz had drawn up — Eileen began her carefully crafted speech. After she was finished, the choir and orchestra would do one more piece together, then each girl would release the balloon she held and the sky would be alive, dancing with yellow and red, a last tribute to Florie.

Jazz had typed up every word of Eileen's speech and she didn't need to listen, so instead, she let her gaze drift from the two empty chairs behind Eileen — reserved for Larry and Renee, who Eileen had personally invited — to the photo of Florie on an easel at the base of the gazebo steps, one of the few photos on Billy's phone that showed Florie out of her film festival costume and makeup. She looked sweet in a baby-blue sweater, her hair down around her shoulders. Billy had caught her off guard and she looked wistful and so young. Not for the first time, Jazz wondered what Florie had been thinking when Billy snapped the pic. Whatever it was, Florie's eyes were bright. Her smile was wide. Her face was tipped toward the sun.

The expression hardly fit with the dark secrets Jazz had discovered about Florie's life, but it was appropriate to the occasion, and important for the girls to see the real Florie instead of the goth vamp whose picture (well, before the city-council-member-and-the-hooker story broke, anyway) stared back at them at the beginning of every local newscast. The girls of St. Catherine's had heard enough about Florie's shortcomings, and as Eileen was about to remind them, there was more to her — more to each and every person there in the park — than just a reputation, good or bad. There is also, always, a spark of the divine.

While she waited for Eileen to wrap up, Jazz quietly made her way over to where the freshmen girls were assembled. One of them, a girl named LaTasha Mills, had always struck Jazz as a little too sensitive, and she saw she was right; LaTasha's cheeks were streaked with tears. Jazz signaled to LaTasha's homeroom teacher for a little extra attention, and joined the girls as they sang the closing hymn. The last note faded, and on Eileen's signal, the girls released their balloons, oohing and ahhing as they sailed into the air. Some of the balloons tangled in the branches of the nearby trees, like oversized yellow and red apples. Many more flew up and over the neighborhood and disappeared into the clear sky.

The ceremony done, the girls and their teachers headed back across the street to school. Jazz stayed behind to handle the wrap-up.

It was a good thing she did, or she wouldn't have seen Billy, who stared at the picture of Florie for a minute, then disappeared into the crowd of neighbors and onlookers who'd gathered at a respectful distance. She wouldn't have seen another familiar face, either, and when she did, Jazz immediately took off in the direction of the tall chain-link fence that surrounded the neighborhood swimming pool.

"Mrs. Brody!" Jazz caught up with her just as Sloane turned toward the sidewalk. "I'm . . ." She hauled in a breath at the same time she scrambled to find the right word that would explain how she felt at finding the suspect's wife at his victim's service.

Sloane saved her the trouble. "Surprised?" She was wearing a hat, sunglasses, an understated gray raincoat, the outfit designed so the media wouldn't notice her. "I thought it was only right for me to be here. For me to . . . acknowledge . . . I don't know if that's the right word." Her slim shoulders rose and fell; her breath trembled. "I needed to do something."

"It was very kind of you. Not to mention brave. If those reporters catch on to the fact that you're here . . ."

Sloane snickered. "They're packing up and leaving," she said, and when Jazz looked over her shoulder she saw Sloane was right. "On to the latest and greatest sensation. By next week, no one will even remember that girl's name."

Jazz wondered if Sloane had already forgotten it.

"You'll still have to live with the story." It wasn't the first time Jazz had thought of the tsunami of consequences resulting from the blackmail, the affair, the murder. "It can't be easy."

Sloane steadied her shoulders. "I've retained the best attorney in . . . know. It was Tate. He's innoce . . .

someone else. It had to be. Someone planted that evidence against Tate." Sloane's voice bubbled with anger, her pale-as-porcelain cheeks shot through with color.

"You're very loyal. After everything they're saying on the news about —"

"You believe that?" The sound that escaped her might have been a snort coming from someone less cultured. "Lies. It's all lies. The media, they're like sharks. They can smell blood in the water and when there isn't any, they toss in some chum just to make things interesting. I hate every last one of them. Almost as much as I hate . . ." Her voice broke.

Jazz gave Sloane time to compose herself, turning to watch, like Sloane did, when Eddie and Frank, the maintenance guys from St. Catherine's, took Florie's photo off the easel. Eddie folded the easel and slung it over his shoulder. Frank carried the picture out of the park.

"I'm just sorry for everything." Sloane's shoulders sagged, her voice clogged with tears. "Obviously I'm angry about what's happening to Tate, but you know, the truth is, I'm sorry for that girl, too. And I'm so sorry about the baby. That poor baby."

"Baby?"

Jazz would liked to ask what Sloane

was talking about, but she never had the chance. Sloane turned and walked up the park path toward the street just as Jazz's phone rang.

"Nick!" Worry pounded at her insides and she barely squeezed the word out. "I need to talk to you!"

He sounded tired. "So you told me in all those voicemails. I've been kind of busy and —"

"Yeah, I know." Jazz watched Sloane cross the street. "And I've got plenty to tell you, but Nick, first I have to know, did something happen to Lalo, you know, that kid Florie was taking pictures of?"

He thought about it for a moment. "Not that I've heard. Why would you ask?"

"Because Sloane Brody was here at the memorial service. She told me she felt bad about Florie, and about the baby. Naturally I thought of Lalo. Could she have meant . . ." The idea was preposterous.

Or was it?

"Nick, could she have been talking about Florie's baby?"

Jazz watched Sloane open her purse and peer inside, no doubt searching for her keys.

"That's weird." Nick must have rapped a pencil against his desktop, because a sound started up, one in perfect rhythm to the frantic beating of Jazz's heart. "Because Brody, when we interviewed him, he told us Florie told him she was pregnant."

"Was she?"

"I've checked and rechecked the autopsy report. I called the coroner just to be sure. No way Florie was pregnant."

"And when . . ." Jazz swallowed hard. "When did Florie tell Brody she was?" she asked.

"That night he told her he was breaking up with her. The night she died. My guess is she was just trying to hang on to him and she was willing to lie to do it."

"So when do you suppose Brody broke the news to his wife?"

Nick didn't answer. Instead, Jazz heard the same *tap, tap, tap.* "Checking the reports," he finally said. "You know, one fact has a way of blending with another and this one —"

When his words cut off, Jazz tensed. "What? What is it, Nick?"

"That whole thing about the baby, it looks like Brody never mentioned it until last night when we interviewed him again. And he swore he never told anyone else, not even his wife."

"And since last night . . ." Jazz's insides clutched. "Has he talked to Sloane?"

"There's no record of a visit or a phone call," he told her. "What do you suppose —"

"Nick!" Jazz was moving before she even realized it, running across the park, toward the street, toward where Sloane Brody's expensive purse seemed to have swallowed her car keys. "Nick, I know who really killed Florie."

Nick said something that might have been "Are you nuts?" but Jazz wasn't listening. Across the narrow street from where Sloane was so intent on searching for her keys she never noticed her, Jazz stopped and held the phone to her side, the call still connected. "Mrs. Brody, wait up! I need to talk to you."

There was certainly nothing threatening about the way Jazz said it, but some deep-seated warning went off in Sloane's head. Her eyes wary, she looked at Jazz. She looked at Jazz's phone. And she took off running.

Her timing was perfect. A truck lumbered by going too fast for Jazz to cross the street in front of it and too slow for her to get around it quickly. She counted out the seconds, cursed under her breath, told Nick, "You've got to get over here to Tremont," and when the truck had finally passed, she was just in time to see Sloane shoot across the street at the far corner of the park and disappear into an alley between a pizza place and a resale shop.

"Jazz!" Nick's voice sounded like it came from a million miles away. "What's going on?"

"She took off." Jazz was already racing after Sloane, and her words bumped along with her breaths. "It's Sloane Brody, Nick. She knew about the baby and if Tate didn't tell her, how could she? She must have been there. In the building where Florie was killed. She must have heard Florie tell Tate she was pregnant. I'm following her —"

"Don't!" Even from the other end of the phone, from whatever bureaucratic desk he sat at, his voice rang with authority, with desperation. Now his words bumped along, too. He was grabbing his coat, heading out of the office, and Jazz heard him call another cop to come along, another car for backup. "If there's the slightest chance she's guilty —"

"She's getting away. I've got to keep an eye on her." That same truck that had stymied her on the street in front of the school made a turn onto the cross street, and Jazz shot in front of it. Safely on the other side, she braced a hand against the corner of a building that housed a women's clothing boutique and looked around, and when she saw the flash of a gray raincoat, she ran in that direction.

"I'm heading down where all the fancy restaurants are," she told Nick. "I bet she knows her way around here." It was, no doubt, exactly why Sloane knew to duck down the alley that ran next to one of the neighborhood's most fashionable spots. It wasn't a part of the neighborhood where Jazz usually hung, but she knew there was a way out of that alley from the back, and her gut told her if Sloane got there first, she would disappear into the warren of buildings there. She had to get to the alley before Sloane did, and she told Nick so.

Her legs pumping and her heart pounding, Jazz came up the alley from the far end, cutting off Sloane just as she was about to race out into the street. Sloane stopped and backed against a wall, fighting for breath. She'd lost her hat somewhere along the way, and her blond hair gleamed in the spring sunshine, a golden halo of knotted mess.

"You were there." Jazz braced her hands on her knees and breathed deep. "You must have been. There's no way you could have known what Florie told Tate otherwise. You were there inside the building waiting for your husband and Florie when they arrived, weren't you? Once Tate left, you killed Florie and then you framed your husband. You . . . you planted the phone at his office. You planted that lanyard you used to strangle Florie in Brody's car. You were getting even, weren't you? Getting even because of the affair."

Sloane shook her head. She pressed a hand to her chest. "Don't be ridiculous. Why would I bother? Why would I care?"

"Why would you care?" Jazz considered the question. "Unless this wasn't the first time and you were sick of playing second fiddle?" Sloane didn't answer. Jazz didn't expect her to. "But your husband, he told me he'd ended it with Florie. That night. You were there in the building. You must have heard him tell Florie. It was over."

"It wasn't over. Don't you get it? It would never be over!" Sloane's mouth twisted. She ripped off her sunglasses and threw them on the ground. "I was there, all right, and I heard what she said. She was pregnant. That little bitch was having the baby . . ." Her voice broke with a wave of emotion that made her double over in pain. "She was having the baby I could never have. I didn't care about the affair. I didn't care about any of Tate's affairs. But a baby . . ." She wept, gagging on every breath, swaying. "That girl . . . that little nobody was having the baby that should have been mine."

Jazz stepped closer to the sobbing woman. "Except she wasn't."

Sloane's head came up. "What?"

"If you knew Florie better, if you knew her like I've come to know her, you would have figured it out. Your husband told Florie they were through and Florie played the only card she had. She told him she was pregnant. My guess is her next move . . . maybe in a couple weeks . . . her next move would have been to ask him for money to pay for an abortion. But see, that was Florie's game. Blackmail. Mrs. Brody, Florie was never pregnant."

Just like that, Sloane's tears dissolved. Her expression hardened. Her skin, streaked with tears and smudged mascara, paled to the color of ice. "Are you telling me I killed that little bitch for nothing?"

Jazz chewed her lower lip. "I guess you did."

If years of good breeding, top-class education, and dealing with the upper echelons of society had taught Sloane anything, it was how to be cool in the face of adversity. Even when the world was falling apart. She shook her shoulders. She raised her chin. She pulled in one long breath and let it out slowly before she clutched her hands at her waist. "No matter who you tell about this, I'll deny it. You know I will. Just as you surely know people are bound to believe me, not you."

"I'm sure that's what you'll try."

"And if the police find out . . ." She got her first indication that they already had when tires squealed out on the street and a siren pulsed through the air. "You can't prove a thing."

"Actually, I can." Jazz lifted her phone and wiggled it in Sloane's direction. "I've been on the phone with the cops the whole time. That's how they know where we are. And they've heard every word."

Jazz thought Sloane had started crying again. That's how the sound started. Like a strangled sob. Then it gained strength and fury and echoed through the alley like the wail of a wounded animal. She came at Jazz, her hands raised, her fingers curled into claws that went around Jazz's neck.

And in the great scheme of things, Jazz supposed she should have been frightened.

Except for the fact that she'd grown up with two older brothers.

Just as Nick and his fellow cops bolted into the alley, Jazz dropped her phone, the better to pull back her right arm and make a perfect fist.

Sloane Brody never knew what hit her.

CHAPTER 22

Nick canceled their coffee date the next day.

Work conflict.

Jazz canceled the week after.

She had to help her mom with preparations for Easter dinner that weekend.

The following Tuesday, Nick didn't bother to either call or text, and Jazz wrote the date off.

It was fun while it lasted, she told herself, but it was never meant to last.

She'd already finished dinner — a tuna sandwich — when her doorbell rang. When she answered and found Nick on the front porch, a brown cardboard box next to him, she couldn't have been more surprised.

"I . . ." She kept one hand on the door and the other on the jamb, balancing herself and every word. "You don't have to apologize for not being able to make it for coffee today. We're both busy. We're always busy. Facts are facts, Nick, and fact is, we're never going to have enough time for each other."

"That's a pretty negative way to think about things." Though she was proud of herself for laying it on the line, for saying what they should have said to each other all along, he dared a smile. "I stopped by to give you a present."

"There wasn't a reward for catching Florie's killer, was there?"

"Sorry. Wish I was bringing you a big, fat check. But hey, you have the satisfaction of having done your civic duty."

"It doesn't feel all that satisfying." A skitter raced over Jazz's shoulders. "What a mess. And what a waste of a life."

"You mean Florie or Sloane Brody?"

She slanted him a look. "Don't tell me you're feeling sorry for Little Miss High Society."

Nick made a face. "Not as sorry for her as I am for her poor sap of a husband." He shook his head. "She knew he was messing around with Florie, and she vowed to get even. I guess she almost did."

"By making him look like the murderer." No matter how many times Jazz thought about it, she still found it inexplicable. "She hated him."

"She hated what he was doing." There was a difference, so Nick was only right in pointing it out. "It wasn't the first affair he'd had."

"But it was the first baby. Or at least what she thought was the first baby."

He nodded. "She couldn't get over it. They've been married something like ten years and a family is all she ever wanted. Never happened. And then . . ."

"Then some kid with black leather clothes and piercings does what Sloane could never do. She gets pregnant with Brody's child. At least Sloane thought that's what happened."

"Florie's last gamble, and it didn't pay off. And though he hasn't admitted it yet, my bet is Brody knew what was up. After we found the murder weapon in his car, he knew his wife was trying to frame him."

"But he never ratted on her."

He shrugged. "He might have eventually. I don't know. Maybe he just couldn't bring himself to do it. You know, he was right on time for dinner that night at the restaurant, just like everyone said he was. Turns out she was the one who was late. That's what got Brody thinking. I guess . . ." He pulled in a breath. "I guess he didn't want to turn her in. He really did love her."

"Well, she had a weird way of loving him back. Framing him!" Jazz shivered. "It's nuts, and I'm glad it's over."

"I'm glad it's over, too, and I'm glad you're not sticking your nose where it doesn't belong anymore. Leave the investigating to the professionals."

She could afford to smile. It had turned out well. "Hey, maybe next time there will be a reward."

"Maybe this will make up for there being no reward this time." He picked up the cardboard box, and Jazz had no choice but to step back so he could walk into her living room. Nick reached into the box and came out holding a puppy.

Black back and tail. Rusty-brown tummy and paws and muzzle, except for the smudge of black straight down the center between his eyes and down to his nose. Wiry coat.

Jazz's heart melted, but her resolve was strong. So was her skepticism. Beware handsome men bearing gifts.

She tucked her hands behind her back. "It's an Airedale."

"Yeah." From the looks of him, the puppy was eight or nine weeks old, a bundle of wiggles and fur, and Nick lifted him up so he could look into the dog's eyes. "Cute, huh?"

Jazz didn't even realize she'd put some distance between herself and Nick — and the dog — until she bumped into the chair that sat catty-corner from her couch.

"Why do you have an Airedale?"

"I've got a buddy who breeds them."

"You don't have time for a dog."

"I don't." Since she'd moved so far away, Nick had to cross the room to hold the dog out to her. "He's yours."

Jazz looked into the puppy's brown eyes. She looked into Nick's blue ones. "What am I supposed to do with an Airedale?"

"Live with him. Love him. Train him. He's going to grow up to be the most kick-ass cadaver dog in the known world. He told me so."

She shook her head. "Airedales are smart, but they're as stubborn as hell. They've got minds of their own. They're tough to train."

Like it was no big deal, Nick shrugged. "Okay." He pulled back his hands and nestled the puppy to his chest and to the red T-shirt he wore with faded jeans. "If you don't think you're a good enough trainer to handle one little dog —"

"I never said that."

The dog let out a tiny yip — half bark, half whimper — and this time, her heart overtook her head.

She tried one last-ditch effort to come to her senses. "He's not Manny."

"He's not." Nick stepped closer. "But

word has it . . ." He bent his ear to the puppy's mouth and pretended to be listening. "Word from the other side of the Rainbow Bridge is that Manny's tired of watching you mope. He says you need a new best friend. Here he is." He put the puppy in her hands.

Jazz juggled him before she got one hand under his wiggly little butt and the other under his front legs. Automatically, instinctively, the puppy folded himself into her chest.

When she looked back up at Nick, her eyes were wet with tears. "Why?" she asked him.

"Because he needed the best home on the planet. Because you need to keep busy and shake away the blues. I dunno, since I've never personally owned a dog, but I've heard it from an expert that there's nothing better for what ails you than a furry body and waggy tail."

It was the mantra she'd always preached. She was surprised he'd been listening.

"I've got food and stuff in the car because I knew you wouldn't be ready for him. And this!" Nick pulled a yellow tennis ball from his pocket and bounced it on the hardwood floor, and the puppy yapped his approval. When Nick went to get the supplies, Jazz got on the floor with the dog and rolled the ball to him. He went after it once, twice, before he snuggled up against her leg and stretched out for a nap.

She scratched one finger over his woolly head.

"Looks like you two are getting along already." Nick set down a bag of puppy food, a fluffy dog bed, and a bag of treats on the couch. "I'm going to leave you alone to get acquainted." He fished his car keys from his pocket and backed toward the door. "Let me know how he's doing, all right? And maybe sometime I can stop by and visit?"

She smiled up a him. "You don't even have to wait for a Tuesday."

ABOUT THE AUTHOR

Kylie Logan is the national bestselling author of The League of Literary Ladies Mysteries, the Button Box Mysteries, the Chili Cook-Off Mysteries, and the Ethnic Eats Mysteries. *The Scent of Murder* is the first in a new series.

The employees of Thorndike Press hope you have enjoyed this Large Print book. All our Thorndike, Wheeler, and Kennebec Large Print titles are designed for easy reading, and all our books are made to last. Other Thorndike Press Large Print books are available at your library, through selected bookstores, or directly from us.

For information about titles, please call:
  (800) 223-1244

or visit our website at:
  gale.com/thorndike

To share your comments, please write:
  Publisher
  Thorndike Press
  10 Water St., Suite 310
  Waterville, ME 04901